The Ninth Life of
Louis Drax

The Ninth Life of
Louis Drax

LIZ JENSEN

BLOOMSBURY

First published in Great Britain in 2004

This paperback edition published 2005

Copyright © 2004 by Liz Jensen

The moral right of the author has been asserted

Bloomsbury Publishing Plc, 38 Soho Square, London W1D 3HB

A CIP catalogue record for this book
is available from the British Library

ISBN 0 7475 7111 2
9780747571117

10 9 8 7 6 5 4 3 2 1

Typeset by Hewer Text Ltd, Edinburgh
Printed in Great Britain by Clays Ltd, St Ives plc

All papers used by Bloomsbury Publishing are natural,
recyclable products made from wood grown in
well-managed forests. The manufacturing processes conform
to the environmental regulations of the country of origin

www.lizjensen.com

For Carsten
with love beyond words

'When we see the brain we realize that we are, on one level, no more than meat; and, on another, no more than fiction.'

Paul Broks, *Into the Silent Land*

WARNING

I'm not most kids. I'm Louis Drax. Stuff happens to me that shouldn't happen, like going on a picnic where you drown.

Just ask my maman what it's like being the mother of an accident-prone boy and she'll tell you. No fun. You can't sleep, wondering where it's going to end. You see danger everywhere and you think, *Got to protect him, got to protect him.* But sometimes you can't.

Maman hated me before she loved me because of the first accident. The first accident was being born. It happened the same way as the emperor Julius Caesar. They stab the lady with a knife till her belly pops, and then they yank you out, all yelling and covered in blood. They thought I wouldn't make it out in the normal way, see. (Also gross.) Plus they thought she would die from it too, like Julius Caesar's mum, and they'd have to put our dead bodies in coffins, a big one for her and a kid-size one for me. Or maybe they'd put us both in the same one, a *two-corpse* coffin and blah blah blah. I bet they make them. I bet you can order them from the Internet for mums and boys with a special bond. Being born was gross; even if you live to be a hundred years old, you and your maman don't get over something like that, but it was just the beginning. I didn't know that though, and nor did she.

The second accident was when I was a baby. I was about eight weeks old and I was lying asleep in my cot and suddenly I started getting Cot Death. *Got to protect him, got to protect him,* she went in her head. *Don't panic. Just call an ambulance.* And they told her how to de-suffocate me till they arrived and they gave me oxygen that left bruises all over my chest. She's probably still got the photos. She'll show you if you want, plus the X-rays of my cute little baby ribs, all broken and smashed. Then when I was four I had a fit where I screamed so hard I practically stopped breathing for nine and a half minutes. True story. Not even the Great Houdini could do that and he was an escape artist. He was American. Then when I was six I fell on the tracks of the métro in Lyon. I was 85 per cent electrocuted. That hardly ever happens to anyone, but it happened to me. I survived, but it was practically a miracle. Then I had food poisoning, from stuffing my face with poisoned food. Salmonella and tetanus and botulism and meningitis are just some of the diseases I've had, plus others I can't pronounce but they're in volume three of the *encyclopédie médicale*, you can read about them, they're gross.

— Having a kid like me was a nightmare for her, I tell Gustave. Gustave's an expert on nightmares because his whole life's one. — Every day, she was thinking about all the different kinds of danger, and how to keep me safe.

— You're better off here, says Gustave. — I was lonely before you came, Young Sir. Stay as long as you want. Keep me company.

I'm getting used to him, but he still scares me. His whole head's wrapped in bandages with blood on. If you saw him you'd think he was creepy too; you might even die of fright. But you might tell him things anyway, just like I'm doing. It's easier if you can't see someone's face.

The thing is, I wasn't to be trusted. Lose sight of me for a minute and I'd get myself into trouble. Everyone said having a high IQ made it worse not better.

— They say that cats have nine lives, said Maman, — because their souls cling to their bodies and won't let go. If you were a cat, Louis, you'd have used up eight of your lives by now. One for each year. We can't go on like this.

And Papa and Fat Perez agreed.

—Who's Fat Perez? says Gustave.

Fat Perez was a fat mind-reader who wasn't any good at mind-reading. Maman and Papa used to pay him to listen to me, and get to the bottom of the mystery. *The Strange Mystery of Louis Drax, the Amazing Accident-Prone Boy*. That's what Papa always called it when he was turning it into a story. But it wasn't a funny one. It was deadly serious and it drove Maman to *sheer desperation*.

Hey, Gustave. Listen to what everyone said. Everyone said that one day I was going to have a big accident, an accident to end all accidents. One day you might look up and see a kid falling from the sky.

That would be me.

Kids shouldn't make their maman cry, so that's why I went to see Fat Perez in Gratte-Ciel on Wednesdays. He lived in an apartment by the Place Frères Lumières. You might not know who the frères Lumières were. The frères Lumières were two brothers who invented the cinema, and there's a museum about them and a fountain in the square and a market where Maman went shopping for salad and tomatoes and cheese. I hated tomatoes so much I was allergic to them. And she went to the *charcutier* to buy *saucisson sec* that me and Papa secretly called donkey dick. While she was shopping, Fat Perez and me, we talked about blood and stuff.

—Whatever's on your mind, it's OK to talk about, Louis. I'm here to listen.

Quite often it was vampire bats, because I know a lot about La Planète Bleue and also Les Animaux: leur vie extraordinaire and dead people like Jacques Cousteau and Adolf Hitler and Jeanne d'Arc and the Wright brothers and different diseases and poisons. The world blood-sucking record for a vampire bat is five litres, it sucks it from a cow's neck or buttock after paralysing it with spit called *saliva*. I could tell Fat Perez anything I wanted, because it was just between the two of us and it didn't leave the room. The grosser it was, the more excited he got. His leather chair squeaked.

I always thought that if he ever stopped being all excited by my blood stories, he could just leave a tape recorder in the room with his voice on it saying Tell Me More every few minutes. Then he could go and watch Cartoon Network and spend the money on sweets.

— How many euros does it cost per time?

— That's a question to ask Maman, he says. — Or Papa.

— I'm asking you. How many per time?

— Why's it important to you?

— Because maybe I could do what you do. Earn some dosh.

He smiles his creepy fat smile.

— Would you like to help people, do you think?

That makes me laugh.

— *Help* people? I'd like to sit in a chair and say 'tell me more' and get zillions of euros for it per time, that's what I'd like, it looks like an easy life.

— Do you feel that you'd like to have an easy life, when you grow up?

— Stupid question.

— Why is it stupid, Louis?

— Because I'm not going to grow up, am I?

— What makes you think that?

Does he think I'm a total moron? Does he think I come from the planet Pluto or somewhere humans don't have brains?

— Second stupid question.

— I'm sorry if you think it's a stupid question Louis. But I'm still interested in your answer, he says, with his fat face. — So. What makes you think you won't grow up, Louis?

Don't say anything, don't say anything, don't say anything.

Fat Perez was my biggest enemy but he never scared me the

4

way Gustave does. Gustave'd scare you too, if you met him. Because underneath the bandages he hasn't got a face and sometimes he coughs so hard it turns into being sick and sometimes I think I'm making him up just for someone to talk to. But if I am, I don't know how to stop because if someone's living in your head, how do you get them out?

You can't, is how. You can't, because that's where they live.

There are laws and you go to prison if you break them but there are secret rules too, so secret no one ever talks about them. Here's a secret rule of pet-keeping. If you own a small creature, say a hamster called Mohammed, and he lives for longer than a small rodent's lifespan, which is two years, then you're allowed to kill him if you want to, because you're his owner. This secret rule of pet-keeping has a name, it's called *Right of Disposal*. You're allowed to do it with suffocation, or with poison if you have any, say weedkiller. Or you can drop something heavy on him, like volume three of the *encyclopédie médicale* or *Harry Potter et l'Ordre du Phénix*. Just as long as you don't make a mess.

Visiting Fat Perez was Papa's idea, but it was Maman's headache because she was the one who had to take me there. Papa was busy working up in the clouds, saying *cabin crew, fifteen minutes to landing*, *doors to manual* and studying pressure maps and going on a people-skills course because –

Actually I don't know why. I don't know what a people-skills course is.

Fat Perez's apartment was on the rue Malesherbes in Gratte-Ciel. First you rang the bell and he buzzed you in and there was a stink of *bouillabaisse* on the way to the lift, or sometimes green beans, and you had to go up four floors in a creaky old lift, and you needed to pee every time you got in. Fat Perez said it was about feeling trapped.

— You suffer from mild claustrophobia, he says. — It's not abnormal, it happens to lots of kids and some grown-ups too, this need to relieve your bladder in confined spaces. Just try to hold on.

But every Wednesday I still had to rush to pee as soon as we were in Fat Perez's creepy apartment. The bladder is like a balloon. It's a *muscular bag*, but it pops if you hold on too long, trust me. Before I flushed the toilet I sometimes went out and put my ear to the door of his living room to hear what they were saying about me. Sometimes they'd be arguing, like they were married. But I could never hear the words properly, even using the glass he keeps his toothbrush in that's always got gross green gunk at the bottom.

If you pay someone, they shouldn't argue with you.

When I came out, she'd say, See you later, Louis darling, I'll do my shopping. And then she'd leave so that me and Fat Perez could have our little conversation that cost a whole lot of euros from the cash machine that came from Papa being in the cockpit. Sometimes the stewardess brings him coffee while he is flying. Or sometimes tea but never beer or cognac.

— How's life been treating you then, Louis? goes Fat Perez.

— Papa could get sacked from Air France if he drank beer or cognac.

Fat Perez is old, probably forty, and he has a big fat face like a baby. If you had a pin you could burst it, and yellow gob would splatter out.

— Yes. I believe that's true. Or any alcoholic drink for that matter. They have strict rules for pilots, says Fat Perez. — Now my question, Louis.

Question One is always the question about *how life is treating me*. But sometimes he doesn't ask it, he just waits for me to start but that never works because of the secret rule, called Don't Say Anything, so we just sit there till he can't stand it any longer. I'm much more patient than Fat Perez, because five minutes is the longest he can do before his chair squeaks, and he doesn't know the secret rule because I invented it. When he asks me Question One, if I'm not playing Don't Say Anything, I might tell him Everything's perfect, thank you, Monsieur Perez. Is your diet going well? Or I might make up a story about school, about fights and stuff. Sometimes there's a real thing that happened to someone else, but I tell him it was me. He's such a sucker, because he always believes me or if he doesn't, he pretends to. Pretending makes him even more of a sucker. It makes him a double sucker. Watch this.

— Today I got attacked ultra-violently, I go.

Squeak. — Tell me more.

— In Carpentry. I was making this spiral staircase out of balsa wood, a scaled-down model. Then along came the bullies, eight of them, saying Wacko Boy, Wacko Boy, Wacko Boy. They were all carrying hammers, but one of them, the biggest bully, he had a fretsaw too. He grabbed me by the neck and forced my head into the vice. And then they all got their hammers and started bashing nails into my skull.

— Ouch, says Fat Perez. *Squeak.*

What a creep. What a sucker. We don't even have Carpentry, that's from the old days when Papa was at school. We have IT instead, that's much more useful because you can learn to be a hacker.

— It hurt like hell. And he was just about to saw my head off when the teacher came along. Monsieur Zidane. He's a football champion too. But the worst thing was, it was me he punished. True story.

— Why did he punish you, and not the bullies? asks Fat Perez. — Out of interest.

— Cos bullies always win, and cos my blood made a mess. Football champions don't like clearing up other people's messes, when they've won zillions of trophies and the World Cup. When I got my head out of the vice, I left a trail of blood all down the corridor and into the toilets. Green blood. That pissed him off.

— Why green?

— Because I have leukaemia, and the chemotherapy turns your blood green. Didn't you know that? I thought you were trained.

— Green blood. Leukaemia. Fascinating! Tell me more, he goes. *Squeak.*

He should be called Monsieur Tell Me More instead of Fat Perez. Or Monsieur Stupid Creep Sucker Arsehole.

Anyway I can say anything I want, because all feelings are allowed. Children should feel free to express their feelings even if they are negative. The world is a safe place, blah blah blah.

Ha ha, only joking.

Now pay attention, Fat Perez. My turn to ask questions.

Question One: Does my mum visit you on her own, when I'm at school?

Question Two: When she's telling you things about her and my papa, does your chair squeak?

Question Three: Afterwards, do you sex each other?

And if he was there when I asked that, his chair would go: *Squeak, squeak, squeak.* And if Gustave was there he'd say: *Steady on, Young Sir. Don't waste energy. Keep your eye on the ball.*

— We're going to do something wonderful this weekend, she says. — For our birthday treat.

We've got almost the same birthday, see, just like we nearly had the same death-day when I was born. My birthday is on 7 April, just two days after hers, so we're sort of twins her and me, we need each other, we'd die without each other. So we celebrate them together, on the day in between. I'm nine, and she's forty, which is called The Big Four-Oh. Papa comes down from Paris, where he sort of lives now, with his evil mother called Lucille, and I get lots of presents, and one of them's a new hamster. He's called Mohammed, just like the last one, and he'll live in the same cage and poo in the same jam jar as the last Mohammed. I always call them Mohammed because it's a good name for a hamster, Papa says it's a dynasty.

Mohammed the Third came with a book called *How to Look After Your Small Rodent.*

— Let's hope this one lasts a bit longer, said Papa. — You can take him with you to Paris, when you come to see me and Mamie.

But Maman gave him a funny look because Paris is a bad place.

He's a pale hamster, his fur's paler than the last one and his eyes aren't black, they're dark red, like they're bulging with blood. Maybe because he's scared. The Mohammeds are always scared till they've spent a week in their cage and started to learn the secret rules of pet-keeping. Papa calls their cage Alcatraz, which is a film about a prison where they escaped and blah blah blah.

For Maman's birthday present, I gave her some perfume called Aura that totally reeked, it was worse than cat pee and a dead rat. Papa bought it at the airport for me to give her. He gets a discount. So it was a present from me but I didn't choose it and I didn't pay for it and I didn't get the discount, I just had the thought.

— What a nice thought, said Maman, when she sprayed it behind her ears, and she hugged me and hugged me and kissed me and kissed me, and I could hardly breathe I was coughing so much from it.

It's the thought that counts.

In a year's time I will be The Big One-Oh.

I didn't tell her I didn't actually have the thought, even. I'd forgotten it was her birthday because I was so excited about mine and getting Mohammed the Third. Papa reminded me on the phone and told me to make a card but I was doing a Lego model of a rocket-launcher plus space capsule and I forgot about the card so in the end I just signed Papa's when he came in his new car that's a Volkswagen Passat. I used black wax crayon, which is for vampire bats and death stuff and the swastika.

My maman's very fragile like glass because her life's been very hard, Papa says. That's why she gets headaches and she cries and sometimes screams at me and then says sorry and cries more and hugs me and hugs me and kisses me and kisses me. But Papa's not fragile. He's one of the strongest men in the world. If you met him, he might punch you in the face and give you a bad headache called concussion. He's good at hitting, he could've been a boxer but he wouldn't ever fight dirty, like the man who killed the Great Houdini by punching him in the stomach before he got his muscles ready. Papa works on his muscles at the gym; Pectoral and Abdominal are just two of them but he's got others too, more than most dads. He could be a Killing Machine if he did the training. He just hasn't got time to do the training, that's all. He's too busy flying aeroplanes. It's a desk job, he says. The cockpit is a glorified desk. It's a frustrating life, not as glamorous as you think, *mon petit loup*.

Plus you have to be careful about how you drink beer and cognac, you have to do it in secret because nobody's allowed to know, especially if you've been drinking more ever since Disneyland Resort Paris and you've gone all weird and angry with your wife and your son who are *innocent victims of your frustration and shouldn't be blamed for things that aren't their fault because they're no one's fault but your own and you need to face up to it.*

— We're all going away for the weekend, says Maman. — Out of Lyon, into the countryside. We'll go for a lovely spring picnic down in the Auvergne, you and me and Papa, we'll be a family again.

All smiley with lipstick that's pink.

Papa used to fly on international routes but now he just flies domestically. It's better to fly domestically because that way you don't jeopardise your family life, that's the most precious thing in the world. The birthday card I got, it said: To Our Darling Son. And the one him and me gave her, it said: To a Wonderful Mother. When she read it she did something sideways and twitchy with her mouth and she looked at Papa with a weird face and she said, I suppose Lucille chose this? And she put it next to the card from her maman who sent me one too but I've never met her cos Guadeloupe is far away where they grow mangoes and exotic fruit and blah blah blah.

— There's a wild flower up there, you can find it in the mountains, near Ponteyrol, she says. — It's called Spring Glory and it flowers in April. We can pick some.

— What for?

— To put in a vase. And to give to people, she says — Friends. And she smiles again.

Maman's friends keep changing. They keep changing because one day they have a Major Disagreement, and the Major Disagreement is always about me and she has to fire them because she's on my side, defending me from spiteful people who ask mean questions and say I'm Wacko Boy. That's what mums are for but it's very Isolating. My papa has colleagues. They're other Air France pilots and beautiful stewardesses from other airlines that are rival airlines. And maybe people from the gym. But I bet they think flowers suck. I bet they've never heard of Spring Glory. I've never heard of Spring Glory. Have you heard of Spring Glory?

Oh yeah? What colour is it then?

See? No one's heard of it. She made it up, to get us out of the apartment. She does that sometimes because she gets all cooped up. Mothers need air and space and freedom. They're like birds, if you keep them in a cage they go mad. It isn't just dads that need to fly. Plus they've been arguing on the phone.

— All your fault!

— My fault? Did you say *my* fault?

And she's trying to make everything all right again. That's what women do. *They do Emotional Work.* If they don't do Emotional Work he might stay away for ever and drink beer and cognac in bars and plot how to destroy our family with his evil mother called Lucille, who sent me a birthday card with fifty euros in it and a photo of her and Papa when he was a boy with their dog called Youqui who got run over by a tractor. His legs were paralysed so they had to do Mercy Killing. That's a bit like Right of Disposal but the rules are less fun.

— Now let's see, goes Maman. — I've packed the suitcase. We're spending Saturday night in a hotel near Vichy, then we'll drive back to Lyon on Sunday night. Papa's got the whole weekend off, so we're having a bit of a treat. Now, picnic hamper, thermos . . .

The picnic things all look brand new, maybe it's part of Emotional Work. I've never seen this stuff before, plastic plates and cups and knives and forks, because we've never gone on a picnic before. I've been on picnics, but not with them. With school. On school trips. If you drop litter you have to go back and pick it up. The teachers get you to sing stupid songs and on the way back, someone pukes in the coach. I see what's in the hamper when she puts it in the car boot. I lift the lid of the freezer-box and there's the food, all wrapped in cling film that's dangerous for children because if you stretch it over your face you look cool like a mega-violent criminal but then you suffocate and die. There's *pâté* and *saucisson sec* secretly called donkey dick, and Camembert and grapes and a birthday cake from Pâtisserie Charles. Papa comes and looks too.

— You've really gone to town, Natalie, he says.

And that's what I think too but I don't say anything.

— You're only forty once, says Maman.

Donkey dick, says Papa secretly to me, but not aloud, just moving his mouth.

— Can I bring Mohammed? I go.

— No, *chéri*, says Maman. — Sorry. Out of the question.

But Papa says, Why not, just as long as he stays in Alcatraz, so Mohammed goes in the car too, in the boot with the food even though it's OK to leave him for as long as ten days because he's a low-maintenance pet. And hey, just look at us, we're being a family again, with a mum and a dad and a hamster. And Maman slams the door of the boot and we get in the Volkswagen Passat that has a six-stack CD player and a sunroof and Papa puts on his sunglasses that make him look cool like a gangster, and clicks his seatbelt and starts the car, zzhhmm, and turns and smiles at us, and says 'let's hit the road', like nothing's wrong, like they might love each other again, like there isn't going to be a man in bandages who hasn't got a face, and like nothing terrible's going to happen.

Little boys love sea monsters. If I had a son, I'd take him to see the giant squid that's just arrived in Paris, fifteen metres long and pickled in formaldehyde. I saw a photo in *Nouvel Observateur*: a tubular body with suckered tentacles trailing balletically behind. It made me think of an orchid, or a slender, grasping sea anemone loosed from its moorings and wandering fathoms deep, lost and racked by doubt. The Latin name is *architeuthis*. In years gone by they were dismissed as a sailors' myth, the product of too much time spent on too much ocean, salt-water madness. But now, global warming has blessed the giant squid; its population has gone berserk, and proof of its existence is daily flotsam on foreign shores. Its eyes are the size of dinner plates.

If I had a son –

But I don't. Only grown-up daughters. Sophisticated young women with mobile phones, who have little time for freaks of nature. They're both students in Montpellier. I'd have taken them to see underwater monsters, if they'd shown the inclination. But boys are different. A boy has all the time in the world for a giant squid.

Louis Drax would have loved to see one, I'm sure of it. He kept pet hamsters, but he hankered after more threatening creatures: tarantulas, iguanas, snakes, bats – gothic animals with spikes, scales, scary fur, a potential for destruction. His favourite reading was a lavishly illustrated children's book called *Les Animaux: leur vie extraordinaire*. He knew much of the text by heart.

He had a vivid, eccentric imagination, according to his mother, Natalie Drax. A 'reality problem', was how his psychologist, Marcel Perez, put it in his statement to the police. Louis was a dreamer, a loner. He had difficulty distinguishing fact from fiction. Like a lot of highly intelligent, articulate children, he did badly at school because he was bored out of his mind. He was small for his age, with deep, dark eyes that penetrated you somehow. That's what everyone said. *A weird kid. A remarkable kid. Unbelievably intelligent.* Reading between the lines, you also got the impression that the same people might have added, privately, that he could also be a 'typical only child' – code for spoiled brat. But after what happened, no one dared to speak ill of Louis, whatever reservations they may have had about him.

I have a feeling that the nine-year-old Louis Drax and I would have got on, if we'd met. We'd have discussed curious phenomena of the natural world, and maybe I'd have taught him a few card games: poker, *vingt-et-un*, gin rummy. I was an only child too; we had that in common. I'd have shown him my phrenological chart and waxed poetic on the workings of the human brain. Explained how different parts of it govern different impulses. How jokes and tongue-twisters come from a different place from algebra and map-reading. He'd have liked that. Yes, I'm quite sure he'd have liked that.

But that wasn't going to happen. Things got blown off track for both of us, and now – Let's just say, I see no party balloons on the horizon.

Everyone rewrites history. I've certainly been trying to. My favourite version of Louis' story is the one in which I did the right thing every time, and had the intuition to sense what was really going on. But it's not the truth. The truth is that I was blind, and I was blind because I deliberately closed my eyes to what was there.

Fine weather and death should never go together. But on the day of Louis' final accident, they did: it happened on a lovely afternoon in early April in the mountains of the Auvergne. Cool but with a bright sun. It's wild, extravagantly rugged country, much favoured by speleologists, who come to explore and chart the underground cave systems made by earthquakes and volcanic disturbances millennia ago; deep rifts and fissures that stretch for miles, puckering the earth's crust like scar tissue. The picnic site, near the town of Ponteyrol, was a sheltered spot on a mountainside, scented with wild thyme. I suspect that even the *gendarmes*, busy with photographs and maps, couldn't help noticing how seductive their surroundings were. The roar of the ravine far below is soothing rather than menacing. You could be lulled to sleep by the rush of those waters. Some of the *gendarmes* may even have thought of returning here with their families, one summer Sunday in the future – though they would not have mentioned how they came to know the place, or spoken of the catastrophe that occurred there.

After the accident, the boy's mother was far too distraught to make a proper statement, but as soon as they got the gist of what had happened, the police called for urgent back-up to hunt for the missing father. Then Madame Drax was sedated and the ambulance crew bore her off, along with the wrecked body of her son. She wouldn't let go of his hand. It was still soft, but extremely cold, like refrigerated dough. He had fallen to the bottom of the ravine, where the fast-flowing water had gulped him down, then regurgitated him on an outcrop of stone a little way downstream. That's where they found his drowned body, soaked through by freezing spray. They went through the motions of reviving him, pumping the water out of his lungs and attempting resuscitation. But it was pointless. He was dead.

I have often wondered what Madame Drax felt, when they winched the boy up and she saw the hopeless flop of his wet limbs, the stark whiteness of his skin. What was going through her poor mind? Apparently she screamed again and again, then howled like a wounded animal, barely stopping for breath. They managed to calm her eventually. A storm was beginning to gather; as the ambulance drew away, grey bloated rain-clouds were marshalling themselves on the horizon.

In the ambulance, Natalie Drax became silent, almost composed, according to the policewoman who was with her. I am sure that at this point, as she gripped her son's dead hand, she must have prayed. Everyone becomes a believer in a crisis, calling on a God with whom to cut a last-ditch deal. She'd have prayed that time could be reversed, that this day had never dawned, that all their choices had been otherwise, that all the words that had spilled from them could be unsaid, that the whole episode could rewind and stall. I also believe that on some level Madame Drax must have blamed herself, even then, for what became of Louis. She must have seen it coming. She, of all people, knew what was going on, where Louis was headed, the danger he was in. She had done her best to prevent the inevitable from happening – and perhaps even managed to delay it a little. But she was unable to stop it.

At the hospital, the urgency of making a statement got through to her, briefly, before the drugs sucked her into an artificially deep and dreamless sleep. She told the police what had happened in more detail, in a dead voice that might have come from a machine. And in the same dead voice, she answered all their questions. She was the only remaining witness to the event. The family who found her, screaming, in the road, arrived ten minutes after Louis' fatal plunge down towards the ravine and his father's subsequent disappearance. It was they who had rung the police.

By then the storm had split the sky, unleashing ugly gouts of thunder that crescendoed across the mountains. The lashing rain soon became so relentless that cars pulled in at the roadside, waiting for the worst to pass. In retrospect, it seemed an extraordinary quirk of chance that the ambulance crew managed to reach Louis' body when it did. Two hours later the torrential downpour would have made any attempt impossible; by the time night fell, the police were forced to leave the mountainside altogether.

The next morning, the storm had blown over and the sky was blue again, rinsed of violence. Returning to take more photographs and widen the search, the police retrieved the Draxs' abandoned car, a brand-new Volkswagen Passat parked half a kilometre up the road from the picnic spot; in the boot was a live hamster in a cage, running madly on its little treadmill. They removed the now soaking rug, the picnic hamper, and the rest of the detritus from the picnic area: plates, knives and forks, a thermos of coffee, half a bottle of white wine, three unopened cans of Coke, some sodden napkins and – oddly – a blister packet of contraceptive pills, midway through the cycle. What they missed, I imagine nature would have claimed swiftly enough. Ants would march in determined lines to carry off what the rain had not swept away: tiny grains of sugar and salt, soggy fragments of crisps. Squirrels would discover the peanuts, wasps would buzz angrily over half-dissolved cake-crumbs and flakes of icing. Despite a rigorous search, which included sending frogmen down into the swollen ravine, and checking several kilometres of river downstream, the police could find no trace of the boy's father, Pierre Drax. It seemed that he had simply vanished from the face of the earth, as though swallowed and digested by its volcanic crust.

The fact is that only the three people involved in the tragedy knew what happened on the mountainside that day. Of those, one could never know the full truth. One was hiding from it. And the third was dead. That's how it was. And if it had not been for a miracle, that's how it would have stayed.

There are many beginnings to Louis Drax's story, but the day of his death at the ravine was the point where our existences began, invisibly, to mesh. I later came to see it as the day that marked the start of my ruin, and the probable end of my career. I nearly said 'life'; bizarre, how I can still confuse the two, even after all I've learned. Hospitals – medical environments of any kind – are the strangest places on earth, crammed with miracles, horror, and banality: birth, pain, grief, vending machines, death, blood, administrative memos. Yet for a doctor it's so easy to feel at home in them, more at home sometimes than in your own home, if they are your livelihood and your passion and your reason for –

Well. Until one day something happens, and a man like me comes to realise there is a world beyond the clinic where he works, a whole alternative reality to the one he has lived and breathed for all these years, a reality whose toxic logic can send a man hurtling to the brink, destroying everything he's worked for, respected, valued, cared for, earned, loved. That's when life begins to go awry. Put a magnet to a compass and it loses its grip; it spins and jolts and abandons its allegiance to north. That's what happened to me. When the Drax case came along, it's as if a magnet came and skewed my compass, forcing conventional morality to jump ship. You could try and write it up in the normal way but you'd get stuck. I know, because I've attempted it. It starts simply.

The patient, a nine-year-old male, was pronounced dead on arrival at Vichy Accident and Emergency unit, following a series of catastrophic insults to the cranium and upper body caused by a fall, then drowning. The body was taken to the morgue in preparation for the post-mortem . . .

So far, so normal. But then –

The same night, at eleven p.m. . . .

That's when it stops making sense. It's a simple enough scenario. The boy's stone dead on the slab in the morgue in Vichy

General Hospital, the name-tag round his ankle. The thunder's still crashing outside, with sheet lightning illuminating the sky every few minutes. His heavily sedated mother, Natalie Drax, has been settled in a ward on the second floor, and placed under observation; she is judged to be potentially suicidal.

One of the morgue technicians – his name's Frédéric Leclerc – is cleaning his utensils in a corner; he's about to come off shift. But then he hears a noise. Not thunder, he's sure of that immediately. It's indoors, and it's human; he describes it as 'a hiccup'. So he turns round on his heel, and what does he see but the kid's chest moving. A kind of spasm. Frédéric's only young, hasn't been in the job long. But he knows it's long past the stage where a corpse can have muscle reflexes. To his credit, he doesn't panic – even though he must feel he's in some B horror-movie. He rings upstairs straight away, and they mobilise the resuscitation unit.

But when they arrive, the child doesn't even seem to need it. His heart's beating quite normally, and he's breathing, though it's laboured. So they take him back up to Emergency to identify the broken bones and assess the internal damage. They have to take his spleen out. One of the splintered ribs is threatening the left lung, so they have to manage that, while investigating the skull fractures and working out an intervention strategy. It's looking pretty dismal. But he's alive.

Philippe Meunier, who signed the death certificate, is hauled back in to assess the cranial injuries. I went to medical school with Philippe, where we began as friends. Later, when we both opted for neurology, a certain rivalry developed. He's on the circuit, so we bump into each other once in a while at conferences, where we speak with a hearty brusqueness and mask our latent aggression by slapping one another on the back slightly too hard. We've had our clashes but I'll say this for Philippe: he's a good, thorough clinician. Time being of the essence, he acts quickly to reduce the oedemic process that's started. The scan shows that the injury to the cerebrum is serious, but the brain-stem is intact. The real danger from head injuries comes from swelling, because the skull is a box that keeps the brain trapped. With ventilation and steroids, Philippe reduces the pressure swiftly enough. But the child's still unconscious, hovering between four and five on the Glasgow Coma Scale.

You can't call Louis' return to life a miracle; we're not supposed to talk about them in our profession. A medical screw-up is closer to the truth. But to be honest, my heart went out to Philippe Meunier. Drowning and hypothermia can resemble death, in very rare paediatric cases. Searching for some euphemistic phrase to paper over the cracks, one might perhaps call it an 'unexpected event', or 'the result of a previous misdiagnosis', or even 'a rare phenomenon'. But the bottom line is that the boy came back to life, two hours after being pronounced officially dead. And no one on earth – to this day – knows exactly why. No need to go into how bad it's going to be for the doctors involved – and Philippe wasn't the only one – on the blame front. They're all going crazy, of course. There's a basic reservoir of paranoia in any hospital: that day in Vichy, it burst its banks.

Anyway, someone has to break the news to the mother. But they decide not to – at least, not right away. They don't see any point in waking her, in case the boy dies a second time – a distinct possibility, given the extent of his cranial injuries. This case has 'bad outcome' written all over it. But when she wakes up, a few hours later, wanting to be with the body, he's still in the land of the living – though only just – and they can't delay it any longer. *It seems, Madame, that your son is in fact alive. In rare cases, it's not totally unheard of for . . . We don't completely understand how it . . .* She's wild, overjoyed, tearful, confused – everything at once. Totally overloaded. She's been to hell, thinking her son's dead. The next thing she knows, the doctor's telling her he's a mini Lazarus. She's woken from the worst nightmare of her life.

Or not. Because the son-coming-back-to-life part is the good news. The bad news is that he's possibly going to be what in common parlance is termed 'a vegetable'. At which point Natalie Drax goes very pale and very quiet. I can imagine her state of mind. She'd prayed for a miracle in the ambulance, prayed to a God she'd given up on long ago, never really believed in. And now here, as requested . . .

It's unthinkable. She shudders and blinks.

Despite the refunctioning of his lungs and vital organs, the patient did not regain consciousness, though his condition stabilised and improved. He remained in a comatose state in Dr Philippe Meunier's neurological unit in Vichy for three months, until a sudden fit caused his condition to deteriorate considerably. At this point, according to the normal procedure, his transfer to the Clinique de l'Horizon in Provence was approved.

On 10 July, he arrived as my patient in deep coma . . .

A Portuguese artist's reworking of the Gall/Spurzheim phrenological map hangs on the wall of my office, above the table where I keep my bonsais. With deft brush strokes the artist has transmogrified the skull into a piece of natural architecture, a set of juxtaposed compartments all labelled according to phrenology's vision of the mind's contents: secretiveness, benevolence, hope, self-esteem, time, continuity, parental love, eventuality and so on. Nonsense, but so much more poetic, somehow, than the real structure of the brain, with its interlocking meat-chambers: the frontal, temporal, parietal, occipital lobes, the putamen, the pallidus, the thalamus, the fornix and the caudate. I remember glancing up at my phrenological map on the morning Louis Drax was due to arrive, as though it might hold a clue.

But look, before I plunge further into the story of Louis, let me tell you that I was a different man then. For all my professional success and for all the insight I believed I possessed, I was living on the surface of life. I thought I had seen its innards, taken its pulse, got an idea of its hidden workings. But I hadn't really seen within. Had not yet marvelled. Put it this way: I was a man doing a job I loved – perhaps too much, too intensely – but I had my failings too, my tendencies and my traits and my blind spots or whatever a psychologist would call them. I won't apologise for myself. The fact is that during the terrible summer when the world cracked open, I was who I was.

The day Louis Drax arrived at the clinic began on a bad note, domestically. It was a close, rain-starved July, one of the hottest on record in Provence; every day the temperature soared as high as the forties and the radio and TV blared fresh warnings of forest fires. It seemed that the arson season was starting early. As I sat out on the balcony finishing breakfast in the morning sunshine and skimming the previous day's *Le Monde*, crashing noises came from the kitchen. When I've committed any kind of marital transgression, Sophie has the habit of unloading the dishwasher in a particularly cacophonous way. I knew better than to stir things up further, so at eight o'clock I prepared to leave for the clinic without giving her my usual kiss goodbye. But as I was closing the front door behind me, she flung open the kitchen window and stuck out her head like a cuckoo from a Swiss clock. She'd washed her hair and was dripping water.

— So, am I to expect you home for dinner at eight, or will I once again have the fun of cooking something only to sit on my own and watch it go cold for an hour?

Sophie was referring to the previous evening, when I had returned home to find her sprawled on the sofa, red-eyed, and flanked by greetings cards from the girls, her sister and her mother, wishing us both a happy twenty-third anniversary – an occasion I had totally forgotten, despite the fact that our eldest daughter, Oriane, had rung me the previous week to remind me to 'do something romantic with Maman'. Not only had I failed to do anything romantic, but I had added insult to injury by coming home from work late – dismally, shockingly late, even by my own standards. I'd been recounting the content of an editorial in the *United States Journal of Neurology* to my patients and lost track of time.

— It's just so humiliating! Can't you show just a *shred* of romance? Sophie had wailed, as she cleared away the uneaten dinner she'd prepared. — I'm beginning to wonder why we don't just go our separate ways, Pascal. You'd rather lecture comatose people about neurological theory than have a conversation with your own wife. Look at the two of us, rattling around in this big empty house like a couple of . . . I don't know. *Pointless marbles.*

Sophie never shies away from reality, and I recognised she had struck a note of truth. I felt bad, and said so – but my apologies fell on stony ground. It wasn't an easy time in our marriage. Once upon a time we had been happy. We had children early, made a good family. Then . . . well. A typical marriage perhaps: radiant moments, small losses of faith, nagging doubts, resurgences, complacency. For the last few months the public library in Layrac, which Sophie ran with characteristic zeal, had been threatened with cutbacks. With both our daughters now installed at the *fac* in Montpellier, Sophie was feeling frustrated and unfulfilled.

I loved my wife, as far as I knew. But how far *did* I know? The empty nest had highlighted a lack, not just for her, but for me too. Emotional and physical. (Why is it so hard, I wondered, for a woman to grasp that a man needs the comfort of a female body from time to time? That it's unfair to make a man sleep alone every time he rattles her cage?) That burning summer, even before the arrival of Louis Drax, things seemed to be spiralling downward.

My walk to work takes five minutes, door to door. A light morning mist hung in the bright air, with something feral in its scent, as when the hunting season is in full spate. *Life*, I thought. It smells of life. I love breathing in that mixture of pine resin and sea salt. It stirs the brain, puts the turbulences of marriage in perspective. Sophie was always mollified by flowers, especially if they came in the form of a highly expensive bouquet with cellophane and ribbons, so as I made my way to work through the olive groves, I resolved to drop in at the village florist's on the way back from work and make us both feel better. As the clinic came into view up ahead, stark white and bright in the sun, bleached concrete and stainless steel grafted on to the nineteenth-century stone shell of the former Hôpital des Incurables, my heart lifted. By the time the automatic doors slid open to welcome me and I inhaled the first gush of chilled air, I was on a high.

Part of my excitement was about the new patient they were bringing me. It may sound strange to say this about somebody who appears to be irredeemably comatose, but I was looking forward to meeting the Drax boy. I don't read the home pages of the paper closely, so I knew nothing about his accident at that stage, but I'd certainly heard about his bizarre return to life on the medical grapevine, though swift PR work in Vichy had ensured that part of the story never reached the papers. Hiccuping corpses don't do a hospital's image any favours. Given his medical history, I was intrigued about the state I'd find the boy in. Might I be the one to discover a sign of hope, where others – Philippe Meunier in particular – had failed? In my field, you can't help fantasising about trouncing everyone's expectations by producing an unexpected recovery. I spend much of my time doing just that.

I'm an optimist, when it comes to coma. These people are capable of more than it appears. Those who awake – often in an agonisingly slow, incomplete way – can occasionally recall intensely lucid dreams, almost like hallucinations: long, involved fantasies about people they could never have known or met in real life; scenarios so much more vividly alive and compelling than the dim, humdrum noises that filter through to them from the ward. There have even been cases – rare, I will admit, and much-disputed – of a comatose twin telepathically communicating with his identical sibling or a mother 'hearing' the voice of her unconscious child, clearly, in her head. Not all brain activity can be picked up by a machine. We fool ourselves if we think it can be.

So I had my usual optimism when it came to Louis Drax, though when I read his notes in more detail, I must admit that my heart sank a little. He'd had a fit the week before, which had led to his transfer here. According to the latest electroencephalograms, the episode had plunged him into a deeper coma than before, with a diagnosis of Persistent Vegetative State not far off on the horizon. What usually happens to PVS patients is that when they come down with something – it tends to be pneumonia – a doctor like me – in consultation with the relatives – lets nature take its course. It's not unheard of for a patient to emerge from a coma that deep, but nobody holds their breath.

All morning, in my office, I listened out for the crunch of gravel on the driveway, while Noelle buzzed in and out with letters to sign, reminders of appointments, and a fresh memo from the *directeur*, Guy Vaudin, about evacuation procedures in case of a fire threat. Eric Masserot – the father of my anorexic, Isabelle – was arriving later, and I would need to make time for him. A detective with an odd surname had called and would ring back. If I wanted to order new equipment for the physio unit, I must liaise with the new physiotherapist by Thursday at the latest. Had I prepared my talk and my slides for the symposium in Lyon next week? I replied to Noelle's various questions and signed her bits of paper, but my mind stayed on the Drax boy.

It was late morning when the ambulance rolled up the drive. By now the static weather had shifted into something more restless, with the air growing blustery beneath a cobalt sky, making the olive leaves shiver like shoals of fish, dizzy and capricious. There are times when the mistral can drive you mad. Times when it does not fan you, but merely churns the hot air. Today's wind had menace in it, the same menace van Gogh painted over the cornfield the day before he took his life, the kind that starts outside but lodges in your head as soon as you feel its breath. They wheeled him in on a trolley. Age, nine.

Condition, very poor. White-clad nurses on either side, one of them carrying a stuffed toy. And in his wake, the mother, who immediately impressed me with the way she held her small, upright body. Something about her carriage and the tilt of her head announced, 'proud victim'. Madame Drax was petite, with pale hair that hovered somewhere between red and blonde. Her features – fine and delicately scattered with freckles – were too unremarkable to make her striking at first sight, but she had an allure. Something cat-like. As for the child –

The poor boy.

His hair and lashes were dark, but his face was deathly pale. He might have been cast from wax. There was something almost luminous about his skin, which brought to mind those stone carvings of the dead you see in churches, with their tiny, perfect hands and feet, their dreamily closed eyes. His breathing was so shallow that you could barely make out the influx and exhalation of air.

All I knew at that point was that back in April, Louis Drax had technically died as a result of a fall, but that somehow he'd returned from the dead – or at least from a shocking misdiagnosis. Either way, it was so bizarre that it bordered on the grotesque. A medically unusual case, then, with a dismal prognosis in the wake of his fit, according to the notes I'd just read. One to store in one's mental scrapbook perhaps, not much more to me. But I was a different man then. I knew nothing.

And so the man who knew nothing introduced himself to Madame Drax and told her that his job was to do everything he could for her son. And that it was a pleasure to meet her. The first contact is important. I needed this woman's trust if I was to help Louis.

She told me it was a great relief to be here. She had a Parisian accent, and a small catch in her voice. The smile she gave me in return was no more than a twitch. She was wearing a fragrance that I didn't recognise. The hand she gave me to shake felt almost boneless, as though her skeleton had dissolved. What this woman

27

must have suffered didn't bear thinking about. Post-traumatic stress can take many forms. She bore the look of stunned dignity one so often sees on the faces of agonised relatives.

— The pleasure's all mine, Madame. Louis is most welcome here. As you see, this is an open ward. Nine beds are filled at present . . . .

As I spoke, I watched her. I am used to studying faces. There is always the potential for both beauty and ugliness, depending on the emotional currents that swarm beneath. Beneath the mask Madame Drax presented to the world, I imagined the loneliness of unresolved and unresolvable grief – and yes, the shame, too, for pain is alienating – that so many parents suffer in such circumstances.

— He was in a stable coma for nearly three months, she tells me, as we look at the boy's sleeping face, framed by white pillow, white linen, a pure white gown. Tucked beneath his armpit is a toy – a moose, its fur matted with ancient spit. — Then a week ago, he unexpectedly . . . that's why we –

She stops: it seems there is no 'we' any more. No ring on her finger, but a lighter band of skin where it once was.

— That's why Louis and I came here. To you. Dr Meunier recommended you highly.

Our eyes meet. Hers are a pale greenish hazel, the colour of a Provençal hillside after winter rain. Clear and young. It pains me that she seems to be facing this alone, and I feel an urgent need to know why.

— And your husband, is he . . . ?

She looks at me in panic and alarm, and a nervous tic suddenly ratchets away at the corner of her mouth. — You mean you haven't heard about Pierre? About how Louis came to be in a coma? she asks, flustered. — Didn't they . . .

— I've read the medical notes, Madame, of course. Rest assured.

My voice is calm, but I feel a little unsettled. Have I missed something?

28

— But how it happened, the full story . . . you're *not aware?* The police haven't . . . ?

— I believe there was a call from a detective this morning, I said quickly, suddenly remembering something Noelle had mentioned. But I could sense something – was it anger? – boiling up in her. — A fall, I gather? Into a ravine?

But I have triggered an excruciating memory: her face tightens again, and more tears well up. She fumbles in her handbag for a tissue and turns away.

— Forgive me, Madame. I am assuming she will elaborate at this point, but she does not. Instead she smudges at her eyes with the tissue, then all of a sudden blinks, pulls herself together, and changes gear, telling me that she has rented a cottage in the village, on rue de l'Angelus, and wants to start participating in Louis' treatment. What can she do? Can she spend as much time as she wants with him? The cleaning-woman, Fatima, begins to mop the floor by our feet; we shift a little. I explain that she needs to take it easy, and let her son settle. She, too, must settle. All too often, patients' relatives neglect themselves – which doesn't help anyone. She needs to feel as well and happy as she can.

— Is there any activity you particularly enjoy? Something you took pleasure in before the accident?

— I have lots of photographs of Louis. I've been meaning to sort them into albums for years.

— Perfect. And you can show them around. You'll make friends here quickly, among the other relatives.

She looks uneasy. — I haven't really spoken to many people since –

The image of Louis' calamitous accident hangs in the air between us.

— Time to start then, wouldn't you say?

— Yes, I suppose so. It's been very isolating, the whole thing.

— You have family? Friends?

— My mother lives in Guadeloupe. She's been meaning to come over, but my stepfather's very ill with Parkinson's.

— And there's no one else?

— Not really. I have a sister, but we don't see each other. We fell out a long time ago. There is a short silence as we both ponder this. I would like to ask the reason for the estrangement, and for her husband's absence, but don't want to appear tactless.

— Dr Meunier said you had a radical approach. I was glad to hear that, Dr Dannachet. Her mouth twitches again: a small muscle spasm. — Because I think Louis' condition needs radicalism.

I return her smile, with what I hope is humility, and give a small, self-deprecating shrug. Might a woman like Madame Drax be impressed by what she has heard of me? Swiftly, I slap the thought down, but not too soon to feel shame at my own ridiculousness. The trouble with being married to someone like Sophie is that you get daily, affectionate reminders of your own absurdity, and imagine her amused laughter in your head.

— He gives a little flicker of life sometimes, she continues, stroking her son's hair softly. I can see how her love for him is anxious, immensely protective. — His eyelid twitches, or he sighs, or grunts. Once he moved his hand, like he was trying to clutch at something. Things like that, they give you hope, and then . . . All this paraphernalia. She indicates the gastrostomy and catheter tubes emerging from beneath the sheet, attached to silicone bags. She stops, bites her lip. Swallows. She knows he may never emerge.

That this could be where she has brought her son to die.

— I know. Gently, I place my hand on her arm, the way doctors are permitted to. — It's unfortunately all too easy to mistake small movements for a form of consciousness. But believe me, they're not voluntary or purposeful, I am afraid they are just tics, evidence of sporadic, uncontrolled motor function.

As I speak, I stroke the boy's brow and then, gently lift the eyelid: his iris is a dark-brown empty pool against the conjunctiva's pellucid white, motionless in the socket. Not a flicker.

She has heard it all before, of course. Like most of the relatives, she will have spent time reading up on her son's condition, talking to doctors in the field, downloading the latest medical literature from the Internet and devouring personal tales of bereavement, despair, false hopes, and miraculous recoveries. But we must go through the motions. She needs to unwrap the small package of words she has come with, and enact the rituals of need. In return I will give her what rituals I have, such as they are. No machine can bring these people back. It's nature that struggles.

— See the nurse over there with the flowers? I point to a matronly figure who has entered with a huge armful of pink peonies. — That's Jacqueline Duval, the ward sister. Our secret medicine. She's been with us twenty years.

Jacqueline spots us and waves, signalling that she will join us when she has arranged the flowers by Isabelle's bed. She does it swiftly and with style, while keeping up a non-stop flow of talk directed at Isabelle. Just watching her makes me smile. She's better with relatives than I am. That is, she knows how to get through to them, how to say the right thing at the right time, hold back when tact is called for. Many have cried on her shoulder and if the need arose and I could shake off my hierarchic inhibitions, I'd do so myself.

— I've read about your Awareness Accretion theory, says Madame Drax as Jacqueline stands back to admire the peonies. — And Memory Triggers and Lucid Dream States and . . . well, Dr Meunier told me that you believe in things that other doctors don't.

There. She has revealed the truth at the heart of her ritual. And soon, in meagre return, I shall disappoint her by disclosing the bald, depressing truth of mine. But first Jacqueline joins us, shaking Madame Drax by the hand and bending to stroke Louis on the cheek.

— Welcome, *mon petit*. I'm going to spoil you rotten.

Madame Drax looks faintly aghast at the intimacy, and seems

about to say something, then checks herself. But within days, Jacqueline will have won her round. I indicate that we should all move out of earshot, and gesture Madame Drax down the ward towards the French windows. I lower my voice.

— Back in a minute, *mon chéri*! says Jacqueline, patting Louis' arm. — I'm sure you're going to settle in well, *petit monsieur*. And remember, your wish is my command!

The three of us walk down the ward. — What I was about to tell you, in reference to what you have heard of my work, Madame, is that my success rate is not as good as people think, I murmur. — It's a delicate field. So many factors are at play, not all of them physical. So please Madame, don't raise your expectations too high.

We step through the French windows and out to the paved patio that gives on to the garden. As I try to ignore the bluster of that maddeningly hot wind, I am struck again by the vertiginous beauty of this slice of tamed land, its foliage now buffeted by the air's tumult in a tumble of silver and magenta, mauve and white. But Madame Drax does not respond to the garden or the talent of Monsieur Girardeau who we can see in the distance, pulling hanks of dripping algae out of the ornamental pond. Her eyes are derelict. She is not ready to step outside her pain. How can I explain that her own suffering will not help her son, and that it is not an act of abandonment to free herself from it for a fraction of a moment to watch a ladybird or smell a summer rose? What can I do to make that poor tense face soften into a smile? Absurd thoughts. Picturing Sophie's silent sneer, I clear my throat, step back a little from the wind's hot pull, rearrange the thoughts in my head.

— Jacqueline, I was just telling Madame Drax that the recovery rate for someone in Louis' condition is far from high.

Jacqueline nods, shielding her eyes from the sun. I can see that like me, she has not quite got the measure of Madame Drax yet. — But we keep positive, she says. — For everyone's sake, including our own. Optimism is a great restorative. We do our best to manufacture it here.

Later she will tell Madame Drax about her son Paul. Not to depress her, but to ease in the thought that death is sometimes the only way out of this place. Jacqueline came into nursing because of Paul. Twenty-five years ago, when Paul was eighteen, he had a catastrophic motorbike accident. He was in a coma for eight months and then he died. She has been in the same position as all the relatives who come here, fraught, and in a state of suspended mourning. Of the two of us, her human expertise is the greater. But Madame Drax does not seem to be interested in acknowledging Jacqueline's presence. I am the expert, in her eyes.

— But Dr Dannachet, your methods! (Her voice changes pitch; I had not guessed she would be quite this volatile.) — Your *revolutionary methods!*

Jacqueline and I exchange a glance. Madame Drax has read some of those magazine articles about Lavinia Gradin and my other successes, of course ('Pascal Dannachet: Champion of the Living Dead'). But suddenly, I seem to be negating them. Madame Drax looks hurt, betrayed. I have let her down. Yes: fragile. Extremely so.

— My methods aren't really so revolutionary, I say soothingly. — They're practised quite widely. But yes, they seem to have an effect. In some cases. Much of it's to do with faith. Attitude. Psychology. But I really do urge you not to get excited. Don't anticipate too much. I will do what I can; we all will. But the largest part in your son's recovery will be played by his family. By you.

— You need to realise that, Madame Drax, says Jacqueline softly. — Blood ties and emotional bonds can go far beyond anything we can do. He needs to feel your love and your presence. Be there for him, and he'll feel it. He'll know it.

But when Jacqueline touches her arm to reassure her, Madame Drax winces in response, pulling slightly away from the contact as though it might bruise her. This tiny dance of pain shows a struggle going on. You see it often. Too much sympathy and you dissolve. Finally she forces her features back into dignity, and says,

— Of course. That's what I heard. That's how I want it.

Of course she does. Her son is her only child. She has lost everything. She seems very alone. No wonder her face is such a taut, blank mask.

— Tell me, Madame, I say, smiling. — Tell me what sort of boy your son was.

— *Is*, she says. — I think you mean *is*. Not *was*.

Again, Jacqueline and I look at one another – but my ward sister's solid, benign presence reassures me that my tactlessness will be smoothed over. Within a week, Jacqueline will have taken this broken-hearted woman fully under her wing, educated her in the ways of the clinic, and made her a part of the extended family of coma relatives. I have seen her do it time and time again, even with the most traumatised parents.

— Madame, I am sorry. As I think you know, it would be unwise to assume an improvement will be . . . immediately forthcoming. But of course we must never give up hope.

— Do you realise, Dr Dannachet, that he actually came back from the dead? Isn't that quite unusual? I mean, apart from in the Bible –

At this point, I stop her quickly. I don't like the way this is heading. The brittleness of her voice disturbs me.

— It certainly is unusual. Remarkable. But death, you know . . . death is never as definite as people think. There have been other cases of drowning where . . . I mean, there's a thin line. It happens.

I step back, feeling embarrassed, and look desperately at my watch. Time to go. Meeting nearly over. Jacqueline, too, is aware of needing to be elsewhere: she hasn't washed Isabelle's hair yet, she explains. Her father is arriving today while his ex-wife takes a much-needed break from their daughter's bedside. It's his first visit in a year; he lives abroad.

— We'll catch up later, Madame Drax, she says. — Just ask me or one of the ward nurses if you have any questions. And welcome again.

— It wasn't just a fluke, Dr Dannachet, Madame Drax says insistently as we watch Jacqueline's full, cushiony figure heading back inside. — I hope that's not what you're telling me. It wasn't. I know my son. *I know what he's capable of.*

I confess that much as I would like to encourage the poor woman to be positive, I don't really want to go down this road with Madame Drax. People get strange things in their heads sometimes. I watch the progress of a Red Admiral that dances past us, zigzagging across the lavender and settling on a violet lupin.

— Look, please just accept my apologies, I say gently. — And tell me about Louis. I need to get to know him.

Her mouth purses in what I read as acquiescence; all of a sudden, our wrong-footed exchange seems to have exhausted her emotionally. She lowers her eyes for a moment, and then stares through the French windows at her son's bed at the end of the ward, as though drinking in the new situation. Her hair shines in the sun, a fine mesh of copper and gold. I wonder what it would feel like to stroke, then feel a flush of guilt at the inappropriate thought. To quash it, I quickly think of Sophie and the flowers I will choose for her this afternoon. Zinnias. I'll buy her zinnias.

— Louis is an extraordinary boy, she says softly. — An extraordinary boy. We're very close. And the thing is, I don't know how I could live without him. Ever since he was born, we've always . . . communicated. Known what the other one was thinking. Like twins. And now — She is swallowing down huge sobs.

— Yes? I ask gently.

— Well, I'm beginning to think – after what happened – She stops and inspects her hands – small, neat hands, the nails carefully manicured and varnished in pale, shell-pink. A good sign: ravaged though she is, she has not let herself go as so many of them do. Again I notice the pale band left by her wedding ring. — This will sound very stupid, she says. — And superstitious and ignorant, and not the kind of thing you'd expect to hear from anyone – well, anyone educated. But if you knew Louis, if you knew what he's like, and everything he's been through –

— Then what? I ask. I can't help it: tentatively, I permit myself to rest my hands, lightly, on her narrow shoulders, to look her full in the face, to try to read it.

— I've come to believe something about my son. Listen, Dr Dannachet, he just isn't like other children. He never has been. I think –

— Yes?

— I think my son's a kind of angel, she blurts.

And her despairing eyes flood with tears.

Boys shouldn't make their mamans cry. And if their maman does cry, boys should be there to comfort them and say I'm sorry things went wrong, Maman, I'm sorry your heart's in your mouth the whole time, I'm sorry the danger got me and I'm in a place where you can't reach me. I know you tried to stop it. I know you said *Got to protect him, got to protect him*. I know you did. It's not your fault it didn't work.

Boys shouldn't make their mamans cry, especially if they've had a difficult life and *Grand-mère* lives in Guadeloupe that's too far away to visit where they grow papaya that has seeds in it a bit like hamster droppings. And back in the time before Gustave, boys shouldn't spy on their maman because they'll get the wrong end of the stick, they'll start thinking weird things and start inventing stuff just to impress people and it'll end in tears. But sometimes you can't help it because you need to know things and it's not on a CD-ROM where you can click on the picture to make the creatures do stuff, and learn about their Habitat and their Nutrition and Life Cycle and How They Rear Their Young and blah blah blah. But I haven't got the one about humans because maybe they haven't made it yet. So I have to spy on them and listen to them doing secret things like sexing each other (*uh-uh-uh*) or crying or having an argument or a secret conversation about Disturbed Children.

A good way is to use the baby monitor they keep in case you

get Cot Death again in the night, even though you're not a baby any more. You can switch it round so you can listen to what they say when you're in your bedroom eating cereal, the kind with dried raspberries in, and they're in the kitchen having a secret talk. You might not know how the raspberries get like that. They freeze-dry them, it's a special process.

—We should tell Louis the truth, says Papa. —I'm sorry Natalie. But I've been thinking about it a lot lately.

—*And damage him for life?* says Maman.

—You're exaggerating. He has a right to know, and I'd rather he heard it from us. He knows there's something that doesn't fit. It's quite uncanny how he picks up on things. Look at the way he senses all your moods. Anyway, he'd accept it. He knows how much I love him. It won't be a problem.

I put down my spoon. Mohammed's running on his wheel so I put a pencil in to jam it and stop the noise. Because I need to hear but maybe I don't.

—He'd ask questions, says Maman. —You know Louis. One question always leads to another, and then another, and another. Until you get to the one you can't answer.

Her voice is wobbly. *Got to protect him, got to protect him,* she's thinking. She's probably looking in the little mirror now, the one by the sink. That's what she does when she's thinking. It's her thinking mirror.

—So let him. Perez is there. He can help him deal with it.

—Surely you're not saying we should tell him the whole story? About Jean-Luc and –

Her face in the thinking mirror. Scared.

—No. Of course not. Not all of it, obviously.

Papa's probably sitting at the kitchen table, cleaning his Swiss Army knife that Mamie gave him last Christmas, that he calls a Big Boy's Toy. *Eighteen blades, and you don't know what half of them are for.* Her back's to him but he can see her face in the thinking mirror.

—How much of it, then? About how he *came into the world?*

About how you and I met? God, Pierre, I can't believe you'd want to do anything so destructive. Don't you think the poor kid hasn't got enough problems as it is? You know what they call him at school? Wacko Boy.

— That's exactly why I suggested a shrink!

— But it's me who has to take him, isn't it? I'm the one who gets driven half-crazy dealing with him afterwards!

Then I guess she doesn't want to look at her face in the thinking mirror any more, because she's crying again. She cries at least once a day and sometimes twice, because it isn't easy being the mother of a Disturbed Child.

— I'm sorry, Pierre. But I'm just saying – no, I'm *insisting*, Pierre, I'm *insisting* – that we drop the subject. It's best he doesn't know. He'll just get confused and anxious on top of everything else. Think of all the self-loathing. We drop it right here.

Eating isn't allowed in your bedroom. Maybe that's why I stopped chewing and maybe that's why I suddenly couldn't swallow anything. Maybe that's why I had to spit it out into Alcatraz before I took the pencil out of his wheel so Mohammed could run again. But afterwards when I thought about it, I couldn't see the big deal because I already knew where I came from. The doctors had to cut her open like the emperor Julius Caesar's mum, and pull me out with a meat-hook and we both nearly died. So it was all blah blah blah and not even worth spying on. But I wondered about Jean-Luc. Who's Jean-Luc? What's *self-loathing*?

Lots of people – not Maman of course, because she knows I'm not a liar – but other people, thought I was making the accidents up. I wasn't though. Not all of them. Anyway I was lucky, because I never cared if people believed me, especially Fat Perez.

Every Wednesday after school, when all the others are doing *ateliers* or *catéchisme* or watching TV, I'm visiting Fat Perez who's a mind-reader who isn't any good at mind-reading and to punish him you could post some hamster droppings to him in an envelope, except maybe he'd think they were papaya seeds and plant them in a pot because he's so dumb and he'll wait and wait and wait for them to grow but they never will. And sometimes I count aloud just to drive him mad, *un deux trois quatre cinq six sept huit neuf dix onze douze*, or in English, *one two three four five* except then I have to stop because I don't know what comes after *five*.

— Any accidents this week?

— I got a burn from a match cos I was lighting candles. Maman hates me playing with fire, she's scared of fire, she hates candles and bonfires but I love them. And then I got a graze on my knee, falling over in the playground. And then yesterday I got a blister on my hand. It nearly got infected with tetanus. I could've got lockjaw. I've got a plaster, look.

— And how did you get this blister?

I've learned this thing where you make your tongue do a click against the roof of your mouth called your palette, and it feels like time to do it. It's quite a loud one, but he doesn't say anything. — I got it from using a spade, cos I was digging a grave.

— Ah, now tell me about the grave! *Squeak.* — Was it for a small animal you found, maybe?

— If I found a small animal I wouldn't kill it. Not right away.

— I meant –

— I'd keep it alive, in Alcatraz, with Mohammed. If it was a rat I'd probably feed it maggots and then maybe kill it later. After say about sixteen or seventeen days.

And I do another click, a bigger one this time.

— So, tell me. What was the grave for?

— For a human.

— A human. What kind of human?

— A big huge fat man who lives in the rue Malesherbes.

— Ah. And who might that be?

Duh! Fatties are so slow!

— These small accidents you had, says Fat Perez, looking at me

40

with his thinking face. — They weren't bad enough to send you to hospital, were they? I mean, a little burn, a small graze, a cut.

— So? I'm accident-prone. Sometimes the accidents are big and sometimes they're small.

— Let's talk about the big ones. The ones that land you in hospital. I want to ask you something, Louis. Do you enjoy being in hospital?

— I don't like casualty. I hate that part. But the recovery bit, that's OK.

— What's OK about it?

— You don't have to go to school. They make a fuss of you. She sits by the bed and talks to you like you're a baby again and you can just lie there and listen. And she does anything you want, because she's so glad the danger didn't kill you.

— The danger?

I do the click again, but it isn't such a loud one and my tongue fizzes from it. — There's always danger. You don't have accidents without danger. And then it's good cos Papa brings you big Lego models. They bring you cool meals. Depending on the hospital. The best one's here in Lyon. In Edouard Herriot you can have pizza or lasagne and there's always ice cream for dessert if you want it, because Lyon's the gastronomic capital of France.

— So they say, says Perez.

— Plus they usually have PlayStation or Nintendo.

— Would you like to go back to Edouard Herriot again, Louis? Hospitals can be very comforting places, can't they? Like you say, no school, and lots of people making a big fuss of you.

I do the big click again. My tongue's all right this time.

— Do you think you might sometimes even be a little bit glad when you end up in hospital?

— You're saying I do it on purpose, right?

— No, Louis. I never said that and it's not what I mean.

That's when I start wanting to smash the bowl with water and seashells in that's on the table, and see them skid all over the place in the broken glass and see the look on his fat face.

—Tell me something, Monsieur Perez. Am I a typical Disturbed Child?

He laughs. —There's no such thing, Louis.

—What about now? I ask him when he's finished mopping up the water and broken glass with his dustpan and brush and his gay dishcloth, and put a plaster on his cut and called Maman on her mobile to say we'll need to finish the session early.

—Who were you thinking of when you smashed that bowl, Louis? he goes while we're waiting for her. —Who are you angry with?

Duh, again! He's always on about 'anger'. 'Your anger'. Why can't he find another word in the dictionary? Why can't he use a word like '*loathing*'?

The doorbell buzzes meaning no time left, so that's when I ask him.

—Is it true that there is a pill that ladies can take to stop them having babies? You take one every day from a little packet that's green and has twenty-one little tiny pills in and you keep them in a secret place?

He looks at me like I'm Wacko Boy.

—Yes, Louis, there is. It's called the contraceptive pill. Why do you ask?

—I just wanted to know. It was a bet.

—With someone at school?

—Monsieur Zidane, my teacher. I say there's a pill to stop babies coming, and he says there isn't.

He thinks for a minute.

—Might you be *swallowing* these pills you found, Louis?

And then I pretend to think for a minute, too. Think, think, think. And then I do another mouth click.

—I might be. What happens if you do?

Maman says that children need rules and they need certainty. *Children should be told the truth. Children should tell the truth too, they*

42

should always tell doctors the truth about how they had their accident. They should never make up stories just to make things look dramatic and impress people. You wouldn't believe how hard it is to be the parent of an accident-prone child. Your heart's in your mouth the whole time. Adults do bad things sometimes. If an adult does a bad thing to you, you should tell another adult, one that you can trust. I'll always be here for you, Lou-Lou. I'm sitting by your bed right now, and when I squeeze your hand like this, maybe you can feel it.

— You don't have to listen to her, says Gustave. — You can switch her off. Tell me more of your story, Young Sir.

— There was a thing that happened one day.

— Where?

— Disneyland Resort Paris.

It's winter. On the Weather it said this morning's average temperature is twelve degrees centigrade and this afternoon it will increase to fifteen but there will be winds gusting in from the south to meet the low pressure over northern France. This means a 65 per cent risk of showers tomorrow and Monday so don't forget your umbrella. Disneyland Resort Paris used to be called EuroDisney. But the Euro bit didn't work, Papa says. Only the Disney did. So they got rid of Euro and called it Disneyland Paris and then they said how about calling it Disneyland Resort Paris instead and letting you drink alcohol. And then abracadabra, people came flocking because it says in the brochure it's *an enchanted realm with lots of kingdoms* especially *Discoveryland with Space Mountain and its unique sensations. It's a magic dream that's ideal for the whole family,* even if you're not really a family, just a mum and dad and a boy with a hamster. Me and Papa came on the TGV from Lyon and we're staying in the Hotel Santa Fe for the whole weekend giving Maman and Mohammed a rest because we are both men and sometimes men can be too much of a good thing at a weekend and give you a headache.

In Adventureland, the brochure says, you can *wander through the oriental bazaar from the world of Aladdin, soak up its exotic atmosphere and follow the rhythm of the bongos to the heart of the Caribbean,* so we do that with Christmas decorations everywhere and Papa carries me on his shoulders for a while even though I'm too big and heavy. The World of Aladdin's full of someone's popcorn accident so we start queuing up in the cold for the giant tree from *Swiss Family Robinson* on Adventure Isle. They were a family that got stranded on a tropical island and they had to make a house in a tree. We're just starting to climb the stairs when a lady's voice says — Pierre? Is it you?

And straight away I can feel Papa's hand go tight over mine, like she's going to steal me or something. He puts the other hand on my shoulder and we stop, we don't go up the stairs. The lady's with a man and they have two Chinese girls, younger than me, who look like twins and a fat baby in a buggy who's not Chinese. We're all squished up together and there are people going past us and up the stairs.

— Well, says Papa. — What a surprise.

He looks like he's going to throw up, but he and the lady kiss each other on both cheeks like everything's normal, and then we all get back so the other people can get past.

— And this must be Louis, she says. — Hello Louis.

And she bends down and I kiss her cheeks too and she kisses mine. She smells of vanilla. Her lips are soft and cold from the wind and suddenly it feels like Christmas is tomorrow or the next day, not in two weeks.

The lady looks at me with her eyes that are pale blue, like swimming-pool water, but I don't say anything. I haven't seen her before, so I don't know how she knows my name. Maybe she met me when I was a baby. She's wearing a red coat and red earrings, she has a pretty face and black hair but not as black as the Chinese girls who are giggling like something's funny, maybe my stupid gloves that Maman made me wear, so I take them off and shove them in my pocket. Then their dad who isn't Chinese either shakes Papa's hand.

— Alex Fournier, he says.

—Pierre Drax, says Papa.

I want to know why the girls are Chinese if the mum and dad aren't.

—So you're the famous Pierre Drax.

Papa doesn't look very happy about being the famous Pierre Drax.

—I didn't know you were famous, Papa.

—It's just a joke, says Papa quickly.

The man keeps looking at Papa and then he looks at the lady. And he nods his head like he's working something out, maybe a tricky piece of Lego, and then he says, —Well, I can't say I haven't heard a lot about you, Pierre.

—And these are our children, says the lady all bright and smiley but it's fake, taking Pascal's hand. —This is Mei, and this is Lola, and the baby's Jerôme. He's thirteen months.

—Congratulations, says Papa.

—And how about you? says the lady. —Do you have any more at home?

—No, it's just Louis, says Papa. They look at each other for a long time then, till the lady's husband clears his throat and opens his mouth like he is going to say something, but he doesn't.

—And how is Louis' mother? says the lady.

—Natalie's very well, thank you, says Papa. —She couldn't be with us today.

—Cos we give her a headache, I say. —Cos sometimes men are too much of a good thing.

—What a shame, says the lady, and she looks hard at Papa, and he tells me to put my gloves back on, my hands'll freeze and I say how come her children are Chinese? And he says I shouldn't be rude. But the lady says it isn't rude, he's just curious. They were born in China which is a faraway country, and have I heard of adoption? She expects I have, she expects Maman and Papa have explained all about adoption to me. But I tell her they haven't and that makes the Chinese girls giggle like it's funny I don't know what adoption is and the lady looks at Papa and then at me and then she says very fast, well anyway, she and Alex got the girls from China two years ago and then right afterwards they had a lovely surprise because Jerôme came along.

— Like a bolt from the blue, she says, going all red in the face because she's happy.

— We didn't waste time, says the man, who's happy too. — Three kids in one year!

He looks proud, like he's won the Loto. Like he's saying to my dad, see? I have three and you only have one, and I have two girls and everyone knows that girly Chinese girls are better than Disturbed Boys. Plus we have a cute baby with fat red cheeks and a dummy and a hat that's got bunny ears.

— So now there are five of us, the lady's saying, — which is a bit of a squeeze in the apartment but we hope to be moving soon because I've been offered a new job up in Rheims, and Alex heard just yesterday that he could be transferred too, and they're promoting him to regional manager at the same time, so today we're all having a bit of a celebration.

— Well, I'm so glad things are going well for you, says Papa. — You deserve it, Catherine.

She looks like a nice lady, I don't know why Papa's looking so sick; the more she talks and is happy and laughing the sicker he looks, and then he suddenly looks at his watch as if he is shocked at what time it is.

— I think we'd better be off, *mon petit loup*, he says.

Yeah, blah blah blah. — What about the Swiss Family Robinson's tree? I go. — We can go up it with them.

The Chinese girls are still giggling at me but I don't care, they are just stupid girls plus they are Chinese and they have eyes that are the shape of a leaf and I don't want to play with them anyway because girls suck and I know they're laughing at my gloves even if they're in my pocket.

— The queue's a bit long, says Papa. — We'll go and have some lunch first. I think I saw some candyfloss for sale over there. You can have that afterwards. Nice to bump into you, he

46

says to the lady. — I'm glad things have worked out for you. All the best. Bye!

This time they don't kiss, they shake hands. Him and her and then him and him. The man looks at Papa like Papa's a pickpocket who's thinking of stealing something from him. I'd like to stay and go up the tree with the Chinese girls even if they're still giggling at my stupid gloves and they're stupid girls, but Papa pulls me away – he really tugs my arm so it hurts. If I dislocated it, I'd go to hospital and I'd better not, because I promised Maman that if I felt danger coming I'd tell an adult, one that I could trust, that's what you must always do if you don't feel safe. When I look back I see one of the Chinese girls waving, and the lady and the man are holding hands. Maman and Papa don't do that, or kissing, because kissing's silly *and there are other ways of showing love, like being a responsible provider for your family and not letting them down.* But sometimes I'd like them to.

There's a rubbish bin so I chuck my stupid babyish gloves in while Papa isn't looking. At lunch we have Mexican fast food called tacos that tastes of cardboard with *pommes frites et ketchup* and Papa's face looks weird and he keeps ordering beer and he takes my hand and he says he loves me and I say I love him too but I know something's wrong.

— Who were those people? Who was that lady?

— Just someone I used to know, says Papa. — We used to be . . . friends. Very good friends. Actually – He takes my hand. — I haven't told you this before. Maman thought you didn't need to know, but . . . well, I don't see why you shouldn't know. I used to be married to that lady.

— Married?

— Yes. For three years. A long time ago.

— Oh.

— Louis, I'm sorry to tell you like this. Are you upset?

— No. Why should I be? Because you're married to Maman now. And you wouldn't have me if you weren't married to

47

Maman, would you? You'd have Chinese children and a baby with a stupid dummy and bunny ears.

He doesn't say anything, he just looks at me with his thinking face.

— Yes. Maybe. I don't know what I'd have. And he sighs again.

— But we're not telling Maman about meeting Catherine, are we?

— Aren't we? Why not?

— Well, he says, picking up a *pomme frite* and eating it. — You know Maman.

It's true. Maman's funny about Papa and other ladies. She doesn't like him talking to them. It leads to trouble. *Men let women down. Over and over again. It's what they're programmed to do.* And we eat our *pommes frites* with our fingers for a while and I tell him about this new model aeroplane I want, that's got a one-metre wing-span that makes me knock over my Coke so Papa has to make a wiggly sign in the air to the restaurant lady.

— So what's *adopted*?

The man who's cleaning up is black but he doesn't have stripes on his cheeks from Ritual Torture that's Initiation, like the one in the market in Lyon who sells necklaces with shells, and while he's mopping up Papa tells me that adoption means you get someone else's baby if you can't have your own. The baby's mum and dad can't look after it because they're too poor or they can't cope, so they give the baby to another couple, who can't have children of their own. Those Chinese girls were adopted because Catherine thought she couldn't have children. But then after she and her husband adopted the Chinese girls, she was able to have a baby of her own.

— So it wasn't because she was taking those pills that stop you having a baby?

— No. She wanted to have a baby. You only take those pills if you don't want to.

— Is that why Maman takes them?

He looks at me and frowns.

— She doesn't take them. She takes vitamins and things. Folic acid. All sorts of things. That's probably what you've seen. It's not the same.

— So why don't you and Maman have another baby? I'm sick of hamsters. I'm sick of our family being so small, just you and me and her. Why can't I have a brother?

— We'd like to, says Papa. — We'd very much like to. Believe me, *mon petit loup*. We're working on it.

But his face looks all pale and sick and yellow, like he's Chinese.

If something's late it might mean bad luck. The TGV to Lyon was delayed by four and a half minutes. You don't know about the bad luck till it happens.

— And no accidents! goes Papa in the kitchen telling Maman about Disneyland. She's making pastry in the food-mixer because if anyone says she can't cook, e.g. Lucille, they are a liar.

Maman gives him a weird angry look, because they don't love each other like that lady and her husband with the Chinese children do. Maybe they hate each other. Maybe all they want to do is to get divorced. But they can't, can they? They can't, because of me.

They can't, because I won't let them. You just watch me.

— We met a family at Disneyland, I say. — Papa knew the lady.

She does take those pills. I've seen her getting them out of her make-up drawer and popping one out and swallowing it. She's got lots of packets of them, too many to count, and Dornormyl and Oil of Evening Primrose and blah blah blah. If a boy ate them, he might grow bosoms like a lady because Fat Perez says there's a hormone in them that's a lady hormone. It might give you a sex change like on TV. I saw a programme, it said there's an operation you can have to turn you into a girl to stop you being a rapist. You pay fifty thousand euros and they cut off your dick.

— So tell me about this family, Louis, says Maman. It's her Ice Voice, that's what Papa calls it. *The clink-clonk of ice.* — Who's this lady Papa knows?

And Papa gets up from the table and starts unloading the dishwasher and stacking the plates away in the cupboard.

— She's got two Chinese girls that just giggle. They're adopted. And a baby that isn't, with a stupid bunny hat with stupid bunny ears.

— An ex-colleague of mine, says Papa, getting out the knives and forks. — Someone from Air France.

He crashes the plates.

— Which department?

— Oh, er. Personnel.

— And was she a nice lady? goes Maman.

She is asking me but she is looking at Papa with funny eyes. But he has his back to her, crashing more plates and maybe he's thinking *the clink-clonk of ice.*

— Yes. Very nice. But we had to go. Papa said we had to go. We didn't have to go, though. I wasn't even hungry but we went to this restaurant that was meant to be Mexico.

— I see, says Maman. — Mexico.

She's still looking at Papa, but Papa's checking to see if the glasses are properly clean.

— How about going to watch cartoons for a while, Lou-Lou? goes Papa. And he looks at me and his eyes are sad and if he wasn't practically a Killing Machine you'd think he was being a scaredy-cat.

I don't know why I told Maman about the lady at Disneyland. I didn't say who she was, I didn't say she was called Catherine, I didn't say he was married to her. But maybe she knows because now they're going to argue. While I'm watching *Madeline*, Maman's screaming at him and he's trying to calm her down.

— It was her, wasn't it? You lied! Why did you lie? she yells.
— Why couldn't you just tell the truth, for Christ's sake?

He says something very quiet and low so I can't hear.

— You're going to see her again, aren't you? Throw yourself at her feet. Well, go on. Do it, if that's what you want. Louis and I don't need you.

He says something low again, trying to calm her down, and then I hear her voice too. *If you feel so guilty. Baby. Don't you dare. Wish I'd never. Should have given you both what you wanted. Bleeding heart . . . Made you happy. Have to live with it. Don't blame me. Your mistake, not mine.*

When I'd finished telling him all this, Gustave didn't say anything. You never knew if Gustave was going to answer you or just cough and cough until out came sick or waterweed. But he didn't do anything. He didn't even move. He was having a bad day, there was more blood than usual, bright red, that soaked through the bandages. I thought he might be crying underneath. Did I tell you his whole head is wrapped up like a mummy's? Did I tell you he doesn't have a face? Did I tell you he lives inside my head?

He's been getting worse. He's been telling me about the time he was trapped in a dark place. He got hungrier and hungrier, but there wasn't any food and anyway he didn't have a mouth because his face was all eaten away. The blood's soaking through the bandages and trickling down his neck like a little bright red river. Under the bandages, he's dying.

— Tell me some more of your story, Young Sir, he says. — Before I go.

So I tell him about Fat Perez's dirty secret.

One time I'm there with him in his creepy apartment in Gratte-Ciel and he's gone to his gay kitchen to get me a Coke because I always have to have Coke, I *refuse to co-operate* without Coke and sometimes sweets too. While he's gone I start hunting to see if he's got any new stuff. I look in all the drawers and under cushions because sometimes you find coins and once a ten euro note or some triple-A batteries and you can nick them and he never notices. Anyway this time I find something big and new. Binoculars.

Cool.

I point them out the window and twiddle them till stuff isn't all fuzzy any more. It's snowing outside and you can see the snow-flakes floating down like big bits of torn-up paper. I want to find out where the music comes from, because when you're playing Don't Say Anything you can hear music thumping and a woman shouting things like, 'one, two, three, squeeze those buttock muscles ladies, do we or do we not want those bums to be firm?'

— What are you doing, Louis? says Fat Perez, coming into the room with his big monster body and my Coke.

— Did you put ice in it? Tell me what you use these for and I'll give you them back.

— Yes, three cubes. They're for seeing things from a distance. Such as birds.

— What birds?

— Well in town you can see pigeons and starlings and sometimes a heron, he says. — They come for the koi carp in ponds.

I look at him, he's just a huge blur. But when I twiddle some more I get his face. He's smiling, his hand's reached out wanting the binoculars back. But I haven't finished with them, have I.

— You're a pervert, aren't you? I go. — You look at ladies getting undressed and doing aerobics. You look at their bottoms and their bosoms. Don't you?

— Louis, I think we should get started.

— You look at bare ladies and you play with your dick. You're a rapist.

— A what, Louis?

— A rapist.

He sits down and looks at me like I'm Wacko Boy, like they call me at school. It's the same look. His face is just a blur again when I look at him, a big fat blur. But I can see he's giving me a creepy smile.

— Tell me more about rapists. It's not the first time you've mentioned them. What do you know about rapists, Louis?

He should look it up in the dictionary, shouldn't he. I'm just a boy. Outside the snowflakes are still falling down and down and down and sometimes a bit up, when there is a current of air called a thermal. You could get dizzy watching these snowflakes, that look like torn-up paper. When you get dizzy you fall over. They talked about rapists on TV once, I didn't know what they were then but Maman's face went strange and she and Papa looked at each other and then they both reached for the remote control. Papa got there first and he turned it off and then they both looked at me in a funny way.

— What's a rapist? I said.

— A bad man, said Papa, and he went bright red. And Maman didn't say anything, she just went into the kitchen and started chopping onions to make herself cry.

— I'll never turn into a rapist, I tell Fat Perez. — Because either I'll have bosoms or I'll be dead.

But I'm wrong about the bosoms, because those lady-pills you keep in your pocket and you eat at breakfast and lunch and dinner and a picnic, which don't taste of anything even if you crunch them, they don't work. Because after a few weeks you're still a boy and you don't have bosoms, even tiny ones. So Fat Perez was lying again. He was playing Always Lie, which is one of the secret games grown-ups play. They have lots of games, with Secret Rules just like kids have. There's Vow of Silence which is like the grown-up Don't Say Anything, and there's Extreme Punishment, and there's Pretend You Don't Hate Him. That's very hard to play. You have to be good at Emotional Work.

— Papa isn't my real dad. I'm adopted. I'm an Adopted Child, like someone Chinese.

— Ah, says Fat Perez. — Interesting thought. It's not an unusual thought for a child to have. And your mother?

— She's my real mum.

— How do you know that?

— Because she nearly died when I was being born. They had

to open her up and pull me out and we both nearly ended up in a *two-corpse coffin*, you can order them from the Internet.

— So Maman is your real mother, but Papa adopted you. Did someone tell you that, or is it just an idea that came into your head?

— No one told me.

— So how do you know?

— I just know. He adopted me like someone Chinese. Like Chinese babies whose parents can't look after them so they come to France and live with another family and laugh at other kids' stupid gloves.

— I see. So who do you think is your real father?

— I don't have one.

— Everyone has a real father, Louis.

— Well not me.

He has a long think with squinty piggy eyes. — If you could choose a father, instead of Papa, is there anyone who you might choose, Louis?

I pretend think for a minute too by making my eyes go piggy like his. Think, think, think. And then I say, — Yes, there is, Monsieur Perez. It's you.

He looks like he might puke.

— Really? he says, his voice all weak and croaky.

It makes me laugh my head off. I laugh and laugh and laugh.

— Gotcha!

I can't stop laughing, and the more I laugh the more he hates it but he can't say anything because he's being paid. You know something about Fat Perez? I don't think he can cope with Wacko Boy. When Maman comes, they leave me in the living-room watching *Les Chiffres et Les Lettres* and they talk in his kitchen. And after he's talked for a while she starts using the Ice Voice. So I turn up the volume with the remote control because I hate that voice. I have to keep turning it up louder. When she comes in to get me, she's still in a rage and her mouth's twitching like mad. It does that sometimes.

On the way home in the car, she says that she and Monsieur Perez have had a little talk because he's got some strange things into his head. And that's when I know for sure that Fat Perez was lying. He said that whatever I tell him will never leave the room because it's a secret between him and me.

But look. He told her, see? So he is a liar like all of them and he plays the same games they all play like Pretend You Don't Hate Him that's like a show on TV. They're all acting and I'm supposed to believe in it, like I'm supposed to believe Papa's my real dad. But he's just playing Pretend You're His Dad. And that makes him the biggest fake of all and that's why I won't talk to him on the phone any more when he rings from Paris and that's why I stop writing him letters and I start hating him because he's done a terrible thing, he hasn't got honour, he's let me down very badly.

I used to sleepwalk, as a child. My mother would find me in strange places. The first time I was only four or five; she found me hunting for something out in the garden; when she asked me what I was looking for, I replied that I was looking for 'it'. I was to search for this unidentifiable 'it' in my sleep on later occasions – in the garden, or the neighbour's field, or the nearby beach. Such episodes worried my parents, and they unsettled me too, when I learned of them the next morning. But in a strange way, I also found it fascinating that a part of me could be giving my body orders in my own absence. I never remembered my dreams afterwards, but I always awoke feeling groggy and exhausted, as though I had undergone a huge physical and mental ordeal in order to visit a place beyond maps. Sleepwalking became an increasingly regular feature of my life, and the habit peaked during my adolescence, when the mind and body are evolving so rapidly. During my puberty, those years of daily self-astonishment, sexual fantasy and furtive masturbation beneath the sheets, I sleepwalked almost every night. I never went as far as the beach again, but sometimes I would awake and find myself in a barn belonging to the neighbouring farmer, or in the storeroom where my parents kept antiques awaiting restoration. Surprisingly, I never had any accidents during any of these episodes. My sleepwalking appeared to be completely benign, and we all came to accept it as an idiosyncrasy which I would one day outgrow. And sure enough, I eventually did. By the time I had left home and begun life as a medical student, somnambulism had become a distant part of my mental landscape, faded to ghosthood like the old Polaroid photos of my youth.

But it stirred up an impulse that would not leave me, however blurred the memories became – a curiosity to re-visit that country beyond maps whose contours I had once traced in my sleep, in my restless quest for 'it'. Like anyone who becomes fascinated by the psychiatric side of neurology, I studied under Professor Flanque at the Institut. But ultimately it was the fully unconscious state, rather than the malfunctions of the conscious one, that held the most enduring appeal for me, and so when I left Paris, I decided to specialise in coma. Which is how I ended up in Provence. Apart from Philippe Meunier, who also went into neurology, my contemporaries – the surgeons particularly – have a theory that it's a thankless task, caring for these devastated people. They see what I do as being only a step away from pathology: ministering to humans who are no more than the husks of men and women, living corpses. But they couldn't be more wrong. Even damaged brains can make connections. The mind is more than the sum of its parts.

As soon as I had taken my leave of Madame Drax, I went back to my office. Passing through the small annexe where Noelle works, I caught myself unawares in the small mirror she keeps on the wall, and was vaguely shocked by how severe, how dogmatic my face looked, framed by hair that thinned at the temples. How set in its ways. My eyes, deep-set, suddenly looked sunken. Did I still have what you could call handsomeness, or had age done for me?

I will be dead one day, I thought suddenly. Dead and gone.

One of the four bonsai trees a patient, Lavinia Gradin, had given me – my favourite, the cherry – was looking in need of a trim, so I began pruning it with my little secateurs while I rang Philippe Meunier in Vichy. Philippe had just returned, according to his secretary, from a short convalescent break.

—Back on your feet? I asked when she put me through.
—What did you have?

—What did Michelle tell you? he snapped. He sounded even brusquer than usual, and I felt a nudge of the usual animosity.

—That you were off sick, I said. I hoped he couldn't hear the sound of snipping.

—Just needed to recharge the batteries, he said. —A post-viral thing.

He clearly didn't want to talk about it. Doctors can be cagey when it comes to their own health. Frankly, we hate to succumb to anything. Illness always feels like a defeat of sorts.

—The case of Louis Drax, I said, inspecting a small, shiny, perfect leaf.

—He arrived OK then? asked Philippe heavily. —All in order, I trust?

He sounded more than usually annoyed that I was bothering him.

—No problem. He's settled in the ward.

There was a short silence, in which I contemplated my artistry. I remember feeling a certain dismay when Lavinia Gradin first gave me the trees, as a thank-you gift after her emergence from six years in a coma. Wasn't it, I asked her, a bit like being presented with a pet? But she just smiled and told me to wait. They're like coma patients, she said. They take a lot of time and nothing happens fast but then when they blossom –

She was right: their restrained aesthetic slowly grew on me. But it's a strange passion to have, as Sophie often reminds me. She calls them my *geriatric babies*.

—So how's he doing? asked Philippe bluntly.

—Fantastically active. Jumping up and down all over the place and singing the Marseillaise.

There was another silence, of a different shape, from Philippe's end of the phone.

—Well, what d'you expect? I asked. I found it nettling that Philippe couldn't take a joke. Does something happen when a man hits fifty? — You sent him to me, what more is there to say?

More silence.

— Actually the reason I called is I'm a little intrigued as to the genesis of his condition. This fall he had.

— Charvillefort hasn't briefed you?

— Who's he?

— She. The detective working on the Drax case. Stephanie Charvillefort.

— Not yet. She's called, I believe.

— Well, don't you read the papers? Family Picnic Turns to Tragedy? It even made *Le Monde*, I think. It was on TV too.

Annoyingly, Philippe had now gained the upper hand; disconcerted, I put down my secateurs and reached for pen and paper.

— I must have missed it, I said. — Tell me.

— Well, he muttered. — It's one hundred per cent awful. Detective Charvillefort can fill you in on the details better than I can. But the bottom line is, it seems Louis' fall wasn't an accident. Even though he was a kid who had a lot of accidents. Due to undiagnosed epilepsy, I suspect, but who knows. Anyway according to the mother, he didn't fall into the ravine. He was pushed.

My throat suddenly went unbearably dry, and there followed a little pause, which Philippe did not seem anxious to fill. — As in? I asked, finally, almost against my will.

— By his father.

— *His own father?*

— Yes. So there you have it.

Words deserted me at this point. They seemed to have deserted Philippe too, because we didn't speak for a moment. I fiddled with my pen and looked at the spiky pods on my horse-chestnut bonsai which stands next to the maple. In autumn they burst open and spill glossy chestnuts, small as beads. Next to it, on the other side, my willow.

59

— So where's this father now? I asked finally.

Philippe sighed heavily, as though re-shouldering a burden.
— On the run, apparently. There was a man-hunt, but last time I heard, he still hadn't been found. I don't know what the latest is. When Natalie Drax was here, she was terrified he was going to come after her. She even got herself an Alsatian.

Poor woman, I thought. Philippe must have read my thoughts.
— So how's she doing now? His voice was still oddly tight. (Might it have been more than a virus? Marital problems? Something disciplinary to do with Louis' 'death'?)
— As you'd expect, I suppose. A little tense, but – well. Dignified is the word I might go for. She's taken a house in the village.
— Did she mention Vichy at all? he asked.
— Not as such. Should she have?
— No of course not, said Philippe. — I just wondered.

We talked for a few moments about the prognosis, which we agreed was poor.
— She's in denial, he said.
— Yes, that's the impression I got too. Well, perhaps not all that surprising, given his history of . . . I trailed off.
— Resurrection? We both laughed, a little nervously. — Is she on something? I asked, picturing her desolate, empty face, framed by hair like pale fire.
— I suggested she take something for stress, said Philippe.
— She was in a bad way when Louis first came to us. A bit delusional. The whole case is so freakish. The way he came back from the dead like that. It's the only case I've ever come across. Didn't do me or the hospital any good, I can tell you. One of the trickiest episodes we've had. Required some pretty fancy foot-work.

He'd felt that Natalie needed psychiatric help, he said. But she had refused counselling on the grounds that she wanted to be at Louis' side in case he should emerge from his coma. Then he paused, and although I'd just noticed that both the maple and the willow needed a drink, something told me to wait before reaching for the watering can. Sure enough, when Philippe spoke again, it was in quite a different tone.

— But in fact, Pascal, there's something else. You know how, well. Doctors are faced with dilemmas all the time. His voice was lowered, cagey, rushed. — We've all had them. But sometimes the dilemmas – well, they're not the kind you read about in the literature. Not the kind you find easy to discuss.

— *Dilemmas*, I repeated slowly. Outside, a ragged string of gulls wheeled in the sky, carving a broken white spiral.

— About the best course of action. I'm not just talking about the patients, I'm talking about their loved ones, the relatives and friends who . . .

There was something odd in his voice, something that sounded a little like panic. All of a sudden I was overwhelmed by the suspicion that Philippe had fallen for Natalie Drax, and that she had not returned his interest. That things had gone wrong between them on a personal level. That he had been forced to choose between her and something else. Was that the dilemma he had faced? As Sophie has often remarked, with an unmistakable note of warning in her voice, men our age are always behaving like fools around younger women. I felt sorry for him.

— Philippe, I ventured. — Look, is there something you need to tell me about Madame Drax? Something I should know when dealing with this case? I'm feeling a bit in the dark here. She's – well, she's an attractive woman –

— Do you think so? he barked. — Do you find her attractive?

This was suddenly getting a little too personal.

— Back off, Philippe! I said, forcing a laugh. — Come on, this is the kind of thing we used to joke about.

It's true. We had shared many a drunken evening together in the old days, when we were students and friends. But now, all of a sudden, those days seemed a long way off.

— No, you back off, Pascal, he said. — I mean it. Don't get too involved. Keep them both at arm's length. Take my advice on this one. See Louis Drax as just another case. But keep an eye on him.

— You have to tell me more.

He sighed. — Look, he had a fit, as you know, just a couple of days before I sent him to you. But for no apparent reason. No one was there when it happened. But there was something odd about it.

— Epilepsy?

— A possibility.

— You mean there are others?

— I don't know. Ask Detective Charvillefort. I don't know anything any more. There's something strange about that boy. About the circumstances. Everything.

— Philippe, just tell me –

— No. Look, sorry Pascal – but I need to get back to a patient. Just – well, be careful. Detective Charvillefort will tell you more. Just watch the boy. I must go. Can't wait.

After his hurried goodbye, a mass of questions crowded my mind. I felt annoyed with myself for not having insisted on knowing more. But Philippe had been even more unforthcoming than usual. Perhaps he was glad to have washed his hands of the Drax case. It certainly seemed he was annoyed with me for causing it to resurface – however briefly – in his mind. Meanwhile, now that I knew something of Louis' story, and what his mother had suffered, I couldn't help being impressed by Natalie Drax's ability to muster dignity in the worst of circumstances. I understood her tension, too. Might her husband reappear, down here in Provence? I knew nothing of police procedure, but I was suddenly very aware of the need to know more.

— That detective from Vichy is arriving in half an hour, Noelle announced, handing me a piece of paper. — She'd like to speak to you and Dr Vaudin together in his office, about security. What's he done, this Drax man?

— The information I have is that he pushed his son into a ravine.

— How disgusting, she said, wrinkling her nose, and writing down the name Pierre Drax in capital letters on her notepad. — What's the matter with families these days?

— Call Philippe's secretary in Vichy, and see if she can provide some more background on these accidents Louis had. Whatever she has, from as far back as she can get. And tell Guy Vaudin I think Jacqueline should be at the meeting with Detective Charvillefort. It's her ward as much as mine, and she'll be briefing the nurses.

Unhurried, Noelle got out her moisturiser and started treating her hands.

I shouldn't have been as surprised as I was to hear Louis' story. He wasn't the first victim of violence I'd treated. As often as not, it's some kind of human tragedy – a fight, a car accident, a drunken mishap – that brings my patients to me with multiple contusion, cerebral oedema, skull fractures, brain haemorrhages. Laurent Gonzalez, Claire Favrot and Mathilde Mulhouse have been on the ward so long they now feel like old friends. Kevin Podensac – a blood clot, the result of a bungled suicide attempt – has been here two years. Others, like Henri Audobert, Yves Franklin, Kathy Dudognon, and my anorexic, Isabelle Masserot, are more recent.

I realised that I had time, before my meeting with the detective, to introduce Louis to the others and socialise him a little. When I entered the ward I found Madame Favrot and Eric Masserot there, as well as Kevin's cousin Lotte and my new physiotherapist, Karine. Natalie Drax, Jacqueline told me, had just left. After greeting them all, I sat in my swivel chair and shunted myself to the centre of the ward. Jacqueline perched herself on a trolley where she proceeded to apply lipstick and powder while I addressed my patients.

— We're delighted to have a new arrival among us, I announced. — Of course I hope that he won't need to stay here long. But while he's with us, I would like you all to make Louis Drax feel welcome.

A couple of the relatives murmured to one another at this point. Louis Drax's story would have spread quickly. They may even know more than I did. After introducing each of the patients by name, along with the relatives, I give Louis Drax my little speech about the clinic – which in a darker age was known as l'Hôpital des Incurables, a dustbin where society flung its most hopeless cases. The boy's mouth is slightly open, and there's a small trail of saliva emerging from one corner. I wipe it away. — In the old days, Louis, some people were institutionalised from birth. Those born with severe and unsightly physical defects, or abnormalities of the brain. There were also so-called hysterics, along with syphilitics, deaf-mutes and the criminally insane. Isabelle, our anorexic, twitches and turns, worrying at her feeding tube. Her father pats her hand. — Anyway, I'm thankful to say that times changed, and l'Hôpital des Incurables was eventually re-named. So welcome to the Clinique de l'Horizon, Louis.

I ruffle the boy's hair (how thick it is!), tell everyone to take care of our new arrival, and repeat my daily message to them all: that their chances of recovery are excellent, and that my faith in them is endless. Jacqueline chuckles, and Jessica Favrot smiles wryly. We all talk to them like this. Such one-sided conversations are an inevitability with coma patients. Jacqueline is unstoppable, recounting funny anecdotes about her home life or oddball stories from the newspaper or sometimes, on her more whimsical days, singing old Piaf songs, or Françoise Hardy. I think she maintains a fantasy that her son Paul is still alive, in a secret, invisible bed somewhere on the ward. I can sense it in her. I have even been aware of colluding in it myself. Such are our mechanisms for generating and sustaining hope. I've thought a lot about hope and come to the conclusion that either it's there or it isn't. No in between. You need oceans of it in a place like this, and that is why Jacqueline and I are here.

— Is it really true his father tried to kill him? I heard Jessica Favrot murmur to Jacqueline as I approached her. Jacqueline nodded in the affirmative. — Poor woman, whispered Jessica. — Is she ready to talk?

— I don't think so, said Jacqueline in a low voice, as I ushered her out to the meeting. — I had a try. But there was no getting through.

I wondered, as Jacqueline and I made our way along the cool corridors to Vaudin's office, what Madame Drax made of the clinic. Of the new building so cleverly grafted on to the old, the landscaped garden, the chrome and glass, the muted, quietly luminous colours. Everything designed to induce a state of calm, of acceptance. Could someone like her ever be ready for acceptance?

When we entered Vaudin's smoke-filled office, he was in the middle of devising a flow chart about evacuation procedures in the event of a forest fire encroaching on us. He signalled us to come and admire his handiwork. It was an impressive page of interconnected boxes, colour-coded and packed with detail.

— You'd have thought you could download a thing like this, he said, his eyes gleaming under bushy eyebrows. — Just key in an architectural plan of the building and a local map. But nothing doing. Had to work it out with a pencil.

Jacqueline stifled a laugh. A moment later Detective Stephanie Charvillefort entered. She was a short, heavily built, surprisingly young woman with an open, no-nonsense face, free of make-up. Her eyes were a very bright blue. An intelligent air about her. She reminded me of a magpie. Vaudin introduced himself and then us.

— Louis Drax was technically dead when I first became involved in this case, said Detective Charvillefort, trying to settle into one of Guy Vaudin's uncomfortable designer chairs. — I actually saw the body myself. Medically very unusual, I gather. Mind if I smoke?

— Be my guest, said Guy before I could object, indicating that he would join her. — No point being the boss if you can't break the rules.

Together they lit up and exhaled in unison. I have tried to make the entire clinic a no-smoking zone but Guy has insisted on his office being exempt.

— You're all familiar with the story? she asked. Guy replied that he had read something of it in the paper but had forgotten the details. I confessed I had not, and that all I knew was what I'd heard from Philippe Meunier, which was mostly medical. Jacqueline said she had only heard rumours.

— The reason I'm here is to tell you that if anything unusual should happen – strangers turning up at Reception, or any odd behaviour on the part of any visitors, I want you to ring me immediately. I'll give you my mobile and my home number too. The concern is that Pierre Drax may reappear. Meanwhile, is there a member of staff on duty on the ward at all times?

— Yes, I replied.

— Sometimes two, said Jacqueline.

— When visitors come to see their relatives, what's the procedure for checking them into the premises?

— We have a register, said Guy, and explained the system. Detective Charvillefort tapped her ash into the ashtray before she spoke, and looked out of the window. — I hear you're in for some forest fires, she said. Guy groaned and indicated his flow chart: and she smiled in sympathy.

— So, she said. — The Drax family. I can't go into everything for you, but I can outline what's known publicly, at least. The parents were separated at the time of Louis' accident but were ostensibly trying to make an effort for the kid's sake. Pierre Drax was a pilot with Air France. According to his wife, he was a heavy drinker but hid it well.

— Which he'd have to, if he was a pilot, mused Guy. But I could tell his mind was still on his flow charts. He surreptitiously looked at his watch.

— Anyway, Louis was a bit disturbed, continued Detective Charvillefort, blowing out smoke. — By the way I won't keep you long, Dr Vaudin. Louis was being seen by a psychologist.

He's disruptive at school. No friends, doesn't fit in. They call him Wacko Boy. Anyway it's his ninth birthday, so the father comes down from Paris where he's been living with his mother, and they go on a family outing in the mountains. Now, Madame Drax is the only witness we have. So what comes next – I'm sorry to tell you this – can't be seen as proof of what happened. It's her version. There may be others.

— Guy Vaudin nodded and inhaled, eyes narrowed against the cloud of smoke he'd created. — Of course.

— Anyway, according to Madame Drax, she and Pierre have an argument about Louis. In front of the child. It gets out of hand, and suddenly Pierre's trying to get the kid in the car. Wants to take him to Paris.

— You mean abduct him? asked Jacqueline.

— So it seems, yes. Then when Louis realises what's happening he puts up a struggle, and runs off towards the ravine. The father chases after him and grabs him. Louis tries to fight him off. Pierre Drax becomes furious and sends him over the edge. According to Madame Drax, there was no way it was an accident. It may have been done in the heat of the moment, but we're still looking at an attempted murder.

I really felt quite winded hearing this. Slightly queasy even. I couldn't imagine it at all. A horrible image came to my mind of Madame Drax standing on a mountain peak, screaming into nothingness. I shut my eyes for a moment.

— So my next point is that if Louis should start to show any signs of recovery –

— Unlikely, for now, I interrupted, glad to snap out of my unpleasant trance. — The prognosis isn't good.

— But if he should, we'll need to interview him. He may remember something vital.

— Eventually he may, I said. — But not right away. Some people lose their memories completely, others only ever get it back partially.

— Which is sometimes for the best, added Jacqueline. — In

cases where there might be psychological trauma. We have a boy on the ward who tried to commit suicide. Quite frankly we'd all prefer it if he didn't remember that, if he comes back.

Detective Charvillefort nodded and looked thoughtful. Guy Vaudin was looking at her a little quizzically and I knew that he was trying to guess her age. She didn't look much older than my daughters, but she must have been thirty. Her manner was a little brusque, but she seemed competent.

— What about his history of accidents? I asked.

— Difficult to get to the bottom of that one, she said, grinding her cigarette into the ashtray and reaching for another. I wanted to tell her to stop smoking. Give her a medical lecture on lung cancer and emphysema, order her to nip this habit in the bud. She was too young to die. — His psychologist thought he might be self-harming as a way of seeking attention. But some of the injuries go too far back for that. Louis would have been too young. He may have heard the stories – very dramatic stories, some of them – of the accidents and illnesses he had as an infant, and latched on to the idea of somehow repeating that pattern. But there's also the possibility that one or both of his parents was involved in harming him physically.

She paused for this to sink in. Jacqueline nodded slowly and Vaudin gave an unhappy grunt. I knew that none of us wanted to contemplate this thought. I just continued to stare at the detective. I'd heard what she said but somehow it hadn't got through to the part of my brain that reacts. I needed time to absorb it. I'm slow that way.

— If we're looking at physical abuse, I'm afraid we have to see Madame Drax as a possible suspect too. In the silence that followed, I felt slightly sick, as though the air in the room was too tightly squeezed around us. Vaudin shook his head in disbelief, and Jacqueline looked upset. I got up and opened the window, letting in the cries of distant gulls and the faint roar of traffic from the valley. — It's purely procedural, said Charvillefort, stubbing out her half-smoked cigarette next to

Vaudin's and standing up to leave. — We have to stick to protocol in our job. Just as I'm sure you do in yours.

But as she took her leave of us, I felt uneasy. She had actually told us more about Louis Drax's case than I had expected to hear. Much more. But what was she holding back?

In an unsettled mood, I headed back to the ward with Jacqueline. We didn't talk about what Detective Charvillefort had said. Instead we discussed Isabelle, and her father's arrival. He loved his daughter, it was clear, but his visits had become few and far between. Isabelle's mother was bitter and tense, always keen to take you aside and report on how neglectful her ex-husband was. I sometimes wondered whether Isabelle was hiding from both of them, in her coma. It was a delicate matter to raise with either parent – but Monsieur Masserot, we thought, might be more responsive to the suggestion that as parents they should attempt a semblance of unity.

Jacqueline opened the French windows and allowed the breeze to enter, billowing the white curtains around the beds. Several of the relatives were around and the air buzzed with chatter. I exchanged greetings with Jessica Favrot and Mathilde Mulhouse's sister, Yvette, then introduced myself to Monsieur Masserot, a bullish-looking man who seemed ill-at-ease, over-awed by the whiteness of the place. He sat next to Isabelle, stroking her hair: dark red curls that spread out across the white pillow like the leaves of an exotic fern.

— Her hair was always so alive, he said softly. — However ill she was, her hair resisted it. It was never affected. Isn't that strange, when it's so close to the brain?

I smiled. I didn't want to talk about anything delicate within earshot of Isabelle, so after suggesting he make an appointment with me to discuss his daughter's progress, I rolled my swivel chair next to Louis' bed, where I took hold of his small, clean hand, squeezing it in greeting. He was wearing headphones attached to a Walkman. According to Jacqueline, Madame Drax had been keen to record some new cassettes for him and had prepared one within hours of her arrival. Most of the relatives talked to the patients on cassette as well as at the bedside; all, I think, hated the thought that they might feel lonely and abandoned. Madame Drax had clearly put some music on Louis' tape, because I could hear its tinny rhythm through the headset. As I let it tap against my consciousness, I remembered what Madame Drax had said about her son. *I think he's a kind of angel.* Perhaps you need to be slightly delusional to cope with horrors on this scale. It's hard, I thought, to reproach anyone in Madame Drax's position for choosing to sugar-coat the truth by con-cocting a fairy tale around it. But maybe it's more than that – not just with her, but the others too. Strategy or superstition, or a combination. It's the same impulse that tells you not to speak ill of the dead. Criticise your child when he is at his most vulnerable, and you might kill him. Tell yourself he is an angel, and he might just become immortal.

But it was still puzzling, this talk of angels. The fact was, before his accident, Louis was an actively disturbed child. Behavioural problems, disruptiveness at school, a history of accidents. I tried to picture the small family going on a picnic, and the father suddenly taking it into his head to abduct the boy. I had to shut my eyes, briefly, as I thought of what Drax ended up doing – through pure rage – to his own son. The moral vertigo of it. Imagine his remorse. How immediate, how total, how crushing. We have all had those nightmares in which we do something monstrous, then wake, skin clammy with revulsion. Then comes the wash of pure relief that it was only a dream – followed by an undertow of guilt for having imagined it in the first place. Wasn't it, after all, the uncon-scious expression of a real desire? It's a shameful thing for any parent to have to admit, but there are moments when the flesh of our flesh, the creatures we love most in the world, can fill us with passionate fury. Loathing, even. Is this what happened with Louis' father? A sudden, uncontrollable slam of rage at his son's rejection of him, that blasted the boy off the cliff edge?

Madame Drax entered, wearing her pale, strawberry hair piled high in a chignon and dark lipstick that gave her face a certain drama. She acknowledged the other relatives with a small smile and a brief nod of the head, but no more. Yes, this woman had presence. A certain aloof aura, an *hauteur* that one might think was simply class, if one did not have the suspicion – as I did, for I felt I was beginning to know her a little – that it was actually just pure, agonising loneliness that set her apart from the others. That she needed to tie up her hair and apply that blood-dark lipstick to stop herself from falling to pieces, losing her sanity. She was not ready for the world yet.

— The message is, never give up, I told her an hour later in my office, where I had persuaded her to join me for a cup of coffee before I launched myself once more into writing the talk I was about to give in Lyon. I'd been recounting the story of l'Hôpital des Incurables. — Believe me, we've come a long way from talking about incurability, I reassured her. — We simply don't even accept it as a notion at the Clinique de l'Horizon. However desperate Louis' situation looks, Madame Drax – can I call you Natalie? – we will try to get through to him. Track him down. Coax him out.

Speech over, I smiled and let my eyes wander up to the phrenological map which hangs on the wall adjacent to us. *Memory, moral faculties, reasoning, mental energy, language, love . . .*

— You think he's hiding? she asked softly, her eyes drifting to my bonsai trees. — I didn't think you saw it like that.

— Some of them are hiding, I said. — Others are just . . . lost. You have to prune the taproots as well as the branches, I told her. — It's very delicate.

— They're beautiful, she said. — In a macabre sort of way.

— It's not macabre. It's art more than horticulture. My wife calls them my geriatric babies. But they're much easier than children.

— And more rewarding? she smiled.

— Sometimes.

— You have children?

— Two girls. Grown up.

— Is a brain the same as a soul, Dr Dannachet? she asked suddenly. — I mean, if Louis' brain is damaged, is he still Louis?

— He's still Louis, I said. — In some shape or form. You know, in some cannibal societies, they consumed the brains of their enemies. Literally swallowing the organ that – they thought – housed the soul. Our culture doesn't believe in the soul. We talk about the mind as a social construct. Or as meat that thinks and tells stories, and invents things like the idea of 'soul', to comfort itself. We've ruled out magic.

— I haven't, she said, firmly. She took out an envelope from her handbag. — You asked me about what sort of boy Louis is. And then she spilled dozens of photographs across my desk. — Now you can see. I've got hundreds. I just brought a few.

As I leafed through the pictures, she talked more about her son. His passions, his unusual mind, his interest in animal life, aeroplanes, various heroes. I was touched. You could see an alertness in the boy's eyes, a hunger to know things. Most of the pictures showed Louis on his own; they must have been taken by her. But one in particular struck me, because it showed them together. He was just a baby, held swaddled in her arms. Her eyes looked sad and exhausted, and a little watchful, as though even then, she was having to protect her child from something no one else could see. So different, I thought, from the pictures of Sophie in our old albums: drained, too, but dizzy, euphoric, ecstatic, smouldering with pride. There was another one of Louis as a bigger boy, aged three, with his leg in plaster after a fall from a tree and a big smile for the camera.

She left the most recent one until last. — I nearly didn't have these developed, she said. — It was too painful. Pierre took them, on the day – She stopped. — In the Auvergne.

And there was Louis sitting on a picnic rug with his mother.

She sat behind him, her arms circling him. A birthday cake in the foreground. Nine candles. Happiness.

Natalie was explaining that Pierre's job kept him from home a lot. It had been a lonely existence. She'd wanted to work – in Paris she had studied history of art and worked in galleries – but Louis needed so much attention.

— He kept having illnesses and accidents. It was like there was a curse on him. They say lightning never strikes twice in the same place. But it kept striking Louis.

— I'd be interested to hear more about these accidents, I told her, remembering Philippe's epilepsy theory. — Has Noelle spoken to you about the background files? I want to have a look at everything, so I'll need to know which hospitals treated Louis, with the names of the doctors, if you can remember them. Infuriating, that we still don't have a centralised system in this country. It's taking privacy too far.

She looked uncomprehending for a moment, then rearranged her features. — Yes, of course. It's in that moment that the thought struck me again: she knows he may die – just as I do, and just as Philippe did. At which point I distracted her – and myself, for I do not like to admit such ideas – by talking her through the medical procedures we planned to perform on Louis: physical intervention in the form of massages, water therapy, and general physiotherapy to keep the muscles from wasting. He'd have a twice-weekly session in the exercise room.

— Everyone enjoys that part. It's very sociable, you'll see. The relatives – young siblings especially – do a lot of laughing. It seems to free everyone up. They can even begin to see the funny side. Quite remarkable.

— Given that there isn't one? she said with a small tight smile. I found myself flustered by her directness, her swings of mood.

— I don't believe in pessimism. (How many times have I used that phrase in the course of my career? I feel the cramping inadequacy of it every time). — I believe hope to be part of the process.

— But I know just how bad it is, doctor. Now her voice was flat and weary, with no variation in tone or pitch. I could not imagine her laughing. It was as though what had happened to her had cauterised the muscles that express joy. — And whatever happens, I'll be here for him. I'll see it through. But I want you to tell me something. I know each patient's different, depending on the injury and so on . . . But what I want to know is – She paused to make sure she had my attention: in that moment her eyes seemed to awaken a little, and shine with something that might, finally, be hope. Or was it fear? — If he comes back, how likely is it that he'll remember the accident?

It was an absurd question, given the prognosis, but I tried to stay tactful.

— What a patient does and doesn't remember of their accident is usually the least of one's worries, if they do come round, I told her. — You can never predict what state the memory will be in. In any case – look, I've heard what happened. I spoke to Philippe Meunier. And the detective.

— And what did they say? she asked. There was a pause, during which I studied her face. There was a small muscle twitch, the same one I noticed before – but no expression of discomfort at the mention of Philippe.

— Just – Well, what happened that day. The accident. I had no idea. And I really am sorry. But surely, given the story, it's best that he doesn't remember?

— Yes, she said. — Exactly. I don't want him to. I'd rather his whole memory was wiped than to have him relive that. I'm a prime suspect, you know. Did they tell you that? Can you imagine how that feels?

— No. But it's their procedure. You mustn't take it personally. Do you still . . . I was about to ask about her husband, but she interrupted, agitated.

— I saw Louis fall. I saw his face just as he – She stopped and breathed in deeply, determined to finish. — He didn't fall straight down. He kept hitting the cliff-face and bouncing off it until – It seemed to go on for ever.

Natalie Drax sighed and tilted her whole face to me. Huge tears welled in her hazel eyes, and I couldn't help myself: I stood up and walked around my desk to where she was sitting, and spread my arms wide in an offer of embrace.

She didn't hesitate. She stood up, took a step towards me and collapsed against my chest. I shut my eyes and felt the relief wash over us both. She hugged me desperately, like a child clinging to its parent. I felt immense pity. And then – to my horror – the sudden, unmistakable nudge of sexual arousal. Followed by shame and anxiety, and the realisation that things were taking a wrong turn. In that moment as I held her against my confused heart, and felt the answering beat of hers, I became acutely conscious of the fine line that exists between doctorly compassion and unprofessional behaviour. And I knew that, for the first time in my career, I had crossed it.

What I didn't know then was that there was no going back.

I am not a secretive man by nature, so I am bad at hiding things. And Sophie is a sharp little person who misses nothing. It may have been, once upon a time, one of the reasons I fell in love with her, but with the steady curdling of our marriage, it's become problematic – to me, at least – that I am so transparent to her.

— Tell me about that new patient you were expecting, she says at breakfast the next morning. We are eating outside on the balcony. It's oppressively hot, but the sky is overcast and a net of clouds hangs low on the horizon. As usual, she has a huge pile of books towering next to her, threatening to topple. Kierkegaard, John le Carré, Márquez, a volume of Proust, the new Alexandre Jardin, and *L'Internet et Vous*. She is an omnivore.

— He's called Louis Drax. He's nine years old and in PVS.

Can you get me a book called *Les Animaux: leur vie extraordinaire*? It's one of his favourites, apparently; I'd like to read it to him.

—Is his mother with him? asks Sophie, pouring coffee.

—Madame Drax? Yes, of course she's here. She's his mother.

—Needy? She narrows her eyes, and I raise mine heavenward in annoyance.

—Moderately.

—Husband? she interrogates, adding sugar for herself and milk for me.

—Not here.

—Why not?

—Because he's on the run from the law.

Satisfyingly, that seems to throw her. She fingers the Proust and looks across at the pine forest as though in search of her next question. I drink my coffee peacefully, until a seagull flaps on to the balcony in search of crumbs: I scoot it away with my newspaper.

—Well? Aren't you going to tell me what he's done?

Unhurried, I take another two sips. —It seems he tried to kill his son by flinging him off a cliff, I say.

There. That's wiped the smile off her face. But not for long; she always bounces back speedily from small shocks.

—In the Auvergne? Think I read about it. There was a manhunt.

—Which is still going on. We've had to step up security.

—So, she says, reaching for a croissant. —She's a tragic single woman.

At which point I sigh, fold my newspaper, and get up.

—She simply needs my help, I snap.

—Otherwise known as your saviour complex.

That last remark – *saviour complex* – riled me horribly. Many times I had inwardly fumed at the idea – implicit in that phrase – that compassion is a form of weakness or perversion. Surely it's the opposite? What kind of person can resist offering succour, when someone is silently begging for it?

But Sophie didn't bring up the subject of our wedding anniversary again and later on even said, in an almost conciliatory way, that she'd get me a copy of *Les Animaux: leur vie extraordinaire* if she had one in the library. She's always approved of the fact that I read to my patients, and made sure that the ward was well stocked with audio books. Meanwhile I noticed that she had arranged her flowers – a huge bouquet of zinnias – very beautifully on the hall table, in our largest vase.

The next day the air felt hot but lightweight and strangely electric. The gulls seemed to sense it too, because their cries were shriller, somehow, more raucous than usual, drowning the sound of the cars on the *route nationale* in the valley below. As I walked to work through the olive groves, I felt a vague sense of excitement. I worked intensively all morning on my paper for Lyon, and then joined Guy Vaudin in the canteen for lunch. He was becoming increasingly preoccupied by the possibility of having to evacuate the building, and was keen to explain his finalised flow chart before he met the Fire Chief again to discuss logistics. But despite his claim to be exasperated, I could see that part of him – the part that made him happy administering a place like this – was excited by the planning aspect. He fixed me with his blue stare under wiry eyebrows.

— This Drax case, he said. — Having to lay on extra security's the last thing we need. What did you make of the detective?

— She smokes too much. If the forest fires don't set this place alight, she will.

Guy smiled. — She seemed very young, he said, then lowered his voice conspiratorily. — I got the feeling she was a lesbian. They quite often are, you know.

I couldn't help smiling.

Staff, patients and visitors all eat well at the clinic; by the time I had finished off a terrine of smoked salmon, followed by a mushroom risotto and some plum *clafoutis*, I was ready to settle into my high-backed swivel chair next to Louis' bed and indulge in some conversation. I always relish the tranquillity of such moments. Stroking the boy's cool forehead, it struck me, not for the first time, that my comatose people have a calming effect on me. That they are as much my therapy as I am theirs. If something warned me that being with Louis was another way of being with his mother, I shut it out.

— You can call me Pascal if you like, I told him. — Or Dr Dannachet if you prefer. You're in a coma, Louis. Like sleeping, but deeper. A fascinating place to be. But we don't want you to stay there for ever. You know, Louis, I have quite a few theories about the state you're in. And Isabelle and Kevin and the others. I think that some people stay in their comas because they don't want to wake up. They're frightened of what they might find. Or remember. So they stay asleep. And maybe they only wake up when they've managed to get up the courage. But the world's a good place, Louis. Full of the oddest things. I'd love to take you up to Paris and show you something I read about in the newspaper. A pickled giant squid, fifteen metres long. The Latin name's *architeuthis*.

Occasionally Sophie has asked me difficult questions about what goes on in my head, questions I find myself at a loss to answer. What do I think about, where do my thoughts really travel, when I am sitting with my patients? Why do I feel so convinced that something is getting through? *What attracted me so much to coma in the first place?* She has her own theories, of course, being Sophie and a little cynical about me. Such as: I can lecture them for as long as I like and they won't answer back. I can propound preposterous theories that my peer group refuse to countenance. Or, she argues (conversely), it's because I am in another world myself. Perhaps the latter explanation is closest to the truth. In my sleepwalking years, I learned the existence of another dimension. I do not inhabit it any longer. But somehow, it continues to inhabit me.

Madame Drax arrives, bringing with her some of the electric

dazzle from outside. Her hair is more disorderly today, and her paleness has been replaced by a faint honey glow. More freckles have broken out, scattering her forehead like tiny grains of sand. Provence does everyone good. Then I notice her fingernails. They are much longer than when I saw them last, and painted bright red. False nails, the stick-on kind that my daughters use. For some reason this shocks me. She shakes my hand and kisses Louis, bending to whisper him a greeting that I cannot hear.

— So, she says, shifting slightly, her hand running up and down Louis' forearm. — Is there paperwork to do?

— Noelle's preparing it. Just a few things for you to sign when you leave today, and the rest can wait till next week. Why not take a look around? I suggest. There's a day-lounge where some of the parents sometimes get together and drink coffee; you'll meet all the regulars soon, I'm sure. Madame Favrot is the doyenne of all the mums – she'll make you feel at home. Her daughter Claire's been with us for nearly eighteen years.

But I have once again said the wrong thing.

— *Eighteen years?*

— It happens. But other cases – well, I had one last year. In one week, and recovering the next. Look, see our gardens? You are welcome to walk in the grounds, I say quickly, gesturing hopelessly at the window. — And of course there is plenty going on in the town – we have a cinema in Layrac, you know, and a golf course if that takes your fancy . . .

Trying to recover from my faux pas, I find myself gabbling, and unable to stop: my mouth is running ahead of me. And so I explain that a retirement community such as Layrac is also abundant with chiropodists, medical centres, hunting-and-fishing outlets, and toyshops for indulgent grandparents. A little lacking in nightlife perhaps, but a friendly town, with an excellent swimming pool . . . I blabber on in the same vein a little more, before petering out almost in mid-sentence.

— I'm sure I'll settle in, she says, but the catch in her voice betrays her. I'm blind sometimes. I just don't see things. What

I've missed until now is that all the time I have been gabbling she has been fighting back tears, and now she can hold back no longer. She has sunk into a chair next to Louis and flung her arms across him, kissing his face, pawing at his hands, sobbing openly in front of him. It's a pitiful sight. Despite my edict that there should be no crying on my ward – because misery, you must understand, can leak from one soul to another – I can't bring myself to tell her to leave. And nor can I put my arms around her, as I long to, while we are on the ward. So instead, desperate to get her away, I take hold of her elbow and ease her to her feet. Silently, we walk down the ward together, then out through the French windows and into the intense heat of the summer garden, where in the shelter of a laurel bush, I take out a tissue and gently dry her tears.

— I dream about it every night, she whispers. — The same dream, over and over again. Just like a film. It's always in silhouette, I can't see their faces. It's like I've blanked them out. Two people wrestling with each other. One huge, one tiny, in the distance. And they get too close to the edge. I'm screaming at them. But they can't hear me, I'm too far away. I'm just powerless. Completely powerless. And then he's falling. And that's when I wake up.

Her eyes have glazed over; suddenly, as though becoming aware of herself again, she shakes her head and blinks.

— Forgive me, I ask eventually. — But when it happened – what did your husband do? Afterwards?

— Pierre? She stops and bites her lip, then turns her back on me. Lowering her head, she says in a blank voice: — He went and had a look at what he'd done. But Louis was in the water by then. There was nothing to see.

Although we are outside, and out of earshot of the ward, we are both whispering. She is so small, so frail-looking in that moment against the dark leaves of the laurel bush. Her hair is like gold spun through with copper and honey. I can feel the heat of the sun full on my back.

— He ran away. He just left me there. Screaming for help.

Her voice is flattened out, expressionless as ever. She turns her head slightly; I can see the blood rise in her cheek. Through the glass doors, we have a view of the beds, including Louis'. We can see the boy, too: a small hump beneath the bedclothes. As if prompted by its pathos, she suddenly spins round to face me, her eyes glittering with tears.

— You see what a coward I was married to? she blurts.

— Who would do that to his own son, and then just run away?

I'm about to say something conciliatory, something about how not all men are like that, how her husband must have –

But the words don't come. Instead, I take her perfect oval face in my hands and kiss her. She does not resist; indeed, she succumbs in such a sweet, almost grateful way that I wonder whether the resistance I sensed in her before – a certain coolness, a diffidence, an untouchability – was a figment of my imagination, an idea my conscience cooked up to ward me off. She smells of the same perfume I smelt on her before. It's insistent, sexual. Or is it the sun on my back? How did I come to do this? How did I dare? It's a delirious kiss which I fall into like a sleepwalker. I'm drowning in it.

— I've never done this before, I say pulling back from her gently, still amazed at myself, and wondering if I have shocked her, done the wrong thing.

— Kissed the mother of a patient? she says softly. The tears are still wet on her cheeks; I brush them away softly.

— No.

— I suppose I should consider myself flattered.

— I can't help finding you very attractive.

— Can't help?

— I've been fighting it, I confess. — Should I – carry on?

— What? Finding me attractive, or fighting it?

— Fighting it.

— Yes. Certainly for a little while. I'm not really ready for anything. I'm sure you understand.

But she doesn't resist as I lean to kiss her again. Deeper this time, and once again I am in another world, where I am drowning. Drowning –

Until something halts me. I cannot explain what it is, this bad feeling, this strangely amorphous dread that creeps up on me and tells me that something's wrong. Is it Philippe Meunier's warning, or my own vague guilt about Sophie, or is it something else? A distant noise? An instinct? Something, anyway, that forces my eyes open in the middle of the kiss and makes me look through the French windows and into my ward, where what I see – a swift, decisive movement in the far bed – stops me in my tracks and makes me gasp aloud. I pull away from Natalie, my heart tugging painfully.

— What is it? she asks, alarmed. I open my mouth but can't speak. My eyes are fixed on the ward.

Where Louis Drax is sitting up.

You see what a coward I was married to? Who would do that to his own son, and then just run away?

It's like electricity going through me and I sit up.

They were kissing.

They shouldn't do that, should they? Bad things will happen, and it'll end in tears. The sun's too bright. If you look into the sun, you go blind.

— Where's my Papa?

When I was young, say five or six, I had all sorts of stupid babyish soft toys. Don't laugh, I was just a little kid then, all little kids have babyish animals, especially if they're in hospital a lot and they don't like Action Man because he's a gay loser. When I got older, say seven or eight, I used them for the Death Game. I'd line them all up – Monsieur Pingouin and Rabbit-Face and Pif and Paf that were kangaroos and Cochonette who's actually a moose and a black and white cat called Minette – and they'd take it in turns to die. Sometimes they'd die like heroes in a fight against the Forces of Evil and other times stuff would happen to them, unlucky accidents like drowning or being strangled or maybe they'd look up the names of dangerous drugs and poisons and stuff to die from. You can do that if you have the right books. Fungus books, the *encyclopédie médicale*. Insulin. Chloroform. Arsenic. Sarin gas. Lupin seeds. One swallow and you're dead.

Sometimes Pif and Paf decided to die together. The best time was when Pif put Paf in her pouch and they got into my model aeroplane and flew out of the window and crashed on to the courtyard. Cool. They enjoyed it too, because it was a proper kamikaze stunt.

When a toy animal died we did Funeral Arrangements. All the other animals put the dead animal in a coffin that's a shoebox and made speeches. Sometimes they'd talk about how devastated they were. *I am devastated, I am just so devastated.* But other times they'd laugh. When Cochonette murdered Monsieur Pingouin by putting him in a pretend microwave, he said: I'd do it all over again if I could, because Monsieur Pingouin was evil and I hated him. He deserved to die, he should have his dick cut off.

— Why's it just Pif and Paf? Where's Paf's Papa? I ask Maman when me and the animals have finished all the funeral popcorn.

— Paf hasn't got a Papa, says Maman who's reading a beautiful-lady magazine again.

— Why not? Everyone's got a Papa.

— No they haven't actually, says Maman. And she puts down her beautiful-lady magazine and looks at Papa. He's reading the newspaper, the sports page.

— Why not?

— Because some fathers don't deserve to have children, says Maman. — And others are just pretending to be dads. If they were real men they'd take care of their families, they wouldn't go chasing stupid dreams in the past that were never meant to happen.

Papa is folding up his sports page and walking out and then we hear the door slam and the car starts.

— Where's he going?

— To the airport, says Maman. — And then up into the sky.

And Papa leaves us again. He doesn't come back for a long time, because he's with his evil mother in Paris who's called Lucille or Mamie. She is a bad influence, she treats him like a baby and she spoils him, and he probably believes all the rubbish and slander she tells him about Maman *because she hates Maman because she thinks Maman isn't good enough for her precious boy, that's what she tells Papa, she brainwashes him, and brainwashing your son is the evilest thing a mother can do, no decent mother would dream of doing that, manipulating her own child's feelings.*

After Papa goes we put the TV in the kitchen and I'm allowed to watch it when I'm eating my dinner. Maman doesn't eat dinner because she's always on a diet to stay thin. *Astérix* is on because it's cartoon time and Maman's reading a magazine with a picture of a lady and a man getting married, and it says, THIRD TIME LUCKY FOR DOMINIC.

— Who's Dominic?

— A famous actor.

— Why is it third time lucky for him?

— Because it's his third marriage, and when someone tries to do something and it doesn't work out the first two times, people say third time lucky, to wish them luck.

— How many times have you been married?

She laughs. — Just once.

— And Papa?

She puts down the Third Time Lucky magazine on the table and looks at me.

— Has Lucille been talking to you?

— No. Maybe.

Our secret, Papa said. There's a long wait before she says anything and when she does she says it fast to get it over with.

— He was married once for a very short time to someone he never really loved. He just thought he did. It was a mistake. And then he met me, and I was the one he loved. Far more than he ever loved her.

— But who was she?

— Nobody. There's nothing to say about her. He left her. It was a long time ago. They got divorced. OK?

— So why does he feel bad about it?

She looks at me for a long time, like I'm Wacko Boy.

— Did I say he felt bad about it?

— No.

— So why do you say it?

— I don't know.

I'm still feeling like Wacko Boy. You can't see what's going on in her eyes. They always look the same, like there's nothing inside them. That's how she hides from you.

— Well if he still feels so bad, he should go back to her, shouldn't he? He can't cope with us, and he can't cope with his guilt. You have a father who can't cope.

And she starts flicking through her magazine again and we don't say anything for a while and I'm thinking, *he can't go back to her anyway, because she's married to another man now and they have Chinese girls who are adopted and a fat baby they made all by themselves.* But I don't dare say that to Maman because boys shouldn't make their mothers cry and then *Astérix* finishes and *Tom and Jerry* comes on. It's the one where Tom tries to catch Jerry but Jerry gets away. Ha ha.

— Did you love anyone else before Papa?

Then she stops smiling, so maybe it's not OK, and she gives me a look.

— I thought I did. But I was wrong.

— Why?

— Because he let me down very badly.

Tom's uncle has written him a letter saying he would like to come and stay for a few days. But there's one thing he must warn Tom about: he's scared of mice. So he hopes there aren't any mice where Tom lives.

— How did he let you down very badly?

She sighs. — Have you heard of honour, Lou-Lou? Honour's doing the right thing. But he did the wrong thing. A terrible thing.

Tom has to try and get rid of Jerry before his uncle comes. But as soon as Jerry realises Tom's uncle is scared of mice, he does everything he can to be scary. And on and on in the usual way, Tom getting burnt with the iron and going through the wall and leaving a cat-shape in the plaster. I want to ask her what the terrible thing is that isn't *honour* but I can't because she's looking at me like I might make her cry again, and boys shouldn't make their mums cry, it lets them down very badly. And then Jerry laughs and laughs and laughs, because he has won again. And then the circle comes and inside it says in English, *That's all Folks!*

The Death Game's a good game for an only child to play. Only children need to be *self-sufficient* if they haven't got any friends and their maman's very busy in the apartment reading magazines about how to make it even more beautiful, and what clothes to wear in it, and crying because Papa's abandoned us again. *Some families are too different and too special to be like other people. It doesn't mean they're worse than them though. Actually – this is a big secret, it's not the kind of thing you should go round saying to anyone at school and especially not your teacher – it might mean they are just a little bit better.*

So *shhh.*

Fat Perez says it's normal to have mixed feelings about your parents and it's OK to hate your papa for not being there any more. *Hating people is part of loving them. Everything a child feels, it's OK to feel. All feelings are allowed because the world's a safe place for children. But deep down you know how much your maman and papa both love you.* That's why they decide to spend a weekend together being a family again, and take you on a picnic, isn't it?

A picnic with a surprise.

It was a shame what happened there because maybe I'd nearly finished my miniature spiral staircase from balsa wood, and maybe my teacher Monsieur Zidane was going to reward me for how good it was by taking me out to play a bit of football in playtime. He still kicks a ball about for fun sometimes, he says. It's not just the money he's into, see.

That was going to happen but it never did because we got stuck.

It was a cool place on the mountain. With bushes and a drop to a great big sort of ravine that you mustn't go near. We all sang happy birthday and Maman and me cut the cake and Papa took a photo and we both made a secret wish. I know what her wish was. Her wish was probably that I would be her little boy for ever. My wish was that Papa was my real dad, because if he was, I'd get to keep him.

And then things happened very fast. Something about my secret sweets. Papa saw me eating one and I tried to hide it but I couldn't and he kept shouting questions at me and then they had a row, not a normal row, a much worse one, and it's all my fault because of the secret sweets and they're talking blibber-blobber language and then they're shouting and Maman's doing Emotional Work. She's screaming like mad, and screaming and screaming, *Let him go! Don't you dare touch my son!* And then I've got free and I'm running and running but then –

But then.

Seeing and thinking's the same if your eyes are shut. A room full of bright lights and doctors yelling, and people gliding about like they're on wheels and sometimes you see the sun or the moon or a clock, and sometimes photos of Maman and Papa being happy and pipistrelle bats and sometimes you remember bits of the seven times table, e.g. seven sevens are forty-nine, and Fat Perez's binoculars, and the sound of them sexing in the night *uh-uh-uh* and Youqui in the photo who got run over by a tractor and chewing-gum and the frères Lumières and seven eights are fifty-six and Jacques Cousteau and the Power Puff Girls and the stars and seven nines are sixty-three and then you think of a building that's white and looks like Lego and there's forests all around and you're high up like in a balloon floating above and seven tens are seventy, floating above the land and looking down on this white gravelly road and along it comes an ambulance that makes the dust fly up all around, white dust. And when it stops there's a stretcher and a boy on it who looks dead, and his maman who's trying not to cry, and then there are some voices that sound like they're underwater, and then you see white clouds that are curtains blowing in the wind, and more voices –

— We do our best to manufacture it here.

— Ten millilitres should do it –

— L'Hôpital des Incurables.

— The boys send their love –

— One big, one small . . . I'm screaming at them. Screaming. But they can't hear me or they're not listening . . . Completely powerless. And then he's falling . . . he just left me there. Screaming for help . . .

— *You see what a coward I was married to?*

And then you sit up. *He isn't a coward*, you want to scream, but you can't. And you open your eyes and you know that there she was, just then, kissing a man. A man who isn't Papa. They're far away and it's like they're on TV and the sun's too bright. He's holding her. She's holding him. Then he pushes her away.

— Maman! you yell, but no noise comes out because you're stuck. Stuck watching them until you go blind. And suddenly there's a thousand voices exploding right in your ear and someone's hand's holding the back of your head and you open your eyes but you're still blind and Maman's screaming. — It wasn't his fault! He didn't mean to do it! It was an accident!

Screaming too loud, right in my ear.

— Louis, can you hear me? I'm Dr Dannachet. You're in hospital.

Hospitals suck. You kissed my maman.

— You had an accident. You've been in a coma. Like sleeping, but deeper.

Go away. Stop kissing her.

— But you pulled through. And here you are.

No I'm not. I'm somewhere else. Get away from me, you creep sucker arsehole. Where's my papa? I want my papa.

His hand feels like a million volts of electricity. He's electric-shocking me, and I want to yell *Get the hell off me, you pervert, just leave me alone* but there's no sound. My head's gone like a heavy ball, gravity's made it too heavy for my neck, it might roll off and break my neck and then I'll be in even more trouble. Do you think my maman enjoys having a kid like me?

—I said Louis, can you hear me? You're in hospital. In Provence.

No. No, I can't hear you because I've found the Off button. And Off is best.

And I press it and they're gone.

All except one.

—Hello, Young Sir, he says. —Welcome to your ninth life.

His head's all wrapped in bandages and his voice is croaky like he's swallowed gravel.

L ouis' bizarre seizure changed nothing on the surface of things – but somehow, like a seismic shudder, it rocked us all in unforeseen ways. The worst part of the whole episode, I thought afterwards, was the reaction of his mother. It should have told me instantly that things weren't fitting together the way they should. That something was fundamentally and irredeemably amiss, that an appalling truth was trapped inside her, insisting on release. But I was blind. We all were.

When I caught sight of Louis sitting up in bed, before I even had time to register the fact that he might be waking, I felt a rush of superstitious guilt. *He heard us. He saw us. He knows.* I raced across the garden, up the path – white gravel and dust spitting beneath me – and up the stone steps to the balcony. I was aware of Natalie following somewhere behind, calling out to me to wait, to please explain what was –

But there was no time. I stormed through the French windows to find chaos. The nurses had come running and everyone was crowded round the bed, including several visitors, Isabelle's father among them. They cleared the way as I arrived. When I saw that Louis was still sitting up, I felt a surge of hope.

His small, pinched face was enamel-white and glistened with a marshy, feverish sweat. His dark eyes – huger than I could have imagined – stared straight ahead. I sat on the bed and gently took his face in my hands, levelling my eyes with his. But as I looked into the dark pools of his enlarged pupils, it felt as if I were looking at holes to darkness, no more. Whatever Louis could see, it was not of the here and now. His fixed gaze was pure, unblinking blindness, like the introversion of insanity or the deep alienation you see in torture victims. A massive, involuntary shiver ran through me. Nothing could have prepared us for Louis Drax being capable of such a big, decisive, movement. Or for what happened next.

The child spoke. In a tiny voice, almost a whisper.

— Where's my papa?

The words seemed to echo silently for a moment and then his mother screamed. It was a delayed shock reaction I suppose. There was barely time for anyone to register that the voice we had heard came from Louis, when suddenly Natalie Drax had hurled herself at him, flinging her arms around the child's torso in a frenzied embrace.

— It wasn't Papa's fault! He didn't mean to do it! It was an accident! she wailed.

— Get off! Do you want to kill him? I yelled, wrenching her off. — He has head injuries! Don't touch him!

I gripped her by the upper arm and shoved her – quite violently – down into the chair next to the bed, where she cowered, covering her head with her hands and shuddering like a creature electrocuted. I felt a stab of regret at having acted so harshly, but this was not a time for subtleties. Louis required my attention; his mother would have to fend for herself. Jacqueline had by now quickly assessed the situation and had come to the same conclusion as me: that Natalie Drax, in her current state of hysteria, was a liability, and had to be removed from the ward. Somehow, in the interim, she and Berthe persuaded her to come with them and stand at some distance from Louis' bed.

— Louis, can you hear me? I asked, still unable to believe he had spoken. — I'm Dr Dannachet. You're in hospital.

The boy was still sitting bolt upright on the bed, surrounded by the clutter of bedside furniture and monitors; I held my breath as I waited for more words to come. But nothing did. There was no sign at all to indicate that he had spoken, except that his lips remained slightly parted. They looked dry. I moved to take his face in my hands to look properly into his eyes. For a split second they seemed to flicker with life.

— Yes, Louis! I breathed.

But when I felt the weight of his head become denser, my flash of hope evaporated. Quickly I changed position to protect the back of his skull, and as I did so, I sensed – very distinctly – a swift series of muscle spasms in the neck region as the energy that had flooded into him ebbed out again, like sea water swallowed into sand. He slumped back, his eyes sweeping shut. It was over. He had gone back to wherever he had come from. The whole episode had lasted no more than two minutes, I estimated. Whatever the unexplained seizure that had animated his body was, it had run its course. I felt total defeat. It seemed that something had so nearly happened, and then had not. And then guilt ploughed through me again. If I had been a professional, spending time with Louis on the ward, instead of kissing the child's mother out in the garden – *kissing his mother, for Christ's sake* – would things have been different?

That little voice, asking for his papa. That just isn't the way things happen with coma. Never in twenty years had I –

My thoughts whirled.

Meanwhile Natalie's reaction to her son's seizure had been just as bizarre, in its way. She behaved, I thought afterwards, as if she'd seen a ghost. And perhaps she thought she had.

— You can come back when you are prepared to be quiet, I told her as I fixed his drip. — But for now, please just go home.

— I'm staying with my son.

— No, I said firmly, as Jacqueline patted her arm. I noticed that again Natalie Drax pulled away from the physical contact, as though she had been flayed raw. — Believe me, it's for the best, I said. — You have to trust us. Now try to relax.

— Relax? Natalie's voice was a hoarse, cracked whisper.

— My son nearly comes alive for the second time, and you want me to relax?

Her face, just like her son's, had turned an unearthly white. Against her pallor, her lipsticked mouth was a wound, a bloody gash in her face.

— Come with me now, said Jacqueline. She spoke kindly, but with a firmness that brooked no argument. — We're going to the cafeteria for a coffee. We'll talk about Louis there, and I'll introduce you to some of the other relatives. It's time you talked to them, Madame. And listened. They've seen it all. And so have I. I haven't told you about Paul yet, have I? I think it's time for me to tell you about my son Paul.

And she steered the poor broken creature off.

Appalled though I had been by Natalie Drax's reaction, I could understand it on some level. The mind is delicate. Hers had been assaulted again and again by the unimaginable, the unexpected, the inexplicable and the unfair. And at this point I will confess there was a surreality to the episode that made me want to scream too. It was almost, I thought, as though Louis were a puppet, his body operated by a stranger.

As though the voice that came from those dry lips were not his own.

If you wanted to hide, this would be a good place for it.

— My name's Gustave, says the scary man. — What's yours? But I can't remember anything except Wacko Boy. — None of your business, I tell him.

— I've been waiting for you, he says. — I was hoping you'd come. It can get lonely here. And he reaches out his hand for me to shake but I stay still. *Don't move don't move don't move, don't say anything don't say anything don't say anything.* You shouldn't touch a stranger, or let him touch you, because he could easily be a pervert or a paedophile, plus he looks like a mummy that's a pickled human being and he stinks of the water when she empties a vase out. The bit of mouth I can see is smiling or maybe he's just hungry.

— What shall we call you then? says Gustave. — Everyone here has to have a name. If you can't remember your name, they give you one, or you find one for yourself. Do you think Gustave suits me? I've grown quite fond of it.

He's riddled with germs and bacteria, you can tell. Maman would scream if she saw him. She would scream and say he is a disgusting sick pervert, *get away from my son, don't you touch him, don't you come near him. He's not yours, just get off him, you bastard.*

— Bruno? he goes.

— You must be joking, I say. — You know what I'd rather be, mister, than be called Bruno? I'd rather be dead.

So he tries out more stupid names like Jean-Baptiste and Charles and Max and Ludovic and – this is the worst one – Louis.

— Louis sucks! No way am I ever going to be called that! I'd rather be called Wacko Boy.

— Calm down, Young Sir, he says. — It's just a name. I like it. I think it's a good name. I can see you as a Louis.

And that's when I remember something. *The Strange Mystery of Louis Drax, the Amazing Accident-Prone Boy.* It must be a book I once read.

— Louis Drax, I say. — There used to be a boy called Louis Drax.

Things are different in your ninth life. Your ninth life's much further away than your eighth one, it's a whole new place. It isn't the place Maman's in, *a beautiful place*, she says, *lovely and sunny and hot* and blah blah blah. *Too hot sometimes, they have forest fires nearly every year. People light them. Arsonists.* She keeps whispering stuff in my ear. *Come back, Lou-Lou, come back.* But I'm too far away. *I love you darling. Maman's here for you, my sweet boy* blah blah blah. *And there's a nice doctor called Pascal Dannachet who's looking after you* blah blah blah. She's always whispering, like it's a secret, and me and her are the only people in the world, and singing me baby songs that suck. *Ainsi font, font, font les petites marionnettes. Ainsi font, font, font trois petits tours et puis s'en vont.*

— You don't have to listen, says Gustave. — You can switch her off.

— I'd like to meet an arsonist, I tell him. — I'd like to watch him do it, and maybe help.

She says we can go out in the garden later. They'll strap me into a wheelchair and she'll push me along, just like when I was a baby in a pram. It's a beautiful garden, and all the others are going out too, because there's a breeze today and you can smell the sea and the pine from the forest. *And Pascal Dannachet's a good doctor, one of the best, and he knows what he's doing and he's very hopeful about you, sweetheart, he knows you'll come back, and so do I*, blah blah blah.

And the best thing is, we're safe here. No one knows where we are, no one can find us . . . It's just you and me again, like the old days.

What old days? Blah blah blah.

—Don't listen, says Gustave. —Talk to me instead. Tell me stories.

So I tell him what happened with Fat Perez. How in Fat Perez's room there's a big glass bowl with water and seashells in. It's sitting on the table in front of you. You can look inside it and pretend you're drowning. If you went very small you could be like a hermit crab and go inside one of the shells with just your legs coming out when you needed to go somewhere, like from one side of the bowl to the other.

—So what do you say, Louis? says Fat Perez.

But I'm not answering because I'm too busy stuffing my whole body into one of the shells, a small yellow one, where I can concentrate on the last episode of the Power Puff Girls. The bit after the robot shark attack, before they realise that Buttercup hasn't been swallowed up, because she was in the lab all the time, making a potion to reverse the Laws of Time and give the land back to the animals. I can hear his voice but I can't hear the words. I'm in my shell now. I'm safe here and I can think about Buttercup all I want, and forget about the stuff he is saying.

He is afraid it hasn't worked out between us.

—It's no one's fault. But it's been a pleasure working with you, Louis. I have learned a lot. I think you have learned a few things too. But your mother thinks we should call it a day. I'm sorry, Louis. I'm used to making progress and your mother feels that I haven't. Or at least, not the progress she was hoping I would make with you. The honest thing for me to do at this point is to tell you that your mother feels I have nothing more to offer you.

You wouldn't think I would cry when he says that, would

you? You'd think I would be pleased to get rid of this stupid fat man instead of being a stupid weedy crybaby and shouting over and over again, — NO! Please, Monsieur Perez! No!

But he says he's sorry. — It's your maman's decision. It's over, Louis. No more visits. You don't need me any more.

— Yes I do!

— You'll see.

— No, you're the one who's going to see.

That's what I said to him, before I climbed into the shell with Buttercup the Power Puff Girl.

The next day I wrote Fat Perez a letter and I put some of Mohammed's poo-droppings in. Eight droppings, because I was still eight then, plus some sawdust. I got an envelope and a stamp from Papa's desk and wrote his name, Marcel Perez, and his address, 8 rue Malesherbes, Gratte-Ciel, Lyon, and on the way to school next morning when we were going past the postbox, I said — Maman, look over there. See that dog?

And I pointed to the other side of the road and while she was looking for the dog, I took the letter out of my pocket and put it in the postbox.

— Did you see the dog?

— Yes, he was lovely.

— You really saw him?

— But I couldn't work out what breed he was. A husky, maybe?

— Or a Dobermann. I think he was probably a Dobermann.

But here's the funny thing about Maman. She can see dogs even when there aren't any. Even when you've made them up.

You are a big fat liar, Fat Perez. You told her you didn't want to see me any more. You told her I was too much for you. That's what she told me. Plus you said nothing would leave the room and that wasn't true either. So you suck. I hope you die soon or catch a gross disease.

Louis Drax

All the time I can feel Gustave's eyes staring through a little slit in the bandages. If someone's staring at you but their face is covered in bandages, you don't know if he wants to be your friend or kill you. He won't stop looking at me like I'm his enemy or his son or like I'm living in his head just like he's living in mine.

— Hi, Louis, says Dr Dannachet. — It's a lovely day outside, there's a bit of wind at last. I know you can hear me, Louis. I want you to try and reach us all again. You were trying, weren't you? I know you were. I could feel it.

Don't say anything don't say anything don't say anything.

— Your mother's waiting for you. Have you been listening to the cassettes she's made you? I hope so. I'm looking forward to you waking up. My wife got a book out of her library for you, *Les Animaux: leur vie extraordinaire.* I was just reading about bats. I know you like them. I guess you know the bat bit by heart, don't you? But I was fascinated.

And he starts reading from the bat bit.

— *Did you know that bats are the only mammals that fly? Other kinds of mammals can glide from tree to tree, but bats use their wings in much the same way as birds. These wings are actually flaps of skin called membranes, and they are supported by fingers, front and back limbs and a tail. Bats are to be found all over the world, except in the North and South Pole, but most species are . . .*

But his voice is getting further and further away, and it's hard to listen to. *Tropical or sub-tropical. There are about 1,000 known species. About thirty of these — all insect eaters — are to be found in Europe . . .*

People come along and then they go. You don't know who you'll see and who's going to suddenly disappear. There's a clock on the wall but the time jumps around. Sometimes it's night for too long, and day lasts just a minute, and other times it's for ever and ever.

— What were you doing before? I ask Gustave. He still scares me but I know he can't hurt me. Not by touching me anyway, because he isn't properly real.

— I can't remember. Not completely. None of us can. I had a wife. Her name was . . . Sometimes I remember it. But not today. I just remember being in a dark place. A cave.

— Do you get visitors?

— No. I'm alone. I must have done something bad. Maybe something evil. And you?

— My maman's here but my papa's a pilot. When he comes he'll bring me Lego models and stuff. He's coming soon. He's on his way.

If it was Fat Perez, he'd have asked me a question then. I liked it that Gustave didn't. I wondered what he did to his wife. Maybe he's a rapist. Maybe he forced her to do things she didn't want to do that made a baby she hated who'd be better off dead. Rape is a terrible thing, you can look it up in the dictionary. It lets you down very badly.

And then it's suddenly night-time and there's a thunderstorm and the clock says three.

Adults do stupid things sometimes, you have to believe me, sweetheart. Your father loves you really. He didn't mean to do what he did. Mothers are always there for their children. And one day we'll be free. He'll be out of our lives and we can live together happily ever after.

I wonder if Gustave can hear the same voices as me. Or maybe he hears other ones.

— What happened to you? What happened to your face?

— I don't know, he says. — I don't even remember what I looked like.

— My papa, he has hairy arms like you. Are you tall when you stand up?

— Quite tall, I think.

— So's Papa.

— And your maman? says Gustave. — What's your maman like?

— She's going crazy without me. Some bad things happened to her. She can't always trust men, because some men are bad. I can see how crazy she's going, but the doctor can't see it, no one can, not even Jacqueline. If Papa was here, he'd see it. He knows her like I do. She whispers in my ear the whole time, all blibber-blobber language about how it wasn't his fault and I mustn't blame Papa. She sings me baby songs.

— Blame him for what? says Gustave.

— I don't know. But he must've done a bad thing. He must've let us down very badly.

Did I say that or did I just think it? You can never tell, when you're with Gustave. Then maybe we both go to sleep, because when I wake up he's talking in this whisper I can hardly hear.

— There was water everywhere. It was like a pool or a lake, but it was too dark to see. My face hurt. I could feel it was cut and bruised, and my nose was smashed. I couldn't move my legs and only one arm worked. When you're all alone in a cave you think the strangest thoughts. I couldn't remember anything about the past, except her name. My wife's name. I wrote it on the wall in blood so that I'd remember it. I keep thinking that if I went back there, I could see it. And I'd know her name again and maybe everything would make sense. I wrote my baby's name too. We had a baby.

— How old was it?

— I don't know. Just a baby, I think. A tiny baby.

— Did it have a stupid hat with bunny ears?

— I don't know.

— Well, was it a boy or a girl?

But he doesn't know that either. — Maybe you were a cave explorer and you lost your way and you ran out of supplies. That's why you're so hungry.

— Maybe.

— And maybe I was a boy who fell because he was always having accidents; he was an Amazing Accident-Prone Boy.

— Yes. You were.

I was going to ask him how he knew that but he'd gone again. I knew he'd come back though. Nightmares like that, they go on and on, and you're not the one who decides.

Then some time goes by and Dr Dannachet comes and reads aloud from *La Planète bleue*, and Gustave watches him and doesn't say anything but I know what he's thinking, because I'm thinking the same thing. He's getting tired. We know because we can feel it in his voice and his skin and his bones. Plus he took a Valium. Doctors do that sometimes, if things get to them. Things have been getting to him.

And now he's reading the bit about monster tube-worms that are gross to look at because they're just huge long tubes of slimy flesh, bigger than a grown-up human's arm. One end's a mouth and the other's a butt but only an underwater expert or another tube-worm can tell which is which. They live on the deep-sea bed four kilometres down where it's full of poison. Things happen there that can't happen on land. There's life in places where there shouldn't be life because it doesn't make sense that a creature could survive on poison. But it isn't poison to him. He's completely used to it, he was born there, and if you tried to take him away from it, he might even die.

— Watch, says Gustave.

And Dr Dannachet's suddenly stopped reading and you can hear the book fall on the floor and he doesn't pick it up.

— Now's your chance, says Gustave. — You know what you have to do, Young Sir. Do it now. While you can. He won't feel a thing.

— Will you help me?

— I can't. I have to leave you for a moment now, Young Sir. You have to do this on your own.

And he goes away into a corner of the room where everything's white and starts coughing and coughing and coughing until out comes blood and sick. And while he's over there watching me from his corner, I do the thing we've been thinking about but not saying. Because if you say it, it breaks.

True to her assurance, Jacqueline somehow saw to it that Natalie Drax did not return to the ward that day. That night I stayed in my office late and finished drafting the paper for Lyon. Sophie was out again with Guy Vaudin's wife, Danielle, and a gaggle of other female friends, empowering herself or whatever women do when they're feeling unfriendly towards their husbands. I didn't want to go home through the heat of the olive grove and arrive at an empty womanless house, so, feeling restless and at a loose end, I went back to the coma ward to visit my silent troupe.

The night-nurse told me that Isabelle had been very active again, so I sat with her for a while, holding her hand. When she first came to us her nails were bitten to the quick; now they were long and elegant, manicured and varnished by Jacqueline. A sleeping beauty. She shifted, opened her eyes briefly, gave a light yawn, and then sank back into a torpid state.

After chatting to her for a while – I gave her my thoughts on the new physiotherapist, Karine, who I had just taken on, and was pleased with – I glided from bed to bed, propelling myself in the swivel chair, until I came to Louis Drax. I looked at his soft cheeks, the waxy skin, the parted mouth, the long dark lashes. I stroked his hair. It was sleek and thick, and already seemed longer than when he first arrived. He was motionless. Tonight I would sit with him. Tonight, for his mother's sake, for the sake of the woman whose sad, lovely face was becoming a strange, discomfiting fixture in my heart, I would try to be a good doctor to him. Be there for him, tell him about where he was and what we were trying to do for him here, perhaps even enter his head. He had made a huge effort to communicate. Had even managed a few tiny, astonishing words. Such a sudden, extraordinary impulse does not come from nowhere. Had Louis Drax been more conscious, all along, than I had dared hope or imagine?

The ward was quiet except for Isabelle, who uttered small noises every now and then, and twisted a little. She was the most physically active of my patients, and the closest, I estimated, to recovering consciousness. The nurses reported a marked change in her sleep/wake cycle since her father's arrival; these events are rarely coincidental. Perhaps we were about to see something.

I was still in a state of nervous excitement so I took a Valium and settled myself down with Louis. I read aloud to him from *La Planète bleue*, which Sophie had got hold of for me. It was just the sort of thing I used to read when I was Louis' age, as a devotee of Cousteau. But I was tired, and I could feel my voice becoming weaker and fainter as I charted the life-cycle of a rather unappealing deep-sea creature called a tube-worm. I don't remember the book falling from my hand to the floor.

I don't think I slept long – it felt like seconds rather than minutes – and I woke with a wrenchingly uncomfortable start. I'd had a nightmare. A huge worm was tunnelling its way into my phrenological map, which was wrapped in bloody bandages. It was one of those absurd but somehow plausible dreams, from which you wake and wonder if you really have escaped. I spun the chair and got to my feet quickly: as I did so, I heard the young nurse at the night-desk draw in a breath. I'd surprised her.

— Sorry, Dr Dannachet, she whispered, tiptoeing up to me.
— You gave me a shock. You were so fast asleep.

— What time is it?

— Half past four. I should have woken you before but I didn't dare.

— Why on earth not? It's much later than I thought.

— Sorry. It's just that, well – earlier on, about two hours ago, you were sleepwalking. I heard you're not supposed to wake someone who's –

— What? I felt myself go hot and then very slowly, cold. — Where did I go?

— I didn't really see, but you left the ward. It was around two o'clock. I had to change a bedpan and then I made myself a *tisane* in the kitchen. When I came back, you were walking down the ward, back to Louis' bed. I thought you were awake, but when I spoke to you, you didn't say anything and you looked a bit strange. That's when I realised. I walked you back to your chair and you sat down again, and just stayed asleep.

— Bizarre. Were my eyes open?

— Yes, but it didn't look like you could see out of them. You looked . . . well. You looked blind, Dr Dannachet. Completely blind.

Nobody likes to lose control, especially in front of a junior member of staff. I told Nurse Marie-Hélène Chaillot, who was looking at me anxiously, that she had done the right thing, absolutely and exactly the right thing, as recommended in all the textbooks. I tried to make a joke of it, but inside I was disturbed. What had triggered the episode? Was I somehow *regressing?*

Trying to muster some reason in my half-woken state, I took a couple of paracetamol, thanked Nurse Chaillot and made my way out into the night. The warm air came as a shock after the cool of the clinic, and I instantly felt the pressure of the day's residual heat like a weight on my shoulders. The olive groves shone eerily in the light of an almost full moon, and my shoes caught the dew, reflecting stars. I turned and looked at the clinic, low and flat on the hilltop. Its fluorescence seemed brighter than ever, giving it an aura that buzzed around its outline before dissipating in the starlit sky. It looked like a temple or some other holy structure – a place that could house miracles, a place where miracles hatched and belonged. Yet for once my mind was not soothed by this thought. I inhaled the scented night air deeply, trying to shake off whatever strange miasma had infected me. But it seemed to have crept into my lungs, under my skin. I was almost light-headed with exhaustion.

When I came home, Sophie woke and rolled over under the sheet, sleepy and hot. Our air-conditioning system had broken the previous year, and ever since we'd made do with an electric fan which now spun lazily next to the bed, stirring the heat around rather than cooling the air.

— Nice evening? she murmured.

— I was at the clinic, I told her.

— Briefing Madame Drax? she yawned. — Drying her tears? Feeling excited because she's convinced you're the only person in the world who can save her son?

I wasn't up to arguing. I still felt bleary and groggy.

— I need to sleep.

— Well, the spare room's ready for you.

I was too tired for any discussion of my rights, though her body would have comforted me in the way it always managed to. I thought of telling her about the fact that I had sleepwalked, but something – something aside from her current hostility towards me – stopped me. What it was, I cannot fathom. I simply cannot. I do not understand myself at the best of times, and in those turbulent, heat-stricken days that followed Louis' seizure, I was more disconnected from myself than ever.

I slept badly, and it felt as though what little sleep I got provided the opposite of nourishment. The next morning Guy Vaudin and I ran two more sets of brain scans on Louis and cross-checked them against one another. But nothing we could see made any sense. What happened, we agreed, simply should not have happened. It was a physical impossibility. Like Louis' bizarre return from the dead in Vichy General Hospital, it defied logic.

— Write it up anyway, said Vaudin. — You never know. In

the meantime, I think we should play it down with the mother.

I agreed with him; after her outburst at Louis' bedside, I was becoming increasingly worried about her mental state, and the last thing I wanted was to encourage her 'angel' theory about her son.

— The comatose are not immune to changes of environment, I told her later that morning. She had returned to Louis' bedside suitably contrite, but with a quietly desperate look on her face. There was fear, too. Yes, she was afraid of something. Her own hope, perhaps? It would not be unheard of. Under her thin tan, her face was the same unearthly white I had seen yesterday, as though the episode had drained her of blood. She wore no make-up, and for the first time I noticed fine lines around her eyes. She looked thin and ill, and I wondered whether I should suggest a check-up. — It's not uncommon for them to make a small involuntary movement, shortly after they have been moved to a new bed, I told her, trying to make my voice carry authority. — It means nothing. It should not be misinterpreted – consider it a freak anomaly.

Could she detect the tiny shudder of uncertainty at the back of my voice? Or was her closed-off face merely a sign that she was elsewhere? *In denial*, was the phrase that Philippe Meunier used.

— I'm so sorry Pascal, said Natalie. Her voice was a low, haunted whisper. — About the way I reacted. I was so shocked. Do you understand? I was so sure he was coming back. When he spoke –

— And I'm sorry I pushed you. I didn't mean to. I hope I didn't hurt you.

— You're stronger than you think, she said, drawing up the sleeve of her blouse to show her upper arm. My breath caught in shock as I saw the ugly purple bruise on her skin.

— Did I do that? I whispered, horrified. — I've never hurt a woman before.

Guilt swamped me.

She smiled ruefully. — It's OK. I've had worse. My husband could be quite violent.

I closed my eyes.

— He beat you up?

She looked away and flushed, which I took as a yes. I have never fathomed what attracts people to one another, or how passionate love curdles to poison. Except that sometimes it has to do with sickness, a demented yin and yang of punishment and subjugation, of worst fears dawning, worst impulses fed. I felt my own marriage to Sophie to be solid, healthy – subject only to the usual tidal shifts that happen over the years. Our current phase, which traced a slow arc of mutual neglect – was recent. But did I have it in me to be otherwise?

— I'm not like that, I blurted. — You have to believe me.

— I know, she said gently. I was grateful for the delicacy with which she moved on. — Look, I've made another cassette for him, she said, showing me. The title *Maman 3* was written on it in neat handwriting.

— Good, I said. I was trying to sound normal, but inside I was heaving with panic at the sight of that bruise. — Play it to him. Speak, too. You never know what might happen.

She put the headphones on Louis' ears, pressed the start button, and sat holding his hand, and stroking his hair. All the mothers tend to be very physical. I wondered if it had always been that way between them. Just as I was thinking this, the boy's face gave a small twitch. It probably meant nothing, but Natalie Drax chose to think otherwise because she smiled at me with a hesitant kind of triumph. And despite myself, despite my self-revulsion and the residual rage I still felt over her reaction the day before, I felt some returning warmth towards her. In that brief second I remembered our kiss and her vulnerability in that tiny, explosive moment in the garden, and I forgave her everything and inwardly begged her to forgive me my own disconnected impulses, for an uneasy thought was beginning to stir within me: had I meant to hurt her? Might something small and sick within me be wondering, at this very moment, what her smooth freckled skin would look like with more bruises? I felt cold.

— Thank you, she murmured. — Thank you for all you've done for Louis.

— It isn't much, I said. I still felt contaminated by my own thoughts.

— It's more than you know, she said, and touched my arm lightly with her hand, as she rose to leave.

That small gesture touched me deeply, going straight to the core of my guilt. She had reached out to me at last, on her own initiative, just as I had recognised my own capacity to abuse her trust. As I watched her slight figure moving down the ward and into the corridor, and thought of the bruise on her arm, I realised that it was impossible not to feel an immense sense of pity – and what is pity if not a skewed admiration? – for a woman who asked for nothing. Who appeared, I should say, to ask for nothing. Whose pride perhaps prevented her from articulating her need, but whose whole psyche was screaming to be saved from her own internal hell. Isn't pity one of the higher forms of love? My heart yearned for her, yearned to take away her pain, including the pain I myself might have caused. Call me a middle-aged fool, but what I felt for her, in that moment, seemed sacred.

The heat escalated unbearably over the weekend. We have dangerous summers in Provence, sparked by human madness, fuelled by tinder-dry forests. Two years ago, the whole hillside just a kilometre from the clinic was scorched to blackness; the smoke took days to lift and the fire helicopters circled endlessly above the devastation like furious mosquitoes. By this stage in the summer the heat had become so intense it was almost unbearable to be outside in the daytime. I wondered how Natalie was managing in her cottage. Perhaps she had made friends with some of the other relatives. I hoped so, but could not picture it. Although I hadn't kept a firm eye on her visits, I had the feeling she was spending more time than was healthy with her son. Maybe that's why things had got so out of hand. They were very close, she'd said. The way she touched him – the obsessive stroking of his hair, the way she flung herself at him after his fit – confirmed it. *I don't know how I could live without him.* Touching, but worrying, too. It's all too easy for relatives to identify so closely with their loved ones that they forget about their own needs completely.

All weekend I went about the chores of leisure-time in a trance, counting the hours before I could be back at work and see Natalie Drax again. In the meantime, Sophie and I reached a quiet truce. We ate meals together, discussing domestic topics but otherwise avoided one another. An electrician came to fix the air conditioning. I had a haircut which my barber assured me made me look younger. Sophie tended to the plants, had lengthy conversations with the girls in Montpellier, and read novels, while I thought about Natalie. About what she had gone through and must still be suffering. I saw the bruise on her arm again and again. Its image hovered in my mind like a filthy secret.

I spent Monday working my way through a pile of paperwork and preparing my slides for the talk I was giving in Lyon on Wednesday. I'd asked Noelle not to disturb me, but around four o'clock there was a hesitant knock on my door.

— There's a phone call for you that sounds very urgent, she said. — The mother of Louis Drax. Immediately I told Noelle she had done the right thing to interrupt me, and took the call. Natalie was in tears and could barely speak. She sounded frantic.

— Pascal, I'm at my house. I – her voice choked. — Look, I absolutely I need your help. Can you –

And then she abandoned all semblance of control and broke down completely.

— Please, Pascal! she shrieked. — Something terrible's happened. You've got to come, now! I need you!

I grabbed my keys and flew out.

A dog was barking madly as I opened the front gate. All the way, as I ran through the blisteringly hot olive groves down to the village, I'd been filled with a sense of dread that I would arrive too late. Perhaps Natalie was even more vulnerable than I had imagined. If you are alone in the world, you reach breaking point faster and by simpler routes than those who are surrounded by family, friends, colleagues. And she had none of these. She had a son in a coma and an abusive husband who was on the run from the police. Had she done something stupid? And if so, should I have spotted it coming?

The door had been left on the latch and as soon as I entered, I could hear muffled sobbing. Natalie Drax was on the floor of the kitchen, clutching the telephone and an envelope: a huge Alsatian stood over her, pawing the ground. It barked again as I entered, and she tried to calm it.

— It's OK, Jojo. Quiet now, he's a friend.

She put her arm round the creature and patted it. I don't like dogs, but I did the same. I guessed she had not moved from where she was when she phoned me. I checked her pulse, then hauled her up – she weighed nothing – and walked her out of the kitchen and into the small simple living-room. The dog followed us, its huge bright eyes looking anxious. There was a cage on the side-table containing a hamster which was running madly on its little exercise wheel. It must have belonged to Louis.

— What happened? You haven't taken anything, have you?

— What?

I was relieved to see that she looked genuinely confused by my question.

— I thought –

— Just read this, she said, thrusting the envelope at me. The postmark was local, and her name and address were scrawled on it in the most bizarre handwriting I have ever seen – huge and irregular and so splayed across the page that it could almost have been written by someone blind. There was a childishness about it, a primitivism that sent something cold running up and down my neck.

— I came home and . . .

She broke off, eyeing the letter with fear and disgust. Her shallow, tight breaths were matched by the dog's raucous panting. I wondered how long she had been in this state. I pulled her down to sit next to me on the sofa, and drew out the single sheet of badly folded paper from the envelope. It was plain white, and covered in the same huge handwriting; the effect across a whole page was lopsided, drunken-looking. Whoever had written it had gone to almost comic pains to disguise their real handwriting. And to cause the maximum grief possible.

Dear Maman,

I miss you and I miss Papa too. But I'll be needing a new dad, won't I? Dr Dannachet would like to sex you. But you know what I think? I think you should stay away from him and he should stay away from you. You should stay away from men e.g. Dr Dannachet. I am warning you, Maman. Don't let them come near you. Don't let them kiss you. The danger will come, and bad things will happen.

I love you, Maman.

Louis

I can't have been thinking straight, because my first reaction was one of surprise and bafflement. How could he have done it? How could he possibly have sat up, got hold of pen and paper, and written a letter to his mother, without anyone on the ward being aware of his movements? Even though he'd had that seizure, it was absurd, unthinkable. And yet for the first few seconds after I had read it, I could think of no other explanation. My heart surged with hope – until I caught sight of Natalie's face.

— I thought it was from him too, she said simply. — At first. And then when I realised it couldn't be – there was no way he could get up and do it and post a letter with no one seeing him

. . . but I still kidded myself he'd done it. Somehow. For a couple of minutes I was happy. Overjoyed. But it isn't him, is it?

— Is it his handwriting? I asked gently. — Is it anything like it?

— No. Nothing like.

— So . . .

— It isn't from him. Her voice was flat and dead. — Because it can't be. It's from someone else. There was a long silence as I struggled with my own confusion. — God, can you imagine how sick he is? she whispered at last, burying her face in the dog's fur. — To do something like that? To pretend to be Louis?

I identified misery, fear and disgust in her voice. It was indeed sick. But whoever had chosen to perform this distressing practical joke had read some of my baser thoughts uncannily well. *Dr Dannachet would like to sex you* . . . It was deeply embarrassing. I felt panicky. What the hell was going on?

— But who? I began, and then stopped.

Natalie's hair fell around her face like a pale waterfall, shrouding it. Her small hands were shaking uncontrollably. I noticed that the artificial nails had gone. The real ones looked ragged and chipped.

— There's been no trace of Pierre for three months, she blurted. — Not since the picnic. Back in Vichy I saw him everywhere – well I thought I did. I was in a terrible state back then, quite paranoid. But then after a while . . . it seemed he really had just disappeared off the face of the earth. I was beginning to hope he'd left the country. I even thought he might have committed suicide. She paused. — Well, hoped, actually. But only someone who knows Louis really well would know the kind of thing he'd say.

And yet, why on earth would a man bother to warn his wife off other men by masquerading as his comatose son? Why not threaten her directly? He obviously knew where she lived. Then a strange sensation crawled up my spine as it dawned on me that maybe that's exactly what would happen next. He could be watching us right now.

My heart started to trip over itself in panic. Quickly I glanced at the window; it looked out on to the front garden, beyond which lay the narrow, cobbled village road. I realised with some relief that anyone who wanted to spy on the cottage would have trouble hiding himself. Nevertheless, I stood up and drew the curtains. I was suddenly glad that the dog was with us.

— But I don't understand it. What can he possibly want?

She just sat there for a moment, rocking rhythmically to and fro in her chair. You could see the bones of her jaw working.

— He wants to scare me, she said finally, stroking Jojo and pulling him to her. He licked her hand. — And he wants to scare you too. He must have been spying on us.

— Have you rung Charvillefort?

— Of course not! She's worse than useless!

— What?

— Look, if there's one thing I know, it's that the police can't find Pierre! They're no closer to it now than they ever were. He's playing with them. Stephanie Charvillefort's inquiry into Louis' accident has been a complete disaster. They've bungled everything. All Charvillefort did was interrogate me, and then practically accuse me of pushing Louis over the edge myself. Knowing her, she's going to accuse *me* of doing this. That's how mistrustful she is.

And she slapped the letter in disgust.

— You mean you called no one but me?

She nodded defiantly.

— Get me her number anyway. We have to let her know.

With the kind of numb obedience that comes from shock, Natalie left the room, Jojo padding after her. Sensible of her to get a dog, I thought. She knew the score in a way that others perhaps didn't. She returned with a red address-book filled with phone numbers in small efficient writing. As she handed it to me, the dog growled.

— Good boy, I said nervously, patting his head.

Despite an attempt to appear composed, Natalie was clearly

too shaken to make the call, so I did. When I eventually got through to the Vichy police, it turned out that Detective Charvillefort was giving evidence at a trial, and would not be in until later in the day, but I could leave a message on her mobile. Which I did, before ringing the local police in Layrac. I had met Inspector Navarra on several occasions, at local functions; when I told him about the letter, and its background, I could hear from his voice that he was excited. This isn't a big crime spot, exactly. Apart from seasonal arson attacks, he'd be dealing with drugs, traffic violations, the odd illegal gun, a spot of house theft. But now, suddenly, there was a murderous fugitive on his patch.

—And you're quite sure it couldn't have been written by the boy? By Louis?

—He's been in a coma for over three months. He can't speak, let alone write letters. But it's written in his style, apparently. So whoever wrote it knows him well.

—Does it contain any threats?

Briefly, I explained the content.

—I'll find a way of getting hold of Detective Charvillefort, said Navarra. —But until we know for sure that it's Pierre Drax who wrote it, we have to treat it as a separate case.

When I told Natalie that Navarra was on his way, and a *gendarme* would be keeping an eye on the clinic too, she looked relieved, but distracted. While we waited for Navarra, I tried to get Natalie to tell me more about her husband. But she recoiled from the idea. It was clear she loathed the subject; when she spoke of him, it was with a mixture of fear, revulsion and contempt. She had met him at a difficult time in her life; she had just moved to Lyon from her native Paris – she'd had to get away, something went very badly wrong in her life there. He had seemed like a good man, but he turned out to be selfish and narcissistic. He and Louis never bonded properly. He had an alcohol problem, which – being a pilot – he tried to beat, but when he couldn't, found clever ways to control and hide. He was sometimes violent.

I flushed, remembering the bruise. I edged my eyes towards Natalie's bare left arm. The mark seemed bigger than before, a dark, rancid purple.

Natalie remained distracted when Georges Navarra – a pleasant man with sharp brown eyes – turned up to look at the letter. He greeted us both, and declared it to be very hot. There was a fire burning near Cannes, he said. If you listened, you could hear the helicopters. He patted the dog and asked its name. Funny, the way it seemed to take an instant liking to him. Navarra then sat at the table and spent a long time looking at the envelope.

— Local postmark, he murmured.

He read the letter through, then studied it with intense concentration, in the same way I might inspect a brain scan. All the while he stroked the dog which wagged its tail enthusiastically.

— Very strange, he said, once again holding it up to the light. — And written in ink, too. Who writes in ink nowadays?

— Plenty of doctors do, I said.

— Does your husband own a fountain pen? he asked Natalie. I saw him notice her bruise, and squirmed inwardly.

— What? She sounded far away. — I don't know. Yes, maybe. He never wrote much.

He had more questions, which Natalie answered in the same distracted way; her mind was clearly racing off elsewhere. Yes, she suspected it was written by her missing husband, because he was the only person who could possibly have done it, or wanted to. No, it was nothing like his handwriting and nor was it anything like her son's. Navarra slipped the letter into a plastic bag as he spoke, and then started jotting down notes. While he did this, I thought about the line that Navarra had been discreet enough not to mention.

Dr Dannachet would like to sex you.

It was as uncanny as it was excruciating. The fact was, I had indeed dared to imagine – But now the idea seemed unthinkable.

Criminally inappropriate. Obscenely unethical. Could it be that Pierre Drax's insight into my psychology (perhaps the psychology of any man, or the psychology of embarrassment) was part of his cunning? His way of stopping something from happening between his wife and other men? This made sense to me, if nothing else did. Painfully, he began to rise in my estimation. Was he manipulating me? Watching and laughing?

Navarra finished writing, then sat silent for a moment, tapping his teeth with his biro.

—Best not to sleep here tonight, I think, he told Natalie.

I felt relief at this, and I could see that she did too. Of course she couldn't be left alone if her husband was stalking her. I suggested the clinic. It has two bedrooms set aside for relatives; one was currently occupied by Isabelle's father, but Madame Drax could have the other. We agreed that I would take her there as soon as she had packed a bag, and that she would return to the cottage the next morning to feed the dog. By which time Detective Charvillefort would have been alerted to what had happened, and be on her way from Vichy. When Georges Navarra had gone, Natalie shuddered and sighed.

—I still can't quite believe he did it. It doesn't make sense. It doesn't hang together. But if it is him . . . I mean, who else could it be?

She didn't need to continue. He was probably here, now, in the village, or staying in Layrac. It was unsettling to realise it was a possibility. And even more unsettling to realise that I, too, was being watched. How much did Drax know about me and Natalie?

—I'll pack a bag, she said.

I nearly rang Sophie to say I wouldn't be home for dinner, but resisted because I knew she would put me in the position of making up a lie that didn't hold water, and give me grief. So I let it go. While Natalie was upstairs, I watched the hamster doing something complex to its nest. It seemed to be moving all its bedding from one side of the cage to another. For some reason this bothered me. Why would a small creature take it into its head to rearrange the furniture like that? I glanced at the pile of books on the table. They were mostly the standard texts on coma, but there were a couple of others, of the kind Sophie bought in bulk for the library: *Les Hommes viennent de Mars, les femmes viennent de Vénus, Affirmez-vous!, Le Complexe de Cendrillon*. They looked well-thumbed. Clearly they mattered enough to Natalie for her to have brought them in her luggage. There were photographs of Louis everywhere. A whole wall of them. Maybe too many, I thought. Was she a little obsessional about her son? Or was it just maternal pride? There was something else too: a half-completed model aeroplane. The construction looked quite complicated for a nine-year-old boy. Perhaps it was something he'd done with his father.

— The hamster's called Mohammed, she said, coming back and finding me peering into the cage. — And his home's Alcatraz. That was Pierre's name for it. Louis liked it. She laughed. — Mohammed in Alcatraz.

She left food for the dog, then we got into her Renault. The air was heavy; I wound down my window to try and catch a breeze. Faintly, you could smell smoke. We drove in silence for a while.

— If he wakes up – she said suddenly.

— It's only an if. Don't hope too hard.

I watched her profile.

— But I have to know, she said, changing gear. She drove nervously – a city driver who has found herself in the country and can't gauge its ways. — If he wakes up and remembers what happened, what will it do to him? You must have heard of that American case a year or so ago. The man who went into a coma when he was a child, and came out of it twenty years later. He woke up, and he was able to name his attackers, and they were jailed.

She was speaking with an unusual animation, which made her features seem to come alive.

— But that would be a triumph surely?

— But at what cost? Don't you see? She glanced at me, then back at the road. — His own *father?*

I said nothing. We reached the clinic car-park, where we pulled in. She turned off the engine and we sat in silence for a moment, looking out of the windscreen at the luminous whiteness of the clinic's façade. Mingled in with the evening air and the smoke and the smell of resin from the pine forest, there was the sweet scent of tobacco flowers and jasmine wafting up through the evening heat. The cicadas shrieked and the air felt oppressive with the threat of an imminent storm. You could feel it hatching in your bones, like passion, or dread.

— Look, she said, — I know I overreacted the other day when he sat up and asked for Pierre. And I apologise. But my first thought was to protect him. How can he live with what happened?

Secretly, I had to admit that she had a point – but I saw no use in agreeing with her openly. I looked up at the gathering clouds.

— As I said, it's unlikely he will emerge with his memory intact. And if he does, well, we'll cross that bridge when we come to it.

— Let's go in, she said abruptly. — I don't think we should be sitting here.

Just as Inspector Navarra had promised, there was a policeman in Reception, replacing the usual security guard who was now, he told us, patrolling the building. We went straight to the ward; Louis had not moved all evening, according to Marianne, the nurse on night duty. She said that the policeman had already looked in, and would be visiting at half-hourly intervals.

Marianne looked anxious. — Poor Louis, she whispered. I didn't know.

— Pierre Drax may phone, I warned her. — But if it's him, or if anyone calls and hangs up, or doesn't want to give their name, ring Georges Navarra, and then me. But you'll be quite safe.

The guest rooms were on the fourth floor of the building; I

got the key from Reception and we took the lift in silence. The room was large but bare. Seeing the kettle, she offered coffee. I hesitated, and then accepted. She went to fill the kettle from the tap in the bathroom.

— Natalie, I said slowly, when she emerged. — I'd like you to tell me what happened on the mountain.

She turned to me, flushed, and instantly miserable.

— I don't really like to talk about it, she said quietly, switching on the kettle and sitting down in the armchair opposite me. She looked up and met my eyes frankly. — It's very painful.

— I know. It must be. Forgive me. But – well. You've already told the police. Surely you can tell me? I think I should know, as his doctor. There might be more going on inside his head than we realise. If he does emerge from the coma, his state of mind could affect his recovery.

I could see she was struggling to fight back tears. The kettle began to growl in accompaniment to the gathering wind outside. I breathed in and exhaled slowly, waiting.

— We had an argument. Me and Pierre. Louis hated us arguing, he was trying to stop it.

— How did it start?

— Louis had sweets in his pocket. Pierre saw him eating one. He got furious. He didn't like Louis eating sweets. He said I wasn't bringing him up properly. I didn't even know he'd brought sweets. It was a simple mistake. But Pierre wouldn't let it drop. He went on and on. He was accusing me of all sorts of things. Being a bad mother. Louis couldn't stand it, and he ran off towards the ravine. We both ran after him. Pierre got to him first. He's very strong. He grabbed Louis and started dragging him to the car, saying he was taking him to Paris. Louis managed to get free and run off. But Pierre caught up with him again just by the ravine, and they struggled and . . . I didn't get there in time.

Her eyes met mine, shocked with pain.

— I saw his face as he was falling. His mouth was open like he wanted to tell me something but –

She broke off, and I shut my eyes. I could picture it: the father yelling at his son; Natalie screaming; the boy panicking. But did Louis stumble in the struggle, or was he pushed by a man so angry that he simply hit out at anything that came in his way? I waited for more, but she had fallen into silence. We listened to the thunder, each lost in our own thoughts.

— Louis always sided with me, she said eventually. — Never with Pierre. I told you, they never bonded.

— Why not?

The kettle came to the boil and clicked off. A crack of thunder sounded outside, drowning the cicadas. Natalie shut her eyes and kept them closed as she spoke.

— Maybe they would have done, if Pierre were Louis' natural father. But he isn't.

— What? I asked, incredulous. There was a long pause before she spoke again. Her eyes were still closed, as though she couldn't face seeing my reaction to her words.

— Someone else was.

— But who?

— Another man. Jean-Luc. Who's out of the picture, thankfully. It wasn't meant to happen.

— Oh. I'm sorry. So –

— I met Pierre when Louis was just a few weeks old, and we married and Pierre adopted him. But it didn't work. There were problems. It was very difficult for Pierre to accept Louis as his son. He had . . . well, very mixed feelings. Some very negative ones. All these accidents Louis kept having – well, I began to think they might have been Louis' way of somehow pleasing Pierre. I think Marcel Perez was beginning to think the same thing. The therapy was a slow process. It had its ups and downs, and then – well. It got cut short.

It was now my turn to stay silent, as I absorbed what she'd just told me. It made sense. There was no reason why she should have divulged any of this before, but now she had, a lot began to fall into place. Pierre Drax's negative feelings towards Louis, for a start.

— The police are aware of this? I asked eventually.

— Of course.

But there was still something that didn't fit. It wasn't just that a row that erupted over a packet of sweets – *sweets*, for goodness' sake! – had led to such a catastrophe.

— If Pierre resented Louis so much, I don't see why on earth he'd want to abduct him. What was that all about?

She opened her eyes, almost in surprise, as though it were an absurd question.

— He wanted to punish me. To punish us both. For being so close. For loving each other more than we loved him. For not needing him. For all sorts of reasons that don't even sound like reasons to sane people. But they were reasons to Pierre. Some people need hostages.

I wanted to ask her more about Louis' relationship with Pierre, and indeed about his real father, but I held back. She couldn't take any more, at least not now. She made the coffee, which we drank in silence. I wondered whether she had ever taken the Prozac that Philippe Meunier had prescribed, but I felt I'd probed her enough for one evening. She sat straight-backed and tense, staring at nothing, like someone lost to the world. And to themselves. When I questioned her gently about her family, she said she would phone her mother in Guadeloupe tomorrow, and let her know what had happened without getting her too alarmed.

— I must go now, I told her. — You'll be safe here.

We both stood up, and I went to the door, where I kissed her on both cheeks.

— I feel safe with you, she murmured, and the atmosphere seemed to change colour. She gave me a small sad smile, and in the half-light, the tension seemed ironed out of her. It wasn't conventional beauty that she had. It was an innocence that seemed, at that moment, to be child-like, almost angelic.

Suddenly the unspoken feelings between us were too much to bear, and I tore myself away. But after I left, I had the feeling that a huge, delicate cloud, invisible and lighter than air, was sheltering us both.

By the time I got home the storm had broken. It was after midnight, but the air was still stiflingly hot. I made myself a sandwich in the kitchen, but I didn't have much appetite. I showered and then, not wanting to wake Sophie, padded quietly past our bedroom towards the spare room, but she must have heard me, because the bedroom door opened. She wore an ancient cotton kimono and I could see she had been crying. She took a white square from her pocket and held it up silently, like a flag of surrender. A letter.

— This came for you today, she said. — I opened it. I drew in a breath.

— You opened a letter addressed to me?

— It looked interesting, she said. — Shouldn't I have? You're behaving like you've got something to hide. Have you, Pascal?

That's when I noticed she was drunk.

— Let me see it, I said, snatching it from her.

The envelope was identical to the one Natalie had received. My address, and the same insane handwriting as before. I read it in silence, my heart clenching and unclenching like a panicked fist.

Dear Dr Dannachet,

You should be looking after me, but all you want to do is sex my maman. Stay away from her. Bad things will happen if you don't, I promise you. This is a warning. Keep right away from her.

Louis Drax

I shut my eyes and tried to get my breathing under control.

— I thought you said Louis Drax was in a coma, said Sophie, her voice slurred and nasty with alcohol. I felt myself swaying. *Yes*, I thought faintly. *He is supposed to be.* — You've been with her, she said, not waiting for an answer. — You've been with the kid's mother.

I didn't deny it. I didn't care what she thought, frankly.

— I can see it. I can feel it. I know you, Pascal. She's wormed her way into that stupid bleeding heart of yours. Look at you. It's so . . . it's so undignified. For both of us. We can't go on like this. I can't. I won't. I'm going to Montpellier to stay with the girls for a few days. While you sort yourself out.

I couldn't be kind to her, although I knew that the moment called for it. There was too much distance between us. It had been growing, a centimetre at a time. Now it was a chasm and I could see no way of reaching across it. Nor did I want to. Her drunkenness disgusted me.

— We'll talk in the morning, I said, turning my back on her. — You'd better get some sleep. That's quite a hangover you're headed for.

I left a message on Navarra's phone at the police station. I kept it brief, suggesting we meet in the morning. Afterwards, as I lay in bed under a single sheet in the spare room, I heard Sophie sobbing, but I didn't go to her. I was too tired, and too haunted by the picture of Pierre Drax and the letter he'd sent me. But the hammering rain kept me awake and in the end, almost reluctantly, my thoughts turned to my marriage. The fact was that Sophie and I had lost whatever it was we once shared. We didn't make each other happy any more, not the way we used to in the days when we would dance around the living room, kissing, then pull one another to the floor and make love while the girls slept upstairs. Melanie and Oriane were twenty and twenty-one now, they'd left home. When I applied my mind to it, I realised I admired Sophie, liked her even. But did I love her? It was a question that seemed irrelevant, a question I couldn't answer any more. Something had surely died between us. But it had died so slowly and quietly that it was hard to pinpoint when or even how. Neglect, I suppose. Neglect does that. It makes you go blind.

And besides, I was in love with another woman.

I slept fitfully, haunted by a sense that something was horribly awry, both without and within. Unconscious, I saw scenes that related to my childhood in Bretagne but the dream broke into fragments as soon as I emerged from its grip. I felt strangely powerless, as though emptied of energy. I realised, with dismay, that I had no desire to go to the clinic, despite the pull of Louis and his mother. It was a failure of nerve. The thought of my coma ward and the work I did there suddenly repelled me. Why, I asked myself shakily, was I so committed to coaxing life out of these human husks? And who was the most disconnected from reality, my patients or their doctor? Something inside me crumpled as I considered this. Looking back, I see now that the indefinable dread that swamped me that morning was a premonition of what was to come. But I was on a track, and there was no way off.

I went in to the bedroom where Sophie was still sleeping, clutching a pillow. She looked sweet and crumpled. I was sorry for her, and ashamed of the disgust I had felt the night before. I knew I should wake her before I left, but I couldn't bring myself to. Instead I kissed her lightly on the cheek and was just closing the door when she spoke.

— I'm still going to Montpellier.

— I won't try and stop you.

— Why not?

— Because you want to go. Why waste energy arguing with you? The girls will be glad to see you. I'll call you tonight.

— No. Don't. Don't call me until you know what you want, Pascal. I take it you haven't got a clue what you want?

I didn't say anything. As usual, she was right.

It was only eight, but already the cool brought by last night's storm had dissipated and the sun's heat was piercing. Even the gulls were silent. As I climbed the hill I sniffed the air. Could I smell smoke through the scent of pine and lavender, or was my paranoia making me sense disaster everywhere? It was a relief to enter the reception hall of the clinic. Its whiteness calmed me and gave me a feeling of detachment, the way whiteness always does. I spent a couple of moments watching the TV news; it turned out I had not imagined smoke in the air. Despite last night's downpour, the forest fires were still burning, and the wind was now blowing inland from the sea, spreading the blaze in our direction. But the outside world seemed as unreal as a moonscape. I shivered involuntarily. The air conditioning – too sharply refrigerated after the heat outside – was playing havoc with my blood.

Hoping to ease myself into the day with something non-demanding, I looked in on my new physiotherapist, Karine, who was working with Isabelle. I stood in the doorway and watched for a while, trying to settle. Karine was effortlessly efficient in her role, keeping up a steady flow of conversation and encouragement as she manipulated Isabelle's limbs and demonstrated different features of the equipment to her assistant, Félix. Karine had spent a year in the United States and returned with some interesting ideas. Her predecessor had been a sour-faced man whom I'd never liked. He'd pushed the patients too hard, almost as though his secret aim was to produce a team of comatose body-builders. I'd been glad when he retired to spend more time with his own muscles and left those of my patients alone.

When she saw me, Karine came over and began talking

animatedly about the extra equipment she wanted to order. We were discussing the pros and cons of a new jacuzzi system when we were cut short by the arrival of Isabelle's father, Eric Masserot. Hardly glancing at his daughter, whose arms and shoulders were being massaged, he made his way towards me with a determined step. I had neglected him. I had neglected everyone. I excused myself from Karine, and went to shake his hand, apologising as I did so for not having yet found room in my schedule for him. But we could talk now, I reassured him. The poor man was close to tears. He told me how troubled he was by the state in which he found his daughter. He had been led to believe that when her weight was back to normal, she might stand a better chance of recovery, but although she was moving more than usual, nothing had happened for several months. He worried about her feeding tube. Was she getting enough nutrition? I answered as best I could, and suggested that he talk to his ex-wife about the atmosphere between them. Might it be hampering Isabelle's recovery? Is that what I meant? It was possible, I said. It was an awkward issue to raise, and the encounter – which I did not handle well – distressed me intensely. It highlighted how lax I had become lately. I'd been too preoccupied with Louis and his mother to give the others the attention they deserved; Jacqueline had been picking up the slack, as always, but I needed to start pulling my weight again, before Vaudin or any of the others noticed how absent I had been from the daily life of my patients and their relatives in the week since Louis arrived.

I left Eric Masserot staring out of the window and headed for the ward, where Louis remained under observation in the wake of his sudden spasm. But I didn't go to him. Despite my good intentions towards the boy, he seemed tainted now; it was as if the letters had made me doubt everyone – including him. Absurd, that I couldn't even trust a comatose child. But that's how I felt.

I sat at the ward desk, doing some routine paperwork and

hastily assembling some notes on Isabelle Masserot. But the same question kept nudging at me with an unnerving insistence: Was I losing it? Five minutes later, as if in answer to that very question, Guy Vaudin turned up, looking haggard and anxious. I was immediately on the alert.

— Glad to catch you, he said, taking a chair at the other end of the desk. — I think we need a word. Look, Pascal, he said, scratching the back of his hand. — This is a bit awkward, but – well, Sophie rang Danielle last night. She was very upset. She seems to think you're having an affair with Madame Drax. He sighed heavily. — Should I assume she's right?

— For God's sake, Guy! No!

I felt furious at the misunderstanding. (Christ, we'd kissed once. What's a kiss? Nothing!) What was happening was grotesque, I told him. I explained about the threatening letter sent by Pierre Drax in Louis' name.

— So whatever's happening, it's happening in the head of Pierre Drax. Who has now passed the delusion on to my wife. Who clearly didn't hesitate to ring yours. The police will be here soon; you'll probably need to increase security.

— Yes, he said distractedly. — I know about that. But look, is there anything in what Sophie had to say? She seemed pretty sure about it.

— This is an inquisition!

— It's for your own sake, he said, dropping his voice. We both turned our heads at that moment to check no staff were within earshot. — It doesn't look good, and you know it. It lowers morale, and the other relatives have already noticed that your head's elsewhere. There have been some rumblings, you know. Even Jessica Favrot's had a word, and I know how devoted she is to you. And Masserot isn't happy either. He's come all the way from Spain. This could be a crucial week for Isabelle.

At that moment, Jacqueline came back in, saw the look on Vaudin's face, and immediately turned on her heel and busied herself with something at the far end of the ward. She probably knew about this too. When the phone rang, I was glad of the interruption. Indicating that I must answer it, I signalled to Guy that we would continue the conversation later.

— Think about it, he said as he left.

— It's Detective Charvillefort, Vichy Police. I hear from Georges Navarra that you received a letter too?

Her voice was harried and clipped; she seemed to be clattering on a keyboard as we spoke. I replied in the affirmative.

— If you've spoken to Natalie Drax, you've probably heard that he surprised us again just the other day, I told her. I started to doodle the name 'Charvillefort' on a notepad.

— Yes, I gather. Very interesting. Tell the nurses, extra vigilance, and round-the-clock surveillance. Now are you sure there's no way Louis could have written these letters?

— It's unthinkable.

— But he sat up and spoke, I gather? Asked for his father? So why can't he write a letter?

— Look, we don't understand his seizure. But believe me, with so many people about, he'd never have moved without someone seeing him.

— You say you have properly operative CCTV on the ward?

Damn; my pen was leaking. I felt beleaguered.

Jacqueline had prepared the wheelchairs and was encouraging the relatives to take the patients out for a walk in the garden. I took Louis, who was plugged into a Walkman playing a tape of his mother. The air smelled scorched and drenched at the same time.

Jessica Favrot, spotting my presence, hurried towards me.

— I'm very worried about Natalie Drax, she said.

— In what way? I asked.

— She won't mix. It's strange. She won't let any of us get through. It's so painful for her to suffer like that alone, but it seems like —

— That's what she wants?

— Yes.

— Well, perhaps for now we should respect that, I said. But I could hear the doubt in my voice and so could Jessica. There *was* something wrong, something that rankled, something I suddenly felt I didn't have time to investigate. Excusing myself, I pushed the wheelchair towards the ornamental pond where the fountain was playing tricks with the light, sending tiny rainbows shooting in all directions. Louis and I circled it twice before stopping at a bench where I read a few pages from *La Planète bleue*. I don't know how long I sat there with Louis, just staring at the fountain. It could have been minutes, or hours. My mind felt drained. I tried to imagine what Pierre Drax was thinking now. What his next move would be. Was it really possible he had been watching me and Natalie?

If so, how close was he now?

Suddenly I imagined I felt his eyes on my back, and I hastened back inside with Louis.

After an hour's work back in my office, Jacqueline called to let me know the detective had arrived and was on the ward. And there she was, inspecting Louis like a specimen on a slab. I hovered at a distance, watching her: she wore a mushroom-coloured linen suit, whose jacket she was now removing, to reveal a white shirt and big unwieldy breasts that seemed to steer her movements.

Having hung her jacket over the back of the chair, Stephanie Charvillefort was continuing to give Louis a thorough going-over, not in any medical way, but as one would inspect an object that was deemed to be a piece of evidence. Which I suppose he was, in a manner of speaking. She lifted his hand tentatively, let it drop to see what happened. Someone in a deep coma has no reflexes; perhaps at least she discovered that much then. I quelled my instinct to intervene and watched as she proceeded to blow air on to Louis' face and register the lack of response. Then, lowering her mouth to his ear she asked, quite loudly:

— Louis? Are you awake? Detective Charvillefort here. Can you hear me? I'd like to ask you some questions.

I sped over, cleared my throat, held out my hand. She stood up from her chair and I was struck again by her very bright blue eyes, clean and piercing.

— Do you think Drax is stalking her, then? I asked as we shook hands. She looked up at me coolly, appraising me with those strangely astonishing eyes.

— I'm here to ask you questions, Dr Dannachet. Not the other way round.

She was as unlike Natalie Drax as it was possible to be. No wonder they clashed.

— So fire away, I said politely.

— What do you make of Madame Drax's state of mind?

I motioned to her that we should move; we walked down the ward and stood by the French windows, overlooking the garden.

— She's understandably distraught, I told her. I could hear the annoyance and yes, a certain pomposity, in my own voice. But I couldn't seem to quash either. — I think that her reaction is the normal response of someone who has been under extreme pressure for a number of months, and who is now faced with what may be the final straw.

She looked at me closely. — Do you think she's heading for a breakdown?

— No. I just mean she's in a vulnerable state.

— But *might* she be breakdown material?

Yesterday morning, when I was running through the olive groves, I'd feared she was suicidal, and I certainly agreed with Philippe's diagnosis that she was a strong candidate for Prozac. But I wasn't going to tell Stephanie Charvillefort that. Not in those words.

— I can't see how she can stay under this kind of pressure much longer.

— I'm doing all I can to solve this crime, believe me, Dr Dannachet.

— So where have you got to?

— It's not our policy to disclose details of the investigation to members of the public. I'm afraid.

— I'm aware of that. Nevertheless, if Natalie's life's in danger – if Drax makes his way into my clinic, for example, and tries to attack her, or Louis – or *me* . . .

She and her colleagues were seeing to the security side of things, she replied. She'd talked to Dr Vaudin. There were posters of Pierre Drax up everywhere, and the whole regional police force had been alerted; they had relaunched the manhunt. It was just a matter of time now. I wasn't to worry; they'd get Pierre Drax. Meanwhile his mother Lucille was on her way down from Paris: they'd had to re-interview her after the letters and she wanted to see Louis. But best to keep her and Natalie apart, if that could be organised. According to Madame Drax senior, Pierre Drax should never have left his first wife. Natalie was the worst thing that ever happened to her son, and Natalie returned the compliment. As a result, the grandmother barely ever got to see Louis.

— But she's determined to see him now, Charvillefort finished.

— Pierre Drax was married before? I asked, puzzled that Natalie hadn't told me. What else hadn't she mentioned? But Charvillefort didn't elaborate. Instead she wanted to hear what I knew about Louis' fall into the ravine.

— The version that Natalie Drax told you, she specified carefully.

— Why?

— To make sure it's consistent with what she told us. Madame Drax was at the scene of the crime, and there are no other eye-witnesses unless we catch Drax, or unless by some miracle Louis wakes up and somehow remembers what happened. What are the chances of that in your opinion, Dr Dannachet? As an expert?

— Very small.

— And yet during this seizure . . .

— The seizure was a fluke. I can't pretend to explain it. A strong muscle spasm maybe, a brief return to apparent consciousness – but a very atypical one. Don't hold your breath waiting for Louis to wake up and supply you with a statement. It's not going to happen.

We stand in silence for a moment, pondering the poor boy's plight, and then she resumes.

— So. What did Natalie Drax tell you about her son's accident?

— Very little. There was an argument about a packet of sweets. Then a struggle between her husband and son. Louis was resisting because Pierre suddenly wanted to take him to Paris and he didn't want to go.

— Did she describe where she was standing, in relation to the two of them?

I shook my head. — Should I have asked her to draw me a diagram? I'm sorry, Detective, but it strikes me that this is your work, not mine.

Detective Charvillefort tapped her shoe on the floor.

— I spoke to Guy Vaudin earlier. Your wife rang his, I gather. In a bit of a state. Worried about you and Madame Drax being . . . well, rather close?

I started, horrified. Why the hell had Guy felt the need to reveal *that*?

— Don't worry, Dr Dannachet. It's not for me to pass judgement.

I broke into a sweat. — I don't think you could say we're close, I muttered eventually.

— Perhaps not. But – well, since you have a *certain friendship* with her, and you're also the doctor of her son, I was hoping that you might have some kind of insight which might help us?

— No, I said firmly. — I don't think I have.

There was a small pause. — I would like to ask you to keep an open mind, she said slowly. — If Natalie Drax tells you anything that seems odd or unusual, or if she contradicts something she said earlier, I'd like you to call me. The sweets, for example.

— Sweets?

— The row began over a packet of sweets. Doesn't that strike you as a bit unusual?

— Not if the man's unhinged, no. Lots of family rows begin with the most absurd things, I said stiffly.

— Did you know that Louis is not in fact Pierre Drax's *natural son?* Detective Charvillefort asked slowly, scrutinising my face as she did so. I thought – fleetingly – of telling her that I didn't know. I don't know why; I can't fathom myself sometimes.

— Yes I did, I said eventually. My voice sounded quiet and far away and a huge, greedy worm of anxiety shifted inside me. Charvillefort was still looking at me closely to see how I reacted. And not bothering to hide it. She might as well have brought out a magnifying glass and thrust it right in my face.

— So who's his real father? I asked, in what I hoped was a breezy voice. She smiled.

— You're getting to know Madame Drax, she said. — Perhaps that's a question you should ask her yourself.

— Are you suggesting I spy on her or something? I said with a sudden wash of anger. — Do your work for you?

— No. But you expressed a wish to know more, did you not? There was a small silence. — If she told you Pierre wasn't his real father, she probably also told you that when Louis was a baby, she put him up for adoption, and then changed her mind.

I crossed my arms and immediately regretted letting my body language betray me.

— No. I didn't know that. But I'm not surprised she didn't tell me. It's rather a private thing, don't you think?

— Yes. Of course it is.

— This man Perez, I said. — The psychologist. I'd be interested in talking to him.

— You're very welcome to, she said. — Ring my office and someone will give you his number. But he may say no.

— Why?

— Perez isn't in the best shape, she said. — Louis's therapy didn't work out. It seemed to be fine in the beginning. But Madame Drax wasn't happy, and she ended up firing Perez. After the accident, she went to see him, and accused him of failing Louis. He took it very badly, and gave up practising altogether.

— So what's he doing now?

— Drinking.

My God, I thought. It gets uglier and uglier. I stood up and took my leave of Detective Charvillefort, claiming a heavy workload. As I walked away I could feel her eyes pierce the flesh of my back like lasers.

When I got back to my office, Noelle told me that Georges Navarra had dropped by wanting a handwriting sample from everyone who had been in contact with Louis – all the nurses who worked on the ward, and even Karine, who had only seen him once. Noelle had given her a photocopy of a letter I'd written, and also a New Year's card sent by Philippe Meunier. Everything was going to a police graphologist in Lyon. Oh well, I thought. At least Detective Stephanie Charvillefort was being thorough. I found myself wondering about Sophie. She must have arrived in Montpellier by now. She'd probably be having lunch with Melanie and Oriane at one of their favourite restaurants on the seafront. I pictured the three of them sharing one of their treats: a big platter of shellfish, all claws and shells and wedges of lemon. There'd be white wine, gossip, and to begin with, laughter. The sun on their faces. I wondered when Sophie would tell them, and how much. Everything, I guessed. They didn't have secrets.

I decided to work from home that afternoon to finish my paper there. With Sophie away, I'd have the place to myself and could concentrate better than at the clinic. But that wasn't my only reason for wanting to get out. I took the road that leads through the village rather than the short cut. It was blisteringly hot. As soon as I came to the main square, I headed for the notice-board outside the *mairie*. The air was fierce, making the square buzz with mirages. The wanted poster showed the face of the man Natalie had loved and married. Dark-haired, in his early forties, with the ruins of good looks: strong cheekbones, a high forehead, deep-set eyes. There was power in that face, a power I'd not anticipated. My heart caught. He looked back at me steadily. For a moment I felt a sudden, irrational envy, followed swiftly by a very precise distaste. No, loathing is a better word. This was the man I now loathed, the man who had tried to kill his son, and was now threatening me. Who might be stalking Natalie at this very moment, or contemplating more damage to Louis, or both. Who knew who I was, and understood some of my feelings towards his wife. Who wanted those feelings stopped. I broke into a sweat and turned away, shamed by the sudden fear that swamped me.

Natalie was to spend another night at the clinic; we had agreed that I would drop in to see her after my last ward round. Her hair was once again coiled into a chignon, emphasising the clear, clean oval of her face. She wore the same dark lipstick she had worn once before, and a green dress made of Chinese silk. She looked at me warily, as though slightly embarassed, and smiled nervously. She seemed to have dressed up for me, but although I was aware of it, at least on some level, I was too distracted to feel flattered, or to feel any of the usual attraction. In fact, I felt deeply unsettled. Unsettled by what she hadn't told me, and even by the things she had. Disturbed by the memory of Pierre Drax's face, which seemed to have lodged itself somewhere in my head. And angry: angry with Natalie about things that weren't really her fault, like Sophie confiding in Danielle Vaudin – the direct consequence of which had been to make my interest in her a painfully public matter. I knew I was being unreasonable but I couldn't help it. Much of this must have been visible the moment she saw me, because I hide my emotions badly. She gestured to me to sit in the chair, then settled herself on the bed and began talking at speed. Her tone was apologetic.

— I'm sorry, Pascal. I should have told you more, I know. It's just – well. It was a very difficult time.

— So who is Louis' real father? The question shot out from me, freighted with a blunt anger that took us both by suprise. She turned her head away and twisted her necklace. False nails again. Glass beads, green like the dress. Why had she dressed up for me? For some reason, I found this both puzzling and irritating, like a crossword clue you can't solve.

— He was an ex-boyfriend, she said. Her voice seemed to shake. — I told you his name before. Jean-Luc. After we split up I didn't want anything to do with him but he kept –

She stopped and twisted fully away so that her whole back was to me. Such a small frame, she had, so vulnerable. What was I doing? There was no foundation to my anger, no reason why she should tell me painful things about her past. I felt myself soften.

— It might help to tell me.

— It won't. You have to trust me.

— But if other people know –

— Other people don't know, she said sharply. — And there's a reason for that.

— But as his doctor, I began feebly. — As your friend, I hope . . .

— Look, do I really have to spell it out for you? she blurted, turning to face me. Her eyes looked scorched with pain.

— Yes, I said simply. — Maybe you do. She took a breath, and her face reddened.

— I was raped, OK? Are you happy now? she whispered hoarsely, then collapsed, head bent, her shoulders shaking helplessly. What an insensitive fool I was, not to have figured it out on my own, not to have spotted that her fragility could bring out the worst in a man, as well as the best.

— I'm so sorry, I said, reaching across and squeezing her hand.

— Now you know why I don't want to talk about it. After-wards, it didn't occur to me that I might be pregnant, she said in a flat voice. Her head was still lowered. — Or maybe it did, and I couldn't face the idea, and ignored the signs. By the time I realised, it was too late for an abortion.

— You never reported it?

— There'd have been no point. There never is, not if it's someone you know, someone you once thought you loved. I just wanted to get on with my life. So I went to live in Lyon. I had Louis there. All alone. My mother was in Guadeloupe and my sister didn't want to know.

— It was very brave of you to keep Louis, I ventured gently. — Given what . . . I trailed off, unable to find the right words. Her shoulders shifted and I heard her exhale, as though exhausted.

— Who told you about that?

— Detective Charvillefort.

— She had no right to.

It was obvious that recalling all this was agonising for her. She was almost doubled up in front of me, her hair hanging over her face. I saw goose-pimples appear on her thin bare arms. The bruise was now a sick yellowish-blue, and the sight of it made me shudder with self-disgust.

— So what happened? I whispered.

She sat up slowly and looked me in the face, brushing her hair away from her eyes, which were now red and streaked with make-up. She looked terrible. I felt a huge flood of pity. Or was it love? I couldn't tell, and it didn't matter.

— I was all ready to hand him over, when he was just three weeks old. But then the couple who were going to take him – She stopped for a moment, unable to continue. Gently, I reached out and stroked her hair. Thin hair, brittle and fine as mesh. — I changed my mind about it, OK? That's all. Look, this isn't something I can really bear to –

Tentatively, I leaned over and embraced her. She didn't push me off. She had lost weight; I could feel it. She was no more than a skeleton.

— You didn't like them?

— No, it wasn't that. They were very happy, she whispered. — They were a happy couple, or that's how they seemed. Happy with each other. Happy to be getting my baby. Her voice caught. — Happy happy happy, she said. — They had everything I wanted.

I held her tighter.

— I hadn't really looked at Louis before, she said. — Not in that way. But that's when I started to – I mean as my son. Something that was mine. Someone I could be nice to. Someone I could learn to love in spite of the way I got him. I could be as happy as that woman was to have a baby. And perhaps I'd meet a man who could be happy to be Louis' father. I realised I didn't have to think about how Louis came to be born. I thought, I'll be like them. I'll just love him anyway. And that's what I did. I decided to keep him.

— So when you met Pierre . . .

— I told him everything. And he treated Louis just like his own son – at first. He'd always wanted children.

— None from his first marriage?

She stiffened.

— I suppose it was Charvillefort who told you about Catherine?

— Yes.

— What did she say?

— Nothing. Just that Pierre had been married before.

— Nothing else?

— No. Why?

— Oh, it just feels like my whole life's at the mercy of . . . predators. She looked up then, and her eyes met mine steadily. There was a patch of silence.

— Including me? I asked slowly. — Is that what you're saying? Surely you don't think I would ever –

—I saw the way you looked at me, she said. —When I arrived with Louis. You saw how – broken – I was.

I felt slapped. Was there a tiny splinter of truth in what she'd said? Had I really been a predator? —I'm sorry that's what you think, I mustered, flushing painfully. —Because that's the last thing I meant to be, and it's the last thing I feel I am.

She closed her eyes.

—It's OK. I may be doing you an injustice. If I am, I apologise. I've . . . had a hard time with men, that's all.

Of course she had.

Then suddenly she was smiling, giving me that brisk, false smile I had come to know, the smile that tried to put a brave face on her misery, but failed. My heart hurt for her. There was a short silence as I felt for my next question, unsure of how far I could press her.

—So . . . I mean, when did things start to go wrong? With Pierre and Louis?

—Quite early on. Louis kept having all these illnesses and accidents, he was a difficult baby, and a difficult toddler – he's always been – well, he's been difficult. It meant I couldn't go out to work. Then Pierre started to wonder if Louis' behavioural problems were genetic. He started to resent Louis, and the more he resented him, the more he tried to cover it up by doing boy things together with him. Anyone who saw them together thought he was a wonderful father. And in some ways he was. But under the surface it was a lot more volatile. Then I thought – well, I thought I should get pregnant as soon as possible. Make a baby of our own, to put things right. But we couldn't.

She seemed so sad, and so lost, so needy. I could not resist reaching for her then. And kissing her. I simply could not. And doing so, I sensed that I was giving myself to this woman in a new way, a way I had never known before – for who had ever needed me as she did? I wanted – I was desperate – to make up for all the bad things that men, myself included, had done to her.

All the injustices she had borne so bravely. I wanted to make her world a happy one, I wanted to see her smile, and I knew that if I tried hard enough, if I loved her enough, then I could save her. She must have felt it too, because she allowed me to embrace her and she seemed, in her way, to embrace me back. We lay on the bed, kissing and clinging to one another. I ran my hands through her hair and buried my face in its thin gold mesh. Over and over again, I kissed her arm where I had bruised it, and vowed to myself that this woman would never be bruised again, by me or any other man. Ever. I would make her happiness my mission.

When we made love it was slow, gentle and intense. She cried, but they were tears of release. I felt like crying too. I didn't know what I was feeling. But it overpowered me. I had to leave. I was confused, I said. The speed things were happening –

She smiled. It was OK. She was confused too. Go.

I still hadn't told her that I loved her. Still had barely dared to admit it to myself. But I would. And perhaps one day she might blossom enough to love me back.

After I left her I stayed on at the clinic with Louis, holding his hand and musing over the day's events. I must have fallen asleep at one point because when I woke, the shift had changed.

— You were sleepwalking again, said the nurse. — I just left you to it.

— Where did I go?

She smiled. — It was quite strange. I mean, a bit disconcerting. You were sitting in your chair next to Louis. Then you stood up and came over here to the desk. I was down the other end. I thought you were awake at first, but there was something strange about the way you were walking. And Jacqueline said you did it recently, and warned us that you might again.

— What did I do? Did I just sit there?

— For a while. And then you got the prescription pad and wrote out a prescription. Then you crumpled it up and threw it in the waste-paper basket. And then you got up again and walked back to your chair and stayed asleep again till just now.

— I need to see it.

— Of course. She stopped, looking at me with a quizzical smile. — I was a bit curious, so I read it. I hope you don't mind. You wrote complete nonsense, Dr Dannachet. You'll laugh when you read it.

She fished a piece of paper out of the waste-paper basket and flattened it out before me. One look was enough. I tried to muster a laugh but it wouldn't come.

— Don't tell anyone about this, I murmured. — OK?

I tried to sound calm but I was beginning to sweat uncontrollably. Because although the handwriting wasn't mine, the giant, lopsided lettering was sickeningly familiar.

Insulin. Chloroform. Arsenic. Sarin gas. Lupin seeds.

And I'd filled in the patient's name: Madame Natalie Drax.

She says I'm too young to remember it, I was only eight weeks old. But it looked like Cot Death. I couldn't breathe. Lungs are like two bags made of meat. Breathe air in and the bags get bigger, breathe out and they're smaller. I always slept in her bed, from the time I was born. Babies love to sleep with their mothers and it was just her and me in the big bed.

Papa wasn't there yet. I never told you that before, did I? But you know now. Maybe you even guessed. Sometimes I think you guessed all sorts of things, Lou-Lou. Before Papa came along it was just you and me. You won't remember, because you were too young, you were just a baby. I didn't tell you before because I didn't want to upset you. But I can tell you now, can't I? I can tell you lots of things now.

Anyway, that night I nearly lost you. I nearly lost you so many times, but that was the first time.

Poor Maman. Her heart must've been in her mouth.

She says she woke up, she doesn't know why. It was the middle of the night and everything felt wrong and then she realised I was struggling to breathe because the noises I was making weren't baby noises, they were struggling noises.

I turned on the light and I screamed because I knew I might have rolled on to you in my sleep and squashed you, it might be my fault, I might not be fit to be a mother, just like my sister said. That's the first thing I thought. Your face was blue, your lungs weren't getting enough air. I rang the ambulance right away, and they came and took over. You nearly died in the ambulance. They had to put you on a respirator to get your lungs working again. They took you away and I just sat in the day room, and cried. I cried so much that after a while there were no more tears left, I was completely empty. And then I phoned a man I met when you were really young, just a tiny baby, and he came and comforted me and spent the whole night with me in the day room, waiting to see if you would die. We sat together and he held my hand all night.

And then when the doctor came in he got the wrong idea, he thought we were married. He thought the man was your papa. We laughed about it then but anyway, he did become your papa. Just a few months later we all moved in together in Gratte-Ciel, and later we got married. I thought it was the best thing that could happen for us, because we needed to be a family. We needed a man who would be kind and look after us. It was a shame for Papa's wife but he didn't really love her you see. He just thought he did. It was me he loved, even before he met me. It was me. Me and you.

— I don't get what she's talking about, I tell Gustave. — All this stupid blah blah blah in my ear.

— You don't have to listen, says Gustave. — She won't know.

— She knows everything.

— No, Young Sir. Children think that about mums and dads, but it isn't true.

Then there's Jacqueline, stroking my arm. It feels good. Jacqueline smells of peppermint and she wants to be everyone's mum, even the grown-ups. Her son Paul's dead but she talks to him anyway. Most people don't know you can do that. I didn't know it before, I didn't know anything except what was in the *encyclopédie médicale* and *Les Animaux: leur vie extraordinaire* and stuff. But I'm getting better at knowing things.

— You look like you could do with some fresh air, Pascal, she says, because Dr Dannachet has come in and his name is Pascal. She's worried about him, she thinks he's going a bit mad. — You look terrible. Have you been getting enough sleep?

— Not really, he says.

— I've got the wheelchairs in; how about taking one of them

out for a walk while you're waiting for the detective? Come on. It'll do you good.

— I'm coming too, whispers Gustave. — I'm going everywhere you go, Young Sir. I found a cave map in Dr Dannachet's office, on the wall. We could use it. Look, he says, and he shows me a picture in a frame.

— It doesn't look like a map. It looks like someone's head.

— It's a map, Young Sir. Just trust me.

— Fresh air, says someone. — Lovely day. Hot. *Blistering*.

— I'll take him round the garden, says Dr Dannachet. — Tell his mother where we are, if she turns up. I'll take the Walkman for him.

— The wheelchair's waiting.

— Yes, says Gustave. — We'll go somewhere dark. Just you and me. Somewhere out of the sun. I know a place. It's on the map. It's cold there, like a fridge. You can hear water dripping down. You can hear bats squeaking. You like bats, don't you, Young Sir. I'll take you to the cave and I'll show you where I wrote their names in blood. It's a good place to die.

Outside it's hot and you can hear birds and smell flowers and smoke. It makes you want to turn into a weedy crybaby and we're moving like on wheels and Maman's talking in my ear again, all about how I am her darling baby, she will always love me, what happened to me wasn't anyone's fault, *don't worry sweetheart, they'll find him and they'll put him in prison and then we can live together again and I'll take you to the Red Sea to swim with dolphins and we'll buy a car, a lovely little red sports car just for you and me. You know something, Louis my darling? If you make a choice, and it's wrong, you have to live with it. Everyone has to live with what they've done. You chose, Louis. It was your choice.*

And then her voice goes different. *He scares me, Lou-Lou. He scares me. It's like he's here somewhere. I can feel him thinking bad things. I can feel him making up lies.*

— Just close your ears to her, says Gustave. — You can listen to me instead. Or Dr Dannachet. You can count to a thousand in your head. Anything you want. Just don't listen to her, OK Young Sir?

— My Papa drinks too much beer and wine and cognac, I tell Gustave. — And he jeopardises his family. But I don't care because I miss him. When I think about him it's like drinking hot blood.

— Let's stop here and sit a while, says Dr Dannachet. — D'you know something, Louis? I had a very strange letter, and so did your mother. I wonder if you might know something about it?

— Don't say anything, whispers Gustave.

— No of course not, why would you. Do you think I'm going mad, Louis? Do you think it's a bit unusual that your doctor should be prescribing your mother poison in his sleep?

— Shhh, whispers Gustave. — Don't speak. It's against the rules.

— Anyway, I've brought *La Planète bleue*. Listen here: *In 1998 biologists observed the plundering of a grey whale carcass. First to arrive at the body were swarms of amphipoda, crustaceans just a few centimetres long, which have sharp jaws for cutting into flesh . . .*

And on and on.

— Do you know any good stories? I ask Gustave, while Dr Dannachet's reading.

— I can tell you *Le Petit Prince*. I know it by heart.

— Blah blah blah, too babyish. Papa always wanted to read me that one because it was about aeroplanes.

— And planets, and a boy, and a baobab tree. It's about all sorts of things, says Gustave. — But maybe you've grown out of it now. OK then, here's another. There's a boy and he has a mum and dad who love him. Do you want to hear it?

— No, not that one. It's got a bad ending.

— It doesn't have to, goes Gustave. — You can choose the ending yourself. Anything you want.

— *These were followed by deep-sea fish, many of which were specialist scavengers with an acute sense of smell.*

— It's not easy being the mum of a Disturbed Child, I tell Gustave. — Sometimes the danger was too strong. She couldn't fight it. I know she tried. I know she did.

And I wish I could see his face through the bandages and the land's rocky and it smells of lavender and smoke and if I could open my eyes I'd see olive trees and a garden with gravel and flowers that look like yellow fireworks and maybe the sea and deep-down, underwater creatures.

— *Among them eel-like hagfish, which rip off pieces of flesh by twisting their bodies into a knot to get extra torsion. Next to arrive were sleeper sharks, which took massive bites out of the carcass. Once the first wave of diners had feasted, another group of slower-moving scavengers arrived: brittlestars, polychaete worms and crabs slowly stripped the whale down, leaving only a clean white skeleton such as the one illustrated.*

— I know the picture, I tell Gustave. — It's of some whale-bones on the seabed. A dead thing that's all eaten up by parasites. Live things can be eaten by parasites too. A clever parasite doesn't destroy its host. The host is the thing it feeds off. A clever parasite keeps the thing it feeds off alive for as long as it can, because when the host is dead, the parasite has to find another host and if it can't find another host, it'll die too.

— Let's walk some more, says Dr Dannachet, and he pushes my wheelchair and Gustave limps along too and he doesn't say anything for a long time. And then we stop, and Dr Dannachet says, — Lavender. Can you smell it, Louis?

And I can, it's right in my nose, but I can't tell him.

— She loves you, Young Sir, says Gustave. — She misses you. You can try going back. But it can't be the same. You know that.

— I know, I say, and we move on again.

— When I was in the cave, this is what I dreamed of. Walking in a garden with a boy like you, and my wife, says Gustave. — We were a little family, the three of us holding hands with our little boy in the middle. We'd count to three and then we'd swing him between us. He liked that. All little children like that.

—I know the name of every plant in this garden, says Dr Dannachet. —Every plant and every tree and every shrub. Because of Lavinia. She was a patient of mine, a garden designer. Six years in a coma. We used to read about plants together. She gave me some bonsai trees. I think you'd find them interesting, Louis. It's quite an art, you have to prune the taproots.

He sounds like he's going to cry. Slowly we go all the way round the building. The front entrance is like a Lego model, all white. And it says in big letters in the white stone, La Clinique de l'Horizon and underneath, like in ghost-writing, L'Hopital des Incurables.

—Did you know it was called that? I ask Gustave.

He doesn't say anything, he's good at that, he starts to cough instead, and something comes out of his mouth on to the gravel. It looks like he's been sick but it isn't sick, it's dirty water full of waterweed.

—Yes I did, he says when we are disappearing into the woods and leaving Dr Dannachet behind. —I did know it was called that. I'm incurable, Young Sir. But you're not.

We've left Dr Dannachet behind now. The hospital's far away, like the garden. Gustave's walking ahead of me into the forest and you can see how his head looks all bulgy and white like a light bulb because of his bandages. There are trees everywhere and it's hot, and there might be snakes, it's just the sort of place that adders live. An adder has a dark zigzag stripe along its back and maybe a straight stripe and spots, and its bite can kill a child and seriously affect an adult too, especially the old and frail.

—Let's collect pine cones, he says. —For a fire.

Which is a cool idea so I'm running all over the place collecting them, the biggest ones I can find, and we're putting them all in a pile that gets bigger and bigger, you can stack them together, they hook on to each other and you can put sticks and even branches in too, higher and higher, till it's as tall as me.

— My maman wouldn't like this, I tell Gustave. — She hates me playing with fire.

— And what about you?

— I love it. I'd like to be an arsonist one day. I could kill all my enemies.

He hands me a box of matches.

— Start now.

And I light one and put it right down at the bottom in the dried twigs and branches inside the pile, and the fire creeps about in the pine needles and does sparks and then whooshes up. And we watch it all popping and fizzing with hotness and red light.

— It'll burn all on its own now, says Gustave. — It'll do whatever you want because that's how things are in this place, Young Sir. Come on. We're going to the dark place. The darkest place on earth. But do you trust me, Young Sir? You have to be sure you trust me. People will say I've stolen you, but that's not how it is. You know that, don't you?

And I do, even if I can't see his face, so I take his hand and we walk down the hill together, through the trees.

I went back to my office and sat there for half an hour, trying to think through what had happened. But my mind flailed around as feebly as a blindworm. Dusk was falling and the sunset throbbed fiercely outside, casting a tangerine glow across the pine forest and the vineyards on the slope of the hill beyond. I inspected my bonsais. The maple was doing badly; five leaves hung limp and sickly. Why had I prescribed Natalie Drax ludicrous poisons in my sleep? And written those two letters – *which included one to myself?* Either I was going mad, or Louis Drax was using me. But if he was, who the hell would believe me? Certainly not Natalie. Or Detective Charvillefort.

The security system in the clinic, recently reviewed, required Security to change the CCTV tapes daily, and keep them for a week locked on the relevant ward. The changeover happened at six. I waited until eight, when the nurses were due to swap shifts, then returned to the ward. Both nurses were busy at the far end of the room, so I went to the ward desk. Swiftly unlocking the bottom drawer, I located the current tape, and the previous Thursday's, and slipped them into my pocket. I felt light-headed and oddly unoppressed by what I was doing. Walking home in the gathering dusk amid the insistent shriek of the cicadas, I smelt smoke, stronger than before. The evening heat churned.

The house felt huge and empty without Sophie. I went into the living-room and poured myself a Pernod, then settled myself down to watch that day's tape. I was nervous, though I didn't really know what to expect. Part of me tried to stand back and laugh at the absurdity of my own suspicions. The camera was fixed on a wide-angle view of the ward, with Louis' bed as its central feature. I watched as the black and white images jumped jerkily from frame to frame. Louis lay there as usual, pale and motionless, but you saw occasional movement in the other beds, Isabelle's especially. I fast-forwarded until I saw myself enter the ward, materialise next to Louis' bed, and sit down. The image was a little fuzzy but my gauntness gave me a strange jolt. Was this what I had become? How other people saw me? I pressed play, and watched. I saw myself reach in my briefcase for a book, and start reading to Louis. I fast-forwarded again until I saw the moment when my shoulders seemed to relax and the book slid off my knees to the floor. I sat there with my eyes closed, but nothing happened. The tape showed the night-nurse going in and out and Isabelle moving restlessly. Then suddenly, from one frame to the next, I had got up. Walked over to the desk. Taken paper and a pen and written something very fast, then ripped out the sheet, crumpled it, and hurled it in the bin before returning to my chair. Due to the time-lapse nature of the recording, the whole thing seemed to last only a few seconds. I re-wound and looked again. There was something odd about the way I was holding the pen. An awkwardness I couldn't identify at first, until it suddenly struck me –

I'm right-handed. But I'd been holding the pen in my left. No wonder the script I'd produced looked so extraordinary. I didn't bother watching the other tape. I knew what it would show.

I stood up and felt the blood rush to my head. Swaying as I moved, I reached the bathroom just in time to vomit into the toilet. I cleaned up quickly, brushed my teeth, splashed my face with cold water, my heart banging.

Then I called the girls' apartment in Montpellier. The phone rang for a long time with no answer. Then, just as I was about to hang up, Melanie answered sleepily. When she knew it was me, she launched into a tirade. Maman was in quite a state, she said, and was even thinking of looking for a job in Montpellier. She hoped I was pleased with myself. Was this some kind of midlife crisis or what?

— Can I talk to her? It's important.

— It's one o'clock in the morning, Papa. Anyway, she doesn't want to.

— There's something I need to tell her, I said. — I might be in trouble. At the clinic.

— What kind of trouble? Is it to do with this Drax woman you're obsessed with?

— No. It's to do with her son. The boy. Look, I'm sorry I disturbed you, *chérie*. Tell Maman I rang, and – well, give her my love.

— Your *love*? We're all furious with you, Papa. I could her voice wobble. — Furious, and disappointed, and upset, and –

— I know, I said. — You'll have to bear with me. Life's a mess at the moment. I'm trying to find a way out. Please, Melanie –

She hung up. I poured myself another drink and switched on the radio news. Eight forest fires had swept different parts of Provence. Two were still raging out of control, of which the larger was only ten kilometres away, just west of Cannes.

Everything can change just like that, I thought. A landscape, a marriage, a life.

I didn't know exactly how to proceed. I knew nothing about graphology. It had never seemed like an accurate science to me. Was it possible that the police graphologist could make a connection between the lopsided, drunken-looking handwriting on the two letters written by my sleepwalking, left-handed self, and the everyday handwriting on the sample Noelle had supplied? I had no idea. But I had to assume it was a possibility

– and that therefore the time I had bought myself by taking the CCTV tapes was limited.

The next morning, before I took the train up to Lyon, I checked an address and phone number. I took the tapes with me, the crumpled prescription, and a photocopy of the letter I'd received.

I found it hard to concentrate on my talk on Awareness Accretion at the symposium that afternoon, held in the Sofitel overlooking the Rhône. It didn't go well. There had been a mix-up with my slides, and several were in the wrong order. Normally I rise to the challenge of giving presentations, and often enjoy myself to an almost ludicrous degree. Not this time. It was an ordeal. I stumbled a few times, and at one point dropped a page. Throughout, I felt I was watching myself from a far distance, far but not far enough to be oblivious to the weakness of my performance. For such a well-attended meeting, the applause at the end was decidedly muted. I didn't cope with the questions afterwards well either. I repeated myself or strayed off the point. My mind was elsewhere.

Afterwards I looked out for Philippe Meunier. I'd assumed he would be there, assumed I would have had the chance to ask him more about the Drax case. But he wasn't anywhere to be seen, and when I checked the register, his name did not appear. Frustrated, and hoping that perhaps he would show up anyway, I loitered in the bar, until I was accosted by a woman with whom I'd had a brief affair in my student days. She told me enthusiastically about her career developments and her recent, second marriage to a paediatrician with whom she was very happy. They had five kids between them and were taking them on holiday to California. But I found it hard to concentrate on what she was saying and her dangly earrings annoyed me. She seemed flashy and superficial. I missed Natalie, I realised. I missed her sorrowful face. When I thought of her, my heart twisted with a strange mixture of happiness and pain. Then I remembered the phone call I had tried to make to Sophie last night. I stood up, and felt myself swaying slightly on the plush carpet of the bar. What did I want?

— And how's your marriage? Charlotte asked, as though reading my mind.

— Great, I said vaguely.

Charlotte smiled as though waiting for more, but I didn't feel like elaborating any further on the lie, and nor did I feel like confiding the real truth, so I excused myself. I had no desire to go to the conference dinner. I had too much on my mind.

By seven o'clock I was in Gratte-Ciel, going up the creaky, claustrophobic lift of an ancient apartment block in the rue Malesherbes. I waited a while and had almost given up when the door opened a crack and a man loomed above me in the murk of the hallway. It was clear that Marcel Perez no longer expected any visitors, least of all strangers who took it upon themselves to arrive unannounced. I hadn't anticipated that he would be taller than me, but he was. He was younger, too; in his early forties.

— I'm Dr Dannachet, I told him. — I'm looking after Louis Drax. May I talk to you?

Marcel Perez's strangely boyish face clouded. He had dark greasy hair which fell in a flop across his forehead. There were circles under his eyes, and three days' worth of stubble. He hesitated, just long enough for me to show him the bottle of Pernod I'd bought at the local Casino on my way here. — I bought this for you. Perhaps we could have a drink together?

It worked. I stepped in and followed him through to the small kitchen, where he opened the bottle in silence and poured two glasses, then gestured me to the lounge, where I took one of the two armchairs. So this is where Louis had come for his sessions. It didn't look inspiring. There was evidence of the day's activities that had preceded our aperitif: a bottle of Pernod (I had guessed well) and a half-empty tumbler.

— Sit down, he said, standing the bottle on the table next to an armchair. — Please.

Briefly, I told him what there was to tell about Louis, and said that the prognosis was bad. In short, I didn't expect Louis to emerge from his coma.

— Poor boy, he murmured, then quickly looked away.

— I hear you stopped practising.

— Yes, he said heavily. — I stopped practising.

— Because of Louis? Something about his defeated manner – or perhaps the drink – allowed me to be direct. The man was a wreck.

— No. Because of his mother. She came and saw me after the accident, he said, looking me in the eye in a way that I found unnerving. He took a huge gulp of Pernod and coughed. I watched his Adam's apple struggling. — She said she didn't want it happening to anyone else.

I noticed a pair of binoculars on the window-ledge. On the bookshelves there were books on primitive art and the lives of artists, a few classics – Flaubert featured heavily. A whole shelf was given over to psychology books. But there was an asceticism about the apartment: no art on the walls, and barely anything decorative, except for a pile of seashells.

— Look, I told Detective Charvillefort everything there was to tell, he said. — I answered all her questions.

Despite the fact he was more than half-drunk, I couldn't help noticing that Perez, like Detective Charvillefort, was watching me with a professional interest. I smiled, and drank another slug of Pernod. It was quickly going to my head, but I needed to stay on top of things. I hadn't eaten. I needed to slow down.

— So will you answer mine? I asked him.

— I want to help Louis, he said. — If I can help Louis . . . He trailed off, but he still held my gaze. He was trying to work something out. — Natalie said I should have seen it coming.

— And do you agree?

— Not in the way you think. I admit I got things wrong. I misread the signs. I told Charvillefort that.

— About Pierre Drax, you mean?

— About everything, he said. — About more than you'd know. But in my own defence –

— I'm not blaming you, I said quickly. — That's not what I came for. I don't know if anyone could have prevented what happened. But go ahead.

— The fact is, I was working in the dark. There were things Natalie Drax should have told me. I asked plenty of questions about Louis before he first came to me, but there were some crucial things she didn't tell me. If I'd known then what I learned later, I'd have listened differently to Louis. Every now and then he'd tell me that Pierre wasn't his real father. I just assumed it was a fantasy. But as it turns out, he was telling the truth. He didn't know it was a fact, but he'd overheard bits and pieces, and picked up the vibrations. He had a kind of intuition. He was quite preoccupied with rape, too.

He stopped and looked at me intently, to see if I knew. I nodded slowly.

— So he'd guessed more than anyone realised, Perez finished. — He was a bright kid. If I'd known he'd guessed a thing like that . . . If I'd *known* a thing like that, so much would have fallen into place. But I had no idea until afterwards.

— Did you like him? I asked softly. — I never met him. What was he like?

— Extremely, extravagantly disturbed. He'd tell stories. I never got to the bottom of how much of it was real, or exaggerated, and how much he simply made up to entertain himself and to keep me away from the things that were really bothering him.

— But did you like him?

— I wasn't paid to like him. I found him intriguing and infuriating at the same time. He'd attack me sometimes, smash things up. After we'd finished seeing each other he wrote me a letter.

— A letter?

Something tilted inside me.

— He was fond of writing letters. Perez stood up heavily and went to a desk in the corner of the room. Opening a drawer, he pulled out a folded piece of paper. — But this is the only one he ever sent me. This is a copy. The police kept the original.

I saw that it was classical child's writing: neat, careful, praiseworthy.

— It came with some hamster droppings, he smiled, ruefully.

— Which was a very Louis touch. I showed it to Detective Charvillefort.

You are a big fat liar, Fat Perez. You told her you didn't want to see me any more. You told her I was too much for you. That's what she told me. Plus you said nothing would leave the room and that wasn't true either. So you suck. I hope you die soon or catch a gross disease.

Louis Drax

The anger in it shocked me. Who the hell was this boy? What had been done to him to prompt this level of rage? And by whom?

Perez was wiping his eyes on his sleeve; when he saw I had seen, he shrugged and looked away.

— I got letter from Louis too, I said slowly. My mouth felt dry. — That's why I came here. I didn't just want to ask you questions. I've come to ask for your help.

He turned to me sharply, looking pained. — You got a letter? But he's in a coma.

I pulled out the photocopied letter and the prescription and showed him. I waited while he read them both.

— So, he said looking up. — I don't get this. You'd better talk.

— I used to sleepwalk when I was a child and adolescent. I haven't done it in years. But recently, when Louis arrived, I started to do it again. But I didn't really walk anywhere. I wrote things. I wrote this letter – and another one, to Natalie – and this prescription. I wrote them in my sleep, and I have a tape that shows me doing it.

He nodded slowly, keeping his eyes on my face. I could see the thoughts tumbling over themselves, sense a mounting excitement.

— *Insulin. Chloroform. Arsenic. Sarin gas. Lupin seeds*, he murmured, reading the prescription aloud. Then he banged the table so hard our glasses shook. — It's Louis. There's no question. He was into all sorts of facts. Medical anomalies, poisons. It fits. It's him. It's extraordinary. The letter too. It's him.

Relief swamped me. — I thought I might be going crazy, I confessed.

He nodded. — Of course you did. And you haven't told the detective because you think she won't believe it's really Louis.

It was said matter-of-factly, without accusation.

— Yes.

— Understandable, he said. — But we need to think beyond that.

We talked for a long time. His sudden excitement infected me. I'd been scared of what was happening, baffled and anxious – unable, perhaps, to look past the threat to my own reputation. But now I began to see it from another perspective. It was an opportunity. It signalled hope for Louis – and perhaps redemption for the man who believed he had sent him to his near-death. Although half-drunk, Marcel Perez was quicker and sharper than I had given him credit for.

— You're his conduit, he said. — His way of communicating. He spotted something in you. He needs to tell you something. This is just the beginning of what he has to say. This letter, he said firmly, — is also very typical Louis. A disturbed child with an Oedipus complex. And by the way, he's left-handed.

He paused and seemed to be thinking furiously.

— So what do I do?

— You go back. You spend as much time with him as you can. Sleep on the ward, and wait for him to do it again. He might be closer to consciousness than you thought. And watch Natalie.

— Watch her?

— Yes. Watch her. Even though you've fallen in love with

her, he said softly. It was a statement rather than a question. Quickly, I stood up to leave. — That's the other reason you're here, he continued. — Isn't it? Wasn't Louis right about that?

— That's quite absurd, I said, reaching for my jacket.

But he didn't buy it. He just looked mournful.

— Well, it's not my business, he said with a sigh. — But you need to know that she's more complicated than you think. She needed therapy more than her son did. The parents often do. Natalie came across as someone who had their act together, but – well. She was in a lot of denial. It was her who broke the contract, not me. She was the one who decided to stop Louis coming here. Just when we were really getting somewhere. Looking back, I guess she was terrified that Louis had intuited something that connected him with rape. She didn't want him guessing any more. That's what I think now. At the time I was just puzzled by the whole thing.

— Can you blame her?

— I can understand. But look, he said eventually. — Whatever I think about Natalie Drax and her state of mind, there's one thing you must know. Louis died – nearly died – because of me.

— Is that what Natalie told you?

— Yes. That's what she told me. And she was right.

— Do you really think his father pushed him?

— I got things all wrong, he said slowly. — Louis seemed to have a good relationship with his father. But it was more complicated than I thought. Because of what I didn't know. I've spent hours thinking about it. I always took the view that Louis was causing the accidents himself.

— Do you think he was abused by his father? By either of them?

— I only saw him for a year. I can't say how things might have been before that time. But at the time I was seeing him, I got the clear impression that Louis was doing it to himself. As a way of getting attention from his parents. But I don't know any more. And I don't see any way we're going to find out. Unless Louis wants to tell us.

As we said goodbye he gave a sad alcoholic smile.

—Let me know what happens, he said. —I'll back you up over the letters, if that might make a difference to the police.

I thanked him, and left for the station where I caught the late train to Provence and dropped like a stone into sleep.

I must have been reliving the conversation with Perez in my dreams, because when I woke a couple of hours later, in the cool of the half-empty carriage, I was left with a residue of excitement. Perez had given me optimism, and now I was excited, rather than fearful, about the prospect of finding out more. Of getting through to the boy, and working out what he was really trying to say, and somehow vindicating myself in the process. It would sound mad, far-fetched to my colleagues. I would have trouble convincing Vaudin. But I would have to find a way. Jacqueline would be on my side; of that I was sure. Perez would back me up. By the time the train pulled in at Layrac I had also made another decision. It had made itself, actually, in the wake of my conversation with Perez. For the time being, I shouldn't see any more of Natalie than was necessary professionally. For now, she needed my protection – no more and no less. Before taking it any further, I had to confront my own feelings. Square things with my wife.

I pictured Sophie down in Montpellier, sharing a bottle of wine with the girls, reading Tolstoy in bed and falling asleep with her glasses on. My heart lurched.

When I came home, the house felt empty without her. I thought about phoning the girls again, then stopped myself.

What would I tell Sophie, if I did get to speak to her?

That I was going mad? That a nine-year-old boy was telepathically communicating with me? That I was hopelessly obsessed with Natalie Drax?

I rose early the next morning, and was in my office by seven, having resolved to see no one, put my head down, stay out of trouble and try to diminish, somehow, that strange hold Natalie had on me, which would do neither of us any good. But every time I remembered our lovemaking – the way she had held me and sobbed like a child – I felt faint. I shut myself in my office and told Noelle I was writing a paper, and wouldn't take any calls unless there was an emergency. I actually had a deadline for an article I was submitting to a neurology journal in the States.

And so I wrote. I've always been good at losing myself in work. It was already ten o'clock when Noelle knocked on my door. She looked flustered and shocked.

— It wasn't an emergency exactly, and I didn't want to disturb you. But I thought you'd better know.

— What?

— Well there's been a bit of an incident on the ward. It might still be going on. Jacqueline called; she says you should come. It's one of the relatives. Madame Drax. It seems she's been attacked.

A sudden violence in my chest; I ran. When I arrived, breathless, the ward was in chaos. Vaudin was there, and Charvillefort, and the policeman who was supposed to be keeping an eye on Louis. There was no sign of Natalie. Louis' bedside table had been overturned and a vase of flowers – huge lily and ginger blooms – lay smashed in a puddle of water on the floor, their petals mangled as though trodden underfoot in the skirmish. Jacqueline came and stood next to me by Louis' bed.

— I've moved Kevin, Isabelle and Henri to the physio room; they're listening to music.

— Is she OK?

— Just very shocked, I think. A few cuts from the glass; Berthe's cleaning her up.

— What happened? How did he get in?

— It wasn't him, she whispered. — It was his mother. Lucille Drax.

Relief swamped me, and I shut my eyes briefly.

— She came into the ward but when she saw Natalie she started yelling at her to get away from her grandson. Natalie was sitting with Louis, holding his hand, and she had her back to her; she didn't really understand what was happening until she was attacked.

I listened, first in bafflement and then in anger as Jacqueline described how the older woman had grabbed Natalie by the shoulders from behind, and hauled her to her feet, screaming abuse at her. Natalie had tried to break loose, knocking over the table in the process, and smashing the vase. The policeman had managed to separate them, but it had been quite a struggle.

— And Louis? Any reaction?

— Not a flicker, said Jacqueline.

— Thank Christ.

I shook my head in disbelief, stepping aside for Fatima who had just arrived with a mop. Detective Charvillefort came and joined us.

— Where's Natalie? How is she?

— Georges has taken her back to her room. She's very shocked, of course. But no serious injury.

— It seems violence runs in the family, I said, as we left Jacqueline and headed, by silent mutual agreement, for the French windows.

Charvillefort shrugged. — I don't know. It's more complicated than it looks.

— What do you mean?

— Dr Dannachet, the detective said quietly as we stepped out on to the balcony into the fierce sun. — What I need to convey to you at this point is that when it comes to Natalie Drax, the truth is rather hard to pin down. You don't have all the facts at your disposal.

— And you do, I suppose? Listen, in my experience – I began.

But she cut me off. — Dr Dannachet, I have to tell you that as of yesterday, we have a very interesting new lead. One that we hadn't foreseen. Natalie Drax is being informed of it now.

— What?

— We're waiting for more tests on a piece of evidence, she

said, putting on her sunglasses and looking out across the garden. — It may be nothing, Dr Dannachet. But if it's something, I should know in an hour or so.

The graphologist's report. I flushed, and my stomach whirlpooled slowly. Now was the time to come clean about what I had done, and how I had discovered it. Perez would back me up. But I didn't. Instead, I excused myself, claiming I had a deadline. I left her standing on the balcony, gazing into a landscape flooded by sun. Dark clouds were gathering in the distance.

I sat with Louis.

— I don't know what you're up to, Louis, I said quietly in his ear. — But I'm listening. Talk to me again. OK? I know you're trying to. I'm in trouble. I can help you, but you have to help me too. We have to help each other out of this.

But he just lay there, lashes casting a shadow on his cheeks, the mouth slightly parted, the shallow breathing in and out.

Back in my office, I rang Natalie's room but got put straight through to voicemail. I couldn't blame her for that. I left a brief message saying how sorry I was to hear of the attack, and that I had something I needed to discuss with her, urgently. I left my mobile number for her to ring me back.

— And please take care, I finished.

— I want you to –

I shut my eyes and squeezed tight. Hung up. What did I want her to do, exactly? Love the man who'd written her hate mail in his sleep?

Madame Lucille Drax was in her seventies, with frank eyes and an intelligent face, a physical image quite disconcertingly at odds with the screaming madwoman I had pictured. I felt disturbed by her presence in my office, and a little treacherous for agreeing to a meeting with her, or even allowing her to sit down. But she had every right to visit her grandson and speak to his doctor. She had come all the way from Paris to see Louis. It would have been churlish – and unprofessional – to refuse her a meeting.

— I heard about the incident with your daughter-in-law, I said, as soon as we had shaken hands. I spoke gently but with firmness. — I have to tell you that this kind of behaviour is totally unacceptable on a coma ward. On any ward for that matter.

— I know. I do apologise to you, said Madame Drax. — It was a very stressful encounter to say the least. Natalie tried to stop me seeing my grandson, I do hope you realise that? She told me she didn't want me anywhere near him after Pierre . . . disappeared.

I didn't quite know what to say. I could see that the woman must be under huge personal pressure. — You haven't seen him?

— Of course I haven't, she snapped. I could see she was on the edge of tears. — No one has. And now there's this new evidence . . . I'm sorry. She stopped abruptly and pressed her hands to her mouth. — I'm not meant to say. It's probably a false lead, that's what I keep telling myself. I've been very worried about Pierre. And now I'm even more worried. It isn't like him.

— But given what he did . . .

At this point she stood up and spoke with great dignity and anger. Her voice trembled, but it was strong and utterly convinced. — My son did not try to kill my grandson, Dr Dannachet. He'd be incapable of it. Pierre loved Louis far more than Natalie ever did. You simply have to believe me.

Then she choked. I reached across the desk, put my hand on her arm. I felt immensely sorry for her.

— Please stay, I said, indicating that she should sit down again. I didn't want to argue with her. I felt exhausted. — Let's talk about Louis.

I prepared more coffee – by now I was quivering with caffeine – and we made small talk to clear the air, before I briefed her on the prognosis. Her questions were intelligent and to-the-point. I asked her about the letters. The idea that Pierre might have written them was absurd, she said.

— I agree, I said. I felt guilty. I would have to tell her. But how could I? What words would I use? She'd think I was insane. And so I held my tongue. She would know soon enough. The 'new evidence' could mean only one thing: that the graphologists had found me out. Like Marcel Perez, she confirmed that the letters were typical of Louis. It was 'uncanny'. Only someone who knew Louis very well could parody him like that. He would write to her a couple of times a year, she said. A very idiosyncratic boy, a little eccentric. Loveable, but difficult.

— They were thank-you letters but often he'd write about other things – bats and other creatures, or what he thought about school, or the state of the world. A precocious boy, it was no wonder he didn't fit in anywhere. I often wondered what his real father was like.

I nearly choked on my coffee. Clearly she did not know the story. But she thought she did.

— A nice, very bright young man, according to Natalie's sister.

— I thought she and her sister were estranged.

— They are. But I was curious to know a bit more about the woman my son had married. So I looked up her sister.

— When?

— Four months ago, when Pierre was living with me in Paris.

— So what else did she say about this man?

— Francine? Nothing much. Just that he was nice, and it wasn't fair what happened. I agreed with that. But anyway, if it wasn't for him, I wouldn't have a grandson would I? So I can't exactly complain.

— What do you mean, 'it wasn't fair what happened'? That's a bit of an understatement, don't you think? She looked at me: a long, narrow look.

— There are different versions of that story, Dr Dannachet. The version I heard from Francine didn't tally with the one Natalie told my son. Not at all. She told me – and frankly I never doubted her – that Natalie and Jean-Luc had a relationship, and that –

There was a sharp knock at the door, and it opened swiftly. Detective Charvillefort entered, looking pale and serious.

— Excuse me, she said. — I have to speak to Madame Drax urgently. Dr Dannachet, would you mind if we used your office for a moment? In private?

It was bad timing, and I was annoyed. I'd felt that Madame Drax was about to tell me something important. Something that I might not like, but maybe needed to know. I stepped outside into Noelle's reception area. Noelle was in a talkative mood, clearly fascinated by what was going on.

— The poor boy, she said. — All this fuss, it can't be easy for him.

— He's in a coma, I reminded her.

— Yes, but even so.

Realising she wasn't going to get any information out of me, she proceeded to tell me about her family and their small triumphs. Her younger grandson had just won a swimming medal. I congratulated her. Her older grandson was nearly at the top of his class. Her elder son had just been promoted. I congratulated her again. She thought her daughter-in-law might feel ready to get pregnant again, now their future was looking more secure. I made what I thought were the right noises, but I could barely concentrate on a word she was saying. Just then a terrible wail came from my office, followed by a dead silence and then another wail. Noelle and I looked at one another as we strained our ears for clues. You could just make out the quiet murmur of Detective Charvillefort's voice.

Then the door opened, and Detective Charvillefort stepped out.

— Could I take some tissues? she asked.

Noelle handed her the box in silence.

— What's happened? I asked. But she just gave me a distressed look and went back in.

Five minutes later both women emerged from the room. Madame Drax seemed to be having trouble walking. Her face was streaked with tears, her eyes wild. When Detective Charvillefort offered her hand for support, she grappled for it and then clutched it as though she were drowning.

— I have to take Madame Drax to Vichy, said Detective Charvillefort quietly. — Georges Navarra will be in touch with you very shortly, Dr Dannachet. I think you know what it's about.

And they were gone.

What happened over the next twenty-four hours remains in my memory as a blur of images and conversations, fragments of an anxiety dream I once had but from which I have yet to recover. I mean, really recover, as in heal, forget, forgive, understand, move on. A strange smudge of time whose colour in my mind is the colour of a bloody evening sky, an unhealthy sunset that puts the lid on a day of vexation.

Soon after Detective Charvillefort and Madame Drax senior had left, Georges Navarra turned up looking uncomfortable. He held his body oddly, as though trying to be formal. Which I soon realised he was. When Noelle showed him in he coughed – the kind of cough you make to break the silence rather than to clear your throat – but said nothing. I stood to greet him and shook his hand. Finally he spoke. I was to accompany him to the police station in Layrac for questioning, he said. Noelle, who had been filing some papers in my cabinet, gave a little hiccup of surprise. Excusing herself, she left hurriedly, leaving me alone with Navarra.

— I'm sorry, he said.

I had known, fatalistically, that it would be only a matter of time. But like any theoretical notion that takes sudden, concrete form, the reality of it shocked me. I wasn't being charged with anything, Navarra reassured me. But there was 'an issue' that needed to be cleared up. Concerning the letters. The graphologist's report had arrived; it indicated that it was I who had written the two letters purporting to be from Louis Drax: one to Madame Drax, and one to myself.

— It was done in innocence, I told him. — I mean, when I did it, I wasn't aware. Do you understand what I'm saying? I did it in a state of physical unawareness.

Georges looked at me blankly for a second, before his face creased in worry.

— I don't think you'd better say any more for now, Doctor, he murmured. — Let's just get you to the station.

On the way out, I told Noelle to phone Sophie in Montpellier and tell her I was being questioned. Then I had second thoughts, and told her not to. Then third thoughts. — But don't alarm her, OK?

Noelle winced and gave me a look of indignant despair. It was all too much for her to cope with. She reached for her moisturiser.

We left the clinic. As Navarra drove slowly down the white gravel drive, I saw the gardener, Monsieur Girardeau, surveying the lavender border; as we passed, he plucked a head of lavender and crushed it between his fingers, pensively, then brought it to his face to smell. How I envied him in that moment. When he spotted me in the car as we drove past, he smiled and waved.

— I have to admit I'm surprised, Dr Dannachet, said Navarra, changing gear. — That was quite an act you put on, when you called me about the first letter.

— It wasn't an act. Look, this may be hard for you to grasp, but I wasn't aware of what I was doing. If it was me, I mean. Which still has to be proved, doesn't it? Look, I have a history of sleepwalking. But I mean, why would I write a threatening letter to myself? That's what I can't fathom.

— Sleepwalking, eh? said Navarra. He drove for a while in silence, thinking this through.

— But what about Drax? I asked him eventually. — Surely you're still looking for him?

— No, he said. — No need now, is there?

He turned left on to the road to Layrac, then speeded up to overtake a tractor loaded with logs.

—Of course there is! He's still on the loose, isn't he?

—As a matter of fact, no, he said, turning to look at me as he drove. A sharp, searching look. —Pierre Drax has been found. That's why Detective Charvillefort had to fetch his mother. She's taken her to Vichy to identify him.

—He's been found? But surely that's good news! Surely that –

He interrupted me. —It's a body we're talking about. Pierre Drax's body.

I watched his neat, intelligent profile as we drove on in silence. There seemed nothing more to say. Pierre Drax was dead. Ergo he was not stalking anyone. Was not writing any letters. Was not –

Finally I said, —Suicide?

—I have no idea, he said. —And for now, nor does anyone else.

Layrac police station was small and sleepy, with notices flapping on the notice-board and an air of controlled ruin. In an interview room, Navarra told me, in a stiff, official way, that the police graphologist had identified that the handwriting was written by a right-handed person with their left hand.

—Unfortunately both the CCTV tapes relating to those days have gone missing, he said slowly. Then he stopped and sighed, lowering his voice. —Would you like to speak to your lawyer, Dr Dannachet, or do you think you might be able to lay your hands on them?

I could see he wanted to help me, but I didn't know how to let him; what was the etiquette of my situation? Should I just blurt out the truth? That yes, I had taken the tapes because I knew I had written the letters. But that I had written them in my sleep, guided by Louis? Perez would back me up; he'd said as much in Lyon that night. But could I trust Perez to react the same way sober? Had he even remembered my visit? Might it not be better just to sit tight, talk to my lawyer? Stalled by my own indecision,

I said nothing, until Georges Navarra sighed and excused himself, saying he would leave me to think about things. At one point I heard a dog barking; I looked through the small window and saw Natalie with Jojo; she was walking along the corridor on the arm of a policewoman. She looked red-eyed and broken, smaller and more fragile than ever. I remembered the thinness of her body against mine – skin and bone – and a lump came to my throat. Then the sudden hot jab of tears. I wanted to call out to her, but I knew I couldn't. What would I say? They would have told her about finding her husband's body, I supposed. And they would have told her that I had written the letters, perhaps asked if she wanted to press charges. She'd think I was sick. Unless like Perez, she believed it was Louis communicating. Surely she would. *I think my son's a kind of angel.* Did she realise I loved her? Couldn't she feel it?

See Louis as just another case, Meunier had warned me.

But I hadn't been able to. Then a thought struck me. Philippe must have seen something odd in Louis, for him to warn me off in the way he did. I'd suspected that it was because he had fallen for Natalie. But what if it was something else? I had to speak to him.

— You need to take some time off, said Guy Vaudin, breezing into the interview room and planting his hand firmly on my shoulder. — I spoke to Navarra. I'm sorry, Pascal. I honestly had no idea you were under so much pressure. And with Sophie going off to Montpellier . . .

He didn't need to clarify to me that in his mind, I was having a breakdown.

— It's not what you think, I protested. But I knew it was hopeless.

— Navarra told me your theory. The sleepwalking story. But I'm sorry, I don't buy it, Vaudin said, sighing heavily. — I admire your work, but you've taken a wrong turn here. It's unprofessional in the extreme. Look, I've got a lot on my plate at the moment. Can't stop and talk. But why don't you just take a few days' holiday and write the whole thing up when you get back? Get a bit of perspective on it.

Jacqueline was my next visitor. She arrived with a bag of black grapes and planted them before me. She'd met Vaudin in the street outside and he'd told her about our conversation.

— Louis made you do it, she announced, selecting the best grape and handing it to me with a tin ashtray for the pips. She watched me eat it as though supervising medication. I felt like a grateful invalid.

— But Guy — I began.

— She snorted. — You know what Guy's like. He just wants a quiet life.

— Tell Natalie, I said. — Natalie will believe it. Do it, Jacqueline. Please.

She smiled, but looked doubtful. — Of course, she said, quickly, plucking another grape from the bunch and handing it to me. It was as dark as blood. — The more people who think the same thing, the better. In the meantime, I've been busy. Sophie called me from Montpellier. She'd heard from Noelle. She was quite distressed. I got the feeling she was torn between staying in Montpellier and coming back. What should I tell her, if we speak again?

I understood Sophie's decision to get away from the situation. If she came back now, what would she be coming back to? The same man she had left. A man hopelessly, if uncomfortably, in love with Natalie Drax. The truth was that despite myself, despite all the instincts which urged reason, I had succumbed to something that was out of my control. I hadn't changed. And didn't want to.

— Tell her I'll be fine. I just wanted her to know what was happening, that's all. I thought about Natalie. About the letters. *Stay away from men. Bad things will happen. Insulin. Chloroform. Arsenic. Sarin gas. Lupin seeds.*

Louis had made me prescribe his mother poison. A disturbed child with an Oedipus complex, Perez had said.

Louis Drax, in his coma, wanted his mother dead.

But why? What sort of child would want to punish the mother who loved him? Wish to do further harm to a woman so devastated by circumstance that it was a wonder she was still intact?

After Jacqueline had left I finished off the grapes and arranged the pips on the table in a series of concentric circles. This activity was strangely soothing, and banished all thought.

Gustave picks up a big pine branch with clumps of pine cones on and lights the end with a match till the pine needles are all fizzing with fire and he holds it up in the air and waves so burning sparks come down and you cough from it.

Children need an adult they can trust. That's what Maman says. But who? And how do you know?

— Ever seen a torch like this before?

— No. It's cool.

He's holding my hand like Papa used to do. He's slower than Papa though, because he's got a limp. He's all broken and thin from being hungry all the time, if you pushed him he'd fall over, he isn't any stronger than a boy who's only nine. If we had a fight I might win, I might even kill him by accident. That kind of thing can happen, trust me. Someone gets in a rage and they don't know what they're doing and they're sorry afterwards but then it's too late.

It's dark and you can hear an owl hoot, and smell burning from the forest that's on fire and you can see a red bit glowing if you look down where the hill is, just where we lit our bonfire, far away but maybe moving closer because fire spreads just like a flood, except it can go uphill and water can't, unless it's a giant tidal wave called a *tsunami* that can devastate a whole region e.g. several Caribbean islands. And while I'm walking along with Gustave, holding his hand that you can feel the bones in, I'm beginning to understand something. I need to tell Dr Dannachet because if you feel the danger coming you have to tell an adult, one that you can trust. But he's gone and I don't hear his voice any more. He used to be there, just like in another room, or underwater with the monster tube-worms. But he's gone like a star goes. Papa once told me about stars, there are shooting stars and you might be able to see them but they're not really there, it's just the light that's left behind after they've vanished that you're seeing. But sometimes you see a star really vanish. You can stare and stare at it, and then you blink or you look away just for a second, and it's gone. I must've blinked or looked away and that's how Dr Dannachet disappeared, and the others too, Maman and the nurses. What's happened to l'Hôpital des Incurables? Maybe if I wanted to go back and tell Dr Dannachet the thing I need to tell him, I couldn't. I can feel the danger getting nearer and I'm scared.

— Nearly there, says Gustave. — Just stick with me, Young Sir.

But then he trips on a root and falls over and that's when I see how skinny he is, you can see his ribs, and he lies there to cough up more waterweed and sick and I get even more scared because maybe he's dying faster than I thought, maybe I'm killing him, maybe that's the danger. I try to pull him up but I can't because he's too heavy, so I sit down next to him till he gets his breath back and we can walk again. But this time it's much slower, all his energy's used up like a triple-A battery.

Then maybe we sleep because when we wake up we're in a new place. It's cold and the light's coming back and we're on a slope looking down into a big hole that's dark and creepy, and cold air's coming out of it like a freezing mouth breathing out.

— It's down there, he says. — We'll need to climb. I bet you like climbing, Young Sir.

But I'm scared. It looks too steep for anyone to go down, especially if you're all broken and covered in bandages and your energy's gone. And I don't want to follow him because if we go in, how do we get back out? We don't. This sucks, and I need to talk to Dr Dannachet or maybe even Fat Perez about the danger feeling that's squeezing me like a big snake, it could break your bones. But there's no one, just me and Gustave with his bleeding bandages and if you make a choice it's your choice and no one else's.

— I hate climbing. Climbing sucks.

— Trust me, Young Sir, he says — I'll help you. I'll light one of our torches, look.

And he gets out his matches and he sets fire to the clumps of pine needles on the end of his branch, whoosh, and they crackle and little sparks zing out and fizzle like a firework and his bandages look bright white but the blood on them is dark like earth, like dried-up earth, and suddenly I want to see his face even if he hasn't got one.

— Down here, he says. — I'll go first. Then you. Just follow me, Young Sir. We'll take it slowly, a little bit at a time. Best to go backwards. Feel for footholds.

And he coughs a bit more and when he's finished he crawls to the edge and starts lowering himself down backwards, holding the branch-torch above his head, all flaming and fizzing and spitting out burning needles, and when he calls me, I follow him, even though I'm scared, because I don't know what else I can do, going backwards like he did, clinging on to the rocks and putting my fingers in the cracks – it's cold, it's freezing – to hold on. It's a long way and I'm still scared and the cold air's in my chest and my feet are freezing, I'm freezing all over and shivering – that's from cold but being scared too – and the smoke from the torch comes up and chokes me and makes me cough, and it goes on and on, climbing down and down and down in the almost-dark with Gustave somewhere below and all you can see of him is the fire of the branch-torch, and I'm climbing down into the danger, I can feel it.

— Not much further now! he calls. He sounds like he's far below. — I'm at the bottom, it's flat down here. I'm going to light another torch, Young Sir, and you can see your way better. That's it. Just a few more metres and you're there.

And then I feel his bony hands grip my tummy and he's lifting me down the last bit but then he falls underneath me because he's not strong enough, and then I'm standing on a floor and we're in a cave and the burning branch shows walls all around, white stone like bone, like inside a creepy skull.

— Is this the place?

— Yes, he says. — You can hear water: listen.

And so we listen to it rushing and it sounds like something I heard once before, long ago; Papa having a shower maybe.

— You have to trust me, Young Sir, he whispers. — You have to believe I love you and I would never hurt you.

And then he points to the stone.

— That's where I wrote her name in blood. And my son's name too. See?

And I look. You can't see it at first, it's too dark. And then you can. They're huge letters, all lopsided and croaky, the hugest letters you've ever seen, and you can see the blood's gone dark on the white stone just like the blood on his bandages that he's starting to unwrap, around and around and around like spaghetti Bolognese.

CATHERINE
LOUIS

And I look at the names for a long time and I blink and blink, and then I turn round and there he is. He's taken off his bandages, and there's his face.

Georges Navarra came back after an hour, looking a little happier than before. His eyes had a spark to them.

— What's happened?

— Nothing definite yet, he said. — But I've spoken to Dr Vaudin, and Madame Drax. She's too occupied by other things to press charges. She may change her mind but she's in quite a state, as you can imagine. So it looks like you're in the clear, if the clinic can have the property that you borrowed returned safely. Meanwhile . . .

All of a sudden his hands became busy sorting through the sheaf of papers he had in a loose folder. Among them was a page of *Le Monde*.

— I shouldn't really tell you anything, Pascal, he said. — But I think I can let you see this, as it's in the public domain. He handed it to me, pointed to a headline and left, closing the door behind him quietly.

MYSTERY BODY FOUND IN CAVE. I swallowed. My mouth and throat were dry as I read. In the Auvergne, near Ponteyrol, a team of speleologists had made a macabre discovery: the remains of a male body, on a ledge of rock inside a cave.

It seemed that the cliff from which the man had probably fallen into the ravine was pitted with caves, some three metres above the water level; the whole mountainside in that region of

Ponteyrol was a Swiss cheese. When the water level was high, as happened whenever there was a violent storm, the water level in the river would rise, spilling into the whole cave system and flooding it. The speleologists had assumed at first that the man's body belonged to another cave explorer. But he had no equipment, and was not dressed for potholing. It seemed that the dead man had been sucked into one of the caves by the force of the roiling water in the ravine.

It was a dismal spot, barely mapped and almost impossible to access. Had the speleologists not been making their own detailed exploration of the river and its caves, the body might never have been discovered. It was a big, ragged hole of rock with a small cleft, high above, through which the occasional bar of daylight could enter. It was inhabited by a huge colony of pipistrelle bats. It proved very difficult to get the body out of the cave. It was badly decomposed, and access was awkward. In the end, they had to dig from above, and lower a team down into the cave through a narrow crack. Whatever happened, it appeared that the man did not die right away. There was evidence to indicate that he was still alive when he reached the cave.

The police made the connection between the body and Pierre Drax at once; as soon as the DNA match came back, Pierre's mother had been contacted, and his wife informed of the discovery.

I read the article three times before Georges Navarra returned.

— So if he was alive when he got to this cave, how did he die? What's this 'evidence'? I asked when I had finished reading.

— That's what they're not sure of, said Navarra slowly. — But it seems possible . . . well likely, that he –

He stopped and looked out of the window at the vineyard. The long parallel rows of vines stretched to the far distance over the roll of the hill, lit by blazing sunlight.

— He starved to death, he said quietly. — Pierre Drax starved to death in a cave.

By lunchtime I was free to leave the police station. There was no serious threat contained in the letters, according to Maître Guilhen, my lawyer, to whom I spoke on the phone. Nothing actually illegal had been done; I had borrowed property from the clinic which I was about to return. Natalie Drax was unlikely to press charges, and with the discovery of her husband's body, she had enough on her mind. It would never get as far as court. As for my sleepwalking story, I had best keep quiet about it, or I would look like a madman. He finished on what he called 'a personal note' by saying that it sounded to him as though I needed a break from the clinic, and he was glad to hear that Dr Vaudin had recommended one. Funny, I had never struck him as the eccentric type, he said.

— I'm not, I said. — I treat patients in comas. I have four bonsai trees. I pay my taxes.

— I didn't know about the bonsais, he said. — Should I reconsider my verdict? Listen, take a holiday. Club Med or something. I hear Turkey's nice. Take Sophie.

As soon as my belongings were returned to me, I checked my mobile. There were two messages. The first was from Sophie. Her tone was formal. She didn't understand what was happening but she had a right to know why the police were involved. I should ring her at the girls' apartment and tell her what she needed to know. The second was from Natalie. I barely recognised her voice. She was speaking through angry tears. I was sick. What the hell did I think I was doing. She had trusted me. I was the one she called when she got the letter. And all along, I was the one who'd written it. I was even sicker than Pierre.

I rang her immediately but there was no answer, so I left a long, rambling, absurd message in which I began to explain about the sleepwalking, and Perez, and how sorry I felt for her, and how I wished I could help, wished I could make her understand that it wasn't sickness, it was Louis, Louis who was trying to get through to her, to both of us . . . and how I missed her. I missed her, I missed her. I didn't know what was happening to me, I had tried not to think about her but . . . In the end I hung up, appalled at my own inarticulacy, and the hopelessness of it all. What in Christ's name did I think I was doing?

I went back to the clinic and quietly returned the tapes to the drawer. The ward was almost empty, and the only nurse, Marianne, told me that an emergency meeting was in progress in the conference hall. When Vaudin spotted me come in, he frowned; he had clearly not expected to see me. He was outlining how the fire department had recommended we evacuate the building as early as tomorrow, if the wind continued in this direction. Everyone groaned. It was a precautionary measure, he said. But with the forecast, and the way the winds were sweeping . . .

Vaudin took me aside afterwards and told me that whatever the outcome of the police inquiry, he insisted I take time off, as of now. I was clearly having a personal crisis, and it wasn't good for me to be around anyone at the moment. I should sort myself out. He knew of a good shrink in Cannes. He wrote down a name and phone number and thrust it at me.

— Do it, Pascal, he said. — I want to keep you here, believe me. But you're making it difficult. Take a breather and come back.

— But the evacuation . . .

— We can cope.

On my way out, I looked in on Louis. He wasn't stirring, apart from the tiny rise and fall of his chest. On his face – waxy in the sunlight – nothing. Less than nothing: the blankness of total uncompromising absence. You could see how no one could believe what had happened. Except me, and Jacqueline, and Perez, and perhaps, eventually, his mother. Despite her angry message, I still felt hope. She knew her son like no one else. Knew what he was capable of. *Maybe Louis really did die*, she said. *Maybe he's come back as a sort of angel. Is that possible?*

Surely she knew, inside, what he was up to?

Where was she now? Being questioned, I presumed, and being forced to relive the nightmare on the mountain, reconfigure it to encompass her husband's death. He must have killed himself; of that I felt sure. How could he live with what he had done? I pictured Detective Charvillefort grilling Natalie about it. The same questions repeated over and over again. Natalie by turns tearful and defiant. And alone. I wasn't going to be allowed anywhere near her, I knew that. I didn't want to leave another message. A letter might be a better idea. But in the meantime, there was something I had to do, while I was free to do it.

I drove to Nice, and caught a plane to Clermont-Ferrand, then hired a car and began the familiar drive to that ancient fading belle, Vichy – France's Mecca for the dying, the semi-cured and the hypochondriacal. Lavinia spent three months there after she left the Clinique de l'Horizon, convalescing among the floating denizens, the pampered sick. I visited her regularly, and came to know the city well.

I knew where to find Detective Charvillefort; she would still be at the morgue of the main hospital, and I presumed Madame Drax was still with her. But first there was someone else I had to meet. An hour later, I was strolling through the town. It was cooler than Provence, but a bright sunlight reflected off the walls and glass. Vichy is sadly beautiful. I always loved its genteel whiteness, the faint scruff at the edges of the gleaming modernism, the whiff of spa water and the ancien régime redolent in the streets. I rang Meunier's office from my mobile. He sighed heavily when he heard my voice.

—I thought I might hear from you.

—I want to meet. No, I insist on a meeting.

—Not here.

—Why not?

—It's just not a good idea, he said flatly. —Look, I'll meet you in the Hall des Sources. Go and . . . take the waters and read a paper while I try and make some time. Give me ten minutes to sort something out, OK?

I entered the sulphur-reeking glasshouse, paid my coin and sat among the halt and the lame who were sipping the rancid, lukewarm water from plastic tumblers or their own little china cups. Some were filling thermos flasks. The steaming air seemed to swirl with real and imaginary infection.

Exactly when Philippe arrived I can't be sure, because at first I didn't recognise him. I'd taken the shuffling, shambling man who looked around him vaguely – as though in search of a seat – for another invalid, someone who had only recently left his wheel-chair and was keen to get back to it. He seemed smaller and greyer than I remembered him, like a faded old photo of himself.

—Pascal, he said, giving me a weak handshake. Even his voice sounded faded. Lost.

—Philippe.

We sat down at a small table. Sparrows hopped about us. The stinking vapour rose from the taps, clogging the air around us.

—I've been waiting for you to come, he said. —I thought it might be sooner.

Gaunt. Haggard. He'd aged ten years in six months.

—You have to tell me what happened with Natalie Drax, I said.

He shut his eyes and took a deep breath. I observed him closely, watching for the physiognomical shifts that betray us all. He told me how, during his stay in Vichy, Louis had been making signs of recovery. This had agitated Natalie: she became very preoccupied with what her son's mental state would be if he emerged from his coma, and what he would remember.

—I've had that too, I said. —Hardly surprising.

—She also claimed to be convinced Pierre Drax was stalking her. She said she thought she had seen him on several occasions

– but the thing is, no one else spotted him. He paused as though waiting for me to ponder this, but I was impatient, and signalled for him to continue. — Then one day Louis' condition suddenly deteriorated. No one was with him that morning except his mother. Again, she kept saying she thought she'd caught a glimpse of Pierre – but again, no one else had seen him and the security cameras showed no sign of him entering the clinic. Do you see what I'm saying, Pascal? About dilemmas?

It took a little while for this to sink in.

— Are you saying she actually – she tried to interfere with him? And blame Drax?

— I don't know, he sighed, taking off his glasses and de-steaming them with a corner of his shirt. — But when I saw on the local news yesterday that they'd found his body, I couldn't help wondering. She knows a lot about medicine, more than you'd think. You know how easily it could be achieved. An oxygen block . . . no one would ever know. Nothing can ever be proved.

— So did you confront her?

— Yes. And that's when it blew up in my face. She denied it, and accused me of professional incompetence. There was no proof then that Pierre Drax was dead – we thought he was on the loose. So it was just a hunch on my part, nothing I could back up. She knew that. She said I was slandering her. She got quite hysterical. She said I was trying to frame her. You name it.

— Did you tell Detective Charvillefort?

He met my eye briefly, then looked away. A rotten pall of silence hung between us as we contemplated the implications of his failure.

— You were scared, I said flatly. I could picture it all so easily.

— Of course I was scared, he snapped. — Medically, what happened shouldn't have happened. Easy enough to present it as another mistake on my part. Easy to call it negligence. She knew that, and she played on it. I'd already pronounced Louis dead once, remember. Think how it looked. Not good. Pascal, listen. Listen carefully. This is my career. You'd have done the same.

He looked me in the eye then, hoping to see recognition. But I couldn't give it. I wouldn't have done the same. Ever. I shook my head. There was another silence. Smaller, but tenser. — So you had Louis transferred to my clinic to get rid of her?

I couldn't hide my bitterness. My rage. He reddened, and for a moment I wondered about his heart. If he went into cardiac arrest on the spot, would I help him or watch him writhe?

— You know it wasn't as simple as that, he said pleadingly. — He was heading for PVS. It's hospital policy. She wanted him transferred too. We struck a deal. If I kept quiet, she wouldn't accuse me of negligence. We'd both be rid of each other.

I'd watch him writhe.

— Thanks. Thanks, Philippe. *Thanks!* Several of the invalids were beginning to watch our animated conversation with interest. Instinctively, Philippe and I leaned closer towards one another across the table.

— Look, Pascal, you've got to understand, he said. — I was in a terrible state. I couldn't prove anything. I couldn't cope with her. Her grief, her anger, her strangeness – any of it. The whole thing made me quite ill. I nearly had to take early retirement. I'm sorry, Pascal. I behaved badly. I should have warned you – but I was struggling. I thought I was going mad. Have you ever thought you were going mad?

I stood up sharply, knocking over my chair, which fell with a heavy iron clang. I righted it, and leaned on it heavily for a moment. People were now openly staring.

— I have to go, I said abruptly.

The fact was, I felt that I was going mad right now. I had to get away from here and try and make sense of what I'd heard. The world was shifting around me. But I wasn't going to let it. I had to hang on to the life I knew. The Natalie I knew. My love understood and knew her. My love knew the truth of her. Philippe didn't have that, and couldn't possibly know her the way I did. It was as simple as that. I left him sitting at the table amid the steam and the invalids. My mind raced painfully as I walked towards the morgue. Meunier had suspected Natalie: absurd. And – equally absurdly – said nothing. And what about Perez? *I take the blame for Louis' accident*, he had said. Very clearly. *I should have seen it coming, but I didn't.*

There was only one person on this earth who could stem my anxiety. She had the answer.

I rang her mobile and she picked up right away.

— Tell me you never tried to hurt Louis, I said.

— Pascal, what on earth?

— Just tell me. Just tell me you never tried to hurt Louis. There was a long silence. When she finally spoke, her voice was gentle.

— I'm sorry about the message I left before, Pascal. I was so confused. You can explain why you wrote those letters, I know you can. You've heard that Pierre's dead?

— Tell me you never tried to hurt Louis, I said again. I could hear the harshness in my voice, the cruelty of my need. There was another pause. Longer this time. I tried to picture her face, but I couldn't. Nothing hung together. — Just tell me! I blurted.

— Oh Pascal. I never tried to hurt Louis, she said quietly. There it was in her voice, unmistakably: a tone of forgiveness; forgiveness of the mess I had made of myself, of her, of the us I had so hoped for and so betrayed. Reassurance. Lovingness, even. Yes, I could feel it. My heart slid gratefully back to its normal place. — How could I, Pascal? I love Louis more than anything else in the world! Pascal, come on. How could you doubt that?

— Because I'm an idiot, I told her, smiling foolishly with relief. And I hung up.

I punched in Perez's number, then changed my mind and rang Charvillefort. I noticed my fingers were shaking. Charvillefort said she was still at the morgue with Madame Drax. I told her that I was on my way over. Then, almost with reluctance, I reported what Philippe Meunier had told me. I felt I had a duty to, but at the same time I squirmed with anxiety. What would she read into it? I could sense her listening carefully.

— I'll go and see him now. She said. — I'll need a statement from him. He never told me he suspected Natalie of interfering with Louis, but I did wonder.

I was speechless. — You can't really believe – I didn't mean you to think –

— No. It's not evidence. It's a possibility. A theory. One scenario of many. Don't think I didn't interrogate her thoroughly. But she's always stuck to the same story. Nothing could be proved, and it still can't. Look, Dr Dannachet, now that Pierre Drax's death has been confirmed, I need to talk to Dr Meunier and re-interview Marcel Perez in Lyon. Right now. Could you take Lucille Drax back to Provence for me?

Briefly, we discussed arrangements: of course I would accompany Lucille back to Provence, if she could be booked on the early evening flight I was taking to Nice.

— Good, said Charvillefort, relieved. — She's very distressed, and I think it's better she's with someone she knows. They won't release the body until there's been a full postmortem anyway.

Five minutes later I was at the morgue, a low-slung concrete building connected to the hospital. I found Lucille Drax and Detective Charvillefort waiting in the lobby. The detective seemed harassed; she excused herself to make some phone calls and I was left with Madame Drax. I sat next to her and we stared into space for a moment, watching the comings and goings in the lobby. When I offered my condolences, she seemed to hear the words but not really register them. I recognised that stunned look. I have seen it before on the faces of parents who have lost a child. Their world has collapsed and they have no bearings. She began hunting for something in her handbag, with furious, digging movements.

— We didn't finish our conversation, she said, still digging.

— I'm sorry it had to be interrupted by such terrible news.

— My son was a wonderful man, she said, finding what she was looking for. — A wonderful father.

— I'm sure he was, I said. She pulled a photograph from her bag and showed it to me. It was Pierre Drax being a wonderful father. The proof. Father and son, smiling together at the camera. Louis was holding a model aeroplane high above his head. They looked like a good father and a good son. Proud to be together, proud of their plane.

— How did it fly?

— It crashed, she said with a small laugh. — They all crashed in the end. And she looked away.

— I'm taking you back to Provence, Lucille, I said gently. Louis needs you.

I led her away to the car. She walked stiffly, as though she had aged a thousand years. We drove in silence until we had cleared the city and reached the big curved *route nationale*. My thoughts churned as I remembered the doubts Philippe had planted in my mind. I'd been right to call Natalie right away, right to get her assurance. But for some reason, the doubts were still eating at me. For a horrible, vertiginous moment, I let myself imagine that Natalie had indeed harmed her son. Instantly, fear sliced its way in. A selfish fear, about what kind of creature might do such a thing, and how I might love – could still love – such a creature. And then, a shriller fear: was Louis safe?

— I don't suppose you know about how Pierre and Natalie met, do you? asked Lucille suddenly. The question came as a welcome interruption.

— No, I said.

— It was something I meant to tell you. It shows you – well. It shows you what sort of a man my son was.

— Go on, I said gently. It helped that we were sitting next to one another, free of the need for eye contact. The landscape shimmered before us, the sun casting mirages on the road ahead.

— It was through an adoption agency. Natalie had put Louis

up for adoption, and Pierre and his wife Catherine had been selected as adoptive parents. They couldn't have children of their own, you see. They'd been trying for a long time.

—Go on, I said slowly.

—Natalie had wanted to see who her child was going to live with. But shortly after their first meeting, she pulled out. She changed her mind before any of the papers were signed. Pierre and Catherine were desperate. And then they got a phone call from her. Natalie wanted Pierre to come and see her. Alone. And so he did. He thought he could persuade her to let him and Catherine have Louis after all. But – well. Something else happened. They started seeing each other. At first it was about Louis.

—But then it wasn't?

—Catherine suspected something almost right away. My son didn't behave very honourably, I'm sorry to say. There's something about Natalie that gets to men. Certain men. She brings out the rescuer in them.

The remark reminded me of something Sophie had said. I felt a rush of blood to my face and turned slightly to concentrate on my wing-mirror.

—She rang him one night from the hospital, where Louis was having breathing trouble. Pierre went there and stayed all night in the waiting room with her. That's the sort of man he was. But it was the end of him.

I could feel Lucille Drax fixing me with her clear eyes as she spoke, and I knew she wasn't lying. I could see how it could have happened. I could picture it. Picture myself doing the same thing in Pierre Drax's shoes. Falling, through a mixture of pity and admiration, for a single mother struggling to bring up a child who was the product of rape.

—So Pierre left his first wife for Natalie? I asked. Something seemed to buckle inside me. I felt uncomfortable, although there was no reason for it. Why shouldn't a man leave his wife for a woman he loved, and be a father to her child?

—Eventually. In the end Catherine told him he had to choose and he chose Natalie because she needed him more. My son was a good man. But it ended up being the worst choice he ever made, and he knew it. Look what it led to. I'm still in touch with Catherine. I rang just now and told her. She was devastated. She lives up in Rheims. She got married again and they adopted two little girls from China, and then managed to have one of their own, quite unexpectedly. That really upset Pierre, discovering she wasn't infertile after all. It triggered something in him. Unleashed all the regrets maybe. I guess he couldn't help thinking what a fool he'd been, and that if only he'd stayed with her . . . That's when he began to wonder if Natalie had been harming Louis.

—What? I asked sharply. My heart started to bang fast.

—Harming Louis, she said clearly. I could feel her eyes on me. How much did she know? How much might she have guessed about my feelings for Natalie? Do certain older women have X-ray eyes, that can locate and identify illicit love? It felt that way. She continued slowly, still watching me. — So he insisted on Louis seeing a psychologist. Marcel Perez. Natalie wasn't keen, but she agreed to it. But she fired him after a few months. I don't know how far it got.

She kept her voice level. But I could feel that the effort it took was enormous.

—And the rape? Suddenly, I had to know. I could hear the catch in my throat.

She looked at me steadily. The sign to Clermont-Ferrand appeared and I stepped on the accelerator. Still she said nothing. I could feel her watching me. Could she sense the turmoil I was in?

—But why? I said at last. — Why on earth would someone pretend they'd been raped when . . .

—Pity, said Lucille Drax bluntly. —Natalie knew about pity, and how to work it.

It had a logic to it, the kind of logic that takes you to places you don't want to believe exist.

I hated this. Doubt was blossoming inside me like a crude fungus. I couldn't stop it.

—When Pierre was staying with me in Paris, he confided in me, she went on. —It was such an unhappy marriage – almost from the start. I'd always known something didn't add up about Natalie, so that was when I tracked down her sister. I found out the reason she and Natalie fell out was because Francine knew Natalie had tried to trap Jean-Luc into marriage, and that he'd called her bluff. And that now she was claiming it was rape. Francine told Natalie she knew, and that was the end of that.

—You told Pierre this?

—I felt he should know.

—When?

—Just a week before the picnic.

—So when they went on the picnic, he'd just found out that she'd lied to him about being raped?

—Yes.

—Do you think it came out in the row they had?

—I have no way of knowing, said Lucille. —And nor does anyone.

We drove on in silence as this sunk in. Absurdly, I wanted to cry, or scream, or both.

—I want to know what happened to my son, Lucille managed finally. —He didn't commit suicide. And he would never have harmed Louis.

—So what are you saying? I kept my eyes on the road, which seemed to bulge before me. My perspective felt strange, skewed. Perhaps, I wondered suddenly, I was actually on the wrong road. Driving in the wrong direction. Going nowhere.

—I think she killed him, said Lucille quietly. —That's what I think.

—She said they had a row about sweets, I blurted. —Pierre didn't want Louis eating sweets. (Why did the sweets suddenly bother me so much? Why didn't anything hang together?)

— And Louis? I asked. My throat felt very dry. — Do you think she tried to kill Louis too?

I saw his face as he was falling, Natalie had said. *His mouth was open like he wanted to tell me something.* Something twisted inside me. It can't have happened like that. It can't have. Unless –

— Yes, she said softly. — Yes. I think she tried to kill Louis too.

There was a service station up ahead. I indicated and turned off the slip road. We drove to a quiet corner of the car-park in the shade of some birch trees, next to a play area. We got out and made our way to a picnic table where we sat facing one another. I was sweating. Children were running and jumping all over a complicated system of slides, hanging rubber tyres and tunnels, laughing and screaming. Lucille watched them with dry eyes. Reaching in my pocket, I took out the prescription I had written and handed it to Lucille. She read it in silence, puzzled.

— What does it mean?

I explained the circumstances in which I had written it.

— Arsenic, sarin gas, lupin seeds, she murmured. — That's a lot of poison.

— It's almost like he wants revenge for something, I said. — Don't you think?

I felt like Judas.

— Phone Detective Charvillefort, she said. — Do it now.

— But it doesn't prove – I said feebly. I didn't want it to mean what it might mean. — I wrote it in my sleep. My subconscious might have –

— Phone her, she said harshly. — Now. Or do you want me to?

I got out my mobile and reached Charvillefort right away.

— Listen, I told her. — This is important. You have to keep Natalie Drax away from Louis. You can't let her near him.

— Georges Navarra is with her. But we can't stop her seeing Louis.

— Why not?

— There's no proof, Dr Dannachet. Don't you realise that? There's absolutely no proof!

I sighed and closed my eyes.

— You asked me to tell you what Natalie said about the accident, I said slowly. I hated myself. — She said she saw Louis' face as he fell. His mouth was open as though he was trying to say something.

Across from me, Lucille winced. — You're sure she said that? said Charvillefort sharply. I had to jam the phone hard against my ear to hear her. I could see Lucille tensing. — You're quite sure she said she saw his face as he fell?

— Yes. Quite sure.

— You know that doesn't fit with what she told us, Stephanie Charvillefort said slowly. — She said she was too far away to stop it.

— I know, I said. — She said that too. There was a contradiction. I didn't notice it at the time.

— I'll need you to put that in a statement.

— Of course, I said flatly. — Of course.

— Though it may not be enough to get a conviction. In the meantime, I have bad news, said Charvillefort.

— I don't think I can take any more.

— Well I'm sorry. It's Marcel Perez. He's in hospital with alcohol poisoning. He went on a huge binge. I'm on my way there now, but he may not make it.

You can't see anything in the cave, just the white stone, and Gustave's bloody bandages on the floor like we're standing in spaghetti Bolognese. His hand's growing more and more cold and more and more like bones. But I'm holding it anyway because there's nothing else to hold. I must've always known it was him even when he scared me, even when he said weird things and I could feel the danger all around me. His voice is just a croak now, like it's in my head.

— Once upon a time there was a boy whose mother and father loved him, and one day –

— Blah blah blah.

— And one day –

— I don't want to hear that one, I'm not a baby and I don't want to hear stupid fairy stories for babies cos they suck! I'm shouting but he doesn't shout back. He's quiet.

— How do you know what the story is?

— Cos I've heard it before. It's *The Strange Mystery of Louis Drax, the Amazing Accident-Prone Boy*, blah blah blah. Tell me one that doesn't suck.

— OK. Once upon a time there were two princesses.

— I don't want princesses. I want bats.

— OK. Bats. Once upon a time there were two bats. No, three. Three bats, a male and two females. And one of the female bats was always laughing and the other female bat was always crying, and the male bat had to choose between them.

— To mate with?

— Yes. So he chose the laughing one, but then he had second thoughts. He felt sorry for the crying bat. She seemed to need him more. He thought if he loved her enough, he could stop her crying. But he was wrong.

— Why was she crying?

— Because it made people feel sorry for her, and she liked that feeling, more than she liked jokes or stories or love.

— What happened to her?

— She ended up all alone.

— And the laughing bat?

— She fell in love with another male bat, and they had three bat babies and lived happily ever after.

— And what happened to the male bat?

But Gustave doesn't say anything because I guess the story – which sucked – is finished. He probably knows it sucked, and that I thought it sucked, because most stories suck, if they're about stupid love stuff, even if it's bats. So we just sit there in the cold cave that's like a creepy skull and I'm still holding his hand that's made of bones but there's a warm feeling, like a fizzing fire in your chest, like the pine cones in the forest whooshing up, because you can love someone, even if they're dead, and they can love you too, that's the thing I just found out.

— I have to go soon, Young Sir, he says. — There's going to be a funeral.

I left Lucille on the ward with Louis and went to my office, where I called Jacqueline and asked her to join me. Noelle had already gone home for the day. While I was waiting for Jacqueline, I rang the girls' apartment in Montpellier hoping to reach Sophie, but I got the answerphone. I didn't know what to say so I hesitated and hung up. That felt cowardly, so I rang back and left the briefest message I could.

— Sophie, it's Pascal. We need to talk.

Then, at a loss, I watered my bonsais. They looked dusty and neglected. I wiped a few leaves and sprayed them, but I suddenly couldn't seem to care if they lived or died. Jacqueline knocked, came in, and told me that I looked terrible, and that I shouldn't even be here.

— So where should I be?

— In Montpellier, with Sophie, she answered, rather too quickly. — Have you spoken to her?

— I don't know what to say. I'm in a mess, Jacqueline.

She didn't reply to that, but patted me on the arm in such a quiet, human way that I felt like breaking down there and then. I didn't. Instead, with a painful effort of will, I told her about my trip to Vichy, and what I had learned from Philippe Meunier and Lucille Drax. It wrenched my heart to confess the core of the matter: that I now feared that Natalie Drax – the woman I loved – might have harmed her own child. 'Might have harmed':

saying it aloud made me feel sick, but it had a different effect on Jacqueline. And an instantaneous one.

— *Might have harmed?* Pascal, what you're saying is that *she tried to kill him.*

I'd never seen her angry before, hadn't known how it looked: her mouth went a different shape, the shape I imagined she might use for crying. I'd never seen her cry either. She walked over to the window and looked out.

— There's more, I told her heavily. — Lucille Drax thinks Natalie killed Pierre. I put a laugh into my voice, to show how absurd the idea was. But it sounded forced.

— There's always been something strange about her, Jacqueline said eventually, almost to herself. — She never wanted any contact. Jessica Favrot said it was like she thought she had a monopoly on grief. But I guess she was just scared we'd see through her. It's not something that crosses your mind though, is it? Why would it cross anyone's mind?

— Charvillefort mentioned it, I said, slowly remembering. — Right at the beginning. When we were in Vaudin's office, she said that one of Louis' parents could have harmed him.

— But we didn't want to think about it being her, did we? said Jacqueline. Her back was still to me, I could hear that she was angry with herself. — Everything pointed to her husband. We believed what we wanted to.

But now we had to swivel our thoughts a hundred and eighty degrees. When Jacqueline turned to face me, her eyes were glittering. I could tell she was thinking of her own son, Paul.

— If Natalie's determined to lie about about her role in Louis' accident – and possibly also the death of her husband – then what can we do? she asked simply. — What on earth can we do, Pascal?

I stared at my phrenological chart, losing myself in the chambers of the brain. Where quietly, from nowhere, a very clear and very obvious thought hatched.

*   *   *

Although I wasn't officially at work, I spent the next hour with Isabelle and her parents. Madame Masserot had come down from Paris, at the request of her ex-husband, and it appeared that they had finally reached a shaky truce. Isabelle had responded well to the encouraging atmosphere and there had been a few more small, hopeful signals that she was coming back to consciousness. She had opened her eyes again, and cleared her throat as though preparing to speak. Her mother had combed her hair, and she had protested.

— Like she always did, said Madame Masserot, smiling.

It was good to see her smile at last. I had only sensed that she was a person overloaded by the weight of her own anger, but now I felt a sudden warmth towards her. I congratulated both parents on their decision to put the past behind them, and outlined the ways in which Isabelle's treatment could now be stepped up, then left them by the bedside. Just then Stephanie Charvillefort walked in. She looked exhausted and drained, having spent the last few hours at Marcel Perez's bedside, arguing with the doctors about how soon he was free to leave.

— What? *Leave?* asked Jacqueline, her eyes widening. — But surely he's too ill to –

– I've brought him with me, because I think we need him here, said Detective Charvillefort. — In case Louis wakes up. He wanted to come.

She sounded triumphant, but I detected a quiver in her voice. I wondered how long it had been since she had slept, or eaten anything. By silent agreement, we all headed out of the ward.

— Where is he? I asked.

— In the lobby. I was hoping you could find him a bed.

— I'll see to it, said Jacqueline, and left swiftly.

— About all this, I said to Charvillefort as we walked along the white corridor. — The lack of evidence. I have an idea. Jacqueline thinks it's a good one, and I think Vaudin could be persuaded. And now Marcel Perez is here, he can help too. He'll be useful.

But when I told her what I was thinking of, she looked at me as though I had lost my mind.

— No, she said, stopping to look me full in the face. — Absolutely not.

I was immediately angry. — Why the hell not?

She continued to look at me with those very piercing eyes.

— Because it's insane, Dr Dannachet.

— Surely by now you're willing to try anything? I was feeling desperate. — You don't have many options at this point. We have a boy in a coma, one man dead, and no concrete proof of the slightest wrongdoing on anyone's part. Nothing.

— I can't stop you doing what you want to do, Dr Dannachet, she said finally. — But I can't be part of it. If you go ahead, then I wish you luck.

— Do you have a better idea? I snapped.

— As a matter of fact yes. I'm going to question Natalie Drax again, for as long as it takes. We have new information now. Philippe Meunier's new version of events in the hospital in Vichy, and your account of what Natalie Drax told you about Louis' fall. Two inconsistencies. I think if I confront her with them, she might crack.

I went to find Jacqueline; I found her sitting in the lobby with Lucille Drax and Marcel Perez. The three of them were deep in conversation, I knew that Jacqueline had been telling them what I was planning. Perez looked terrible. He was still attached to a portable drip; he clearly hadn't shaved in days, and his skin exhaled a rancid alcoholic reek. I guessed it would be a long time leaving his system.

— Glad to see you, said Perez.

— Will you help us? I asked.

— We both will, said Lucille Drax.

— Detective Charvillefort says it's insane.

— Maybe she's right, said Marcel Perez. — But what is there to lose?

We all exchanged a nervous smile, and then went in to see

Vaudin. He was on the point of leaving for home, and we caught him off guard.

— You're not even supposed to be here, Pascal, he grumbled, ushering us in. — Didn't I tell you to take some leave?

— I will, I said. — But there's something I have to do first.

Jacqueline, Marcel Perez and I each addressed him, but it was Lucille Drax who did the real persuading.

— I've lost my son, she finished. — My grandson's in a coma. If there's a way of getting him to communicate again, I want to try it. I don't think you can refuse me, Dr Vaudin.

Guy was embarrassed, but gave in to letting us go ahead with what he called 'your experiment'. He would turn a blind eye if it were done while he was off the premises. But there were conditions. It was to be properly supervised. Jacqueline and Lucille Drax were both to be present at Louis' bedside. It must all be recorded on camera, and come to a swift halt in the event of a fire threat. We must do it that night. Leave things any later, and the circumstances would become too chaotic. The forest fires were sweeping closer by the hour, and we might all be forced to evacuate the building whether we wanted to or not. There was no denying the increasingly pervasive smell of smoke that wafted towards us from the forest.

— And remember, he finished. — This isn't officially happening. You're not here, Pascal; you're on sick leave.

So it was agreed: I was to spend the night on the ward with Louis, in the company of Jacqueline Duval, Marcel Perez – who was soon installed, shuffling around in pyjamas – and Lucille Drax.

Georges Navarra called by and told me Detective Charville-fort was still interrogating Natalie Drax.

— Stephanie's very tough, he said. — But so far Natalie Drax is sticking to the version of the story she originally gave the police. She completely denies telling you she saw Louis' face as he fell. She says you invented it.

I felt myself flush with rage. She had said it. I remembered it so clearly. Remembered her misery, the tears she'd shed, the brave face she'd tried to put on, the way I'd melted with pity.

—She's lying.

Then I remembered the firm gentleness of her voice on the phone when I had called her from Vichy. *I never tried to hurt Louis.* She loved him. That was enough for me. Wasn't it? I felt sick at the thought that a part of me had ever doubted her. But sicker still to realise that the doubt lingered, and was deepening, despite everything.

—Good luck with it, said Georges. —For what it's worth, I think it's a good idea. Perhaps if Stephanie Charvillefort doesn't get any further with Madame Drax, she'll change her mind.

But he didn't sound convinced.

We began at six o'clock, as soon as Vaudin had left. I was anxious, even though my role was to be a passive one. I took a 20mg tablet of temazepam, which hit me in a queasy rush, then soaked me up. I lay on the bed that had been installed next to Louis, letting the euphoria wash over me. There was no noise except for the hum of the two respirators that serviced Kevin and Henri; the noise soothed me, and for a beautiful, crystalline moment before sleep overcame me, everything seemed simple and clear and perfect.

The temazepam did its work efficiently; I was fully unconscious, according to Jacqueline, by half past six, when she set the CCTV camera and the tape recorder in motion, and summoned Lucille Drax and Marcel Perez to join her at my bedside. Together the three of them sat in chairs next to the beds where Louis and I lay, and waited. I'd been supplied with paper, a pen and a clipboard. But nothing happened.

Nothing and more nothing. An hour passed, and then two, and the plan that had seemed so inspired began to look like a hopeless act of folly. But they stayed anyway. What choice did they have? More hours limped by, and they fell asleep in turns. By midnight they had sunk into a state of despondency that weighed on them like a cold, unhappy blanket. I had barely stirred, and Louis had remained still, his breathing so shallow it was scarcely detectable, his long lashes casting shadows on his cheeks, his hand curled around the toy moose.

Then at one o'clock, Detective Charvillefort and Georges Navarra returned to the clinic – bringing an exhausted but defiant Natalie Drax with them. She had revealed nothing, and they were quietly desperate. Georges Navarra had persuaded Charvillefort that if Louis was to yield up any information through me, then they should be present, and observe the reaction of his mother. Faced with her own failure to make Natalie confess, Stephanie Charvillefort had finally agreed. Natalie would watch the CCTV link from a separate room, supervised by Georges Navarra, who would stay with her throughout and monitor her reactions – with a CCTV camera for back-up. God only knows what Natalie was going through at that point. Maybe just surviving. I can picture how she might simply shut something off inside her, suffocating any urge towards introspection. When I imagine her eyes – as I do, in those times when a tidal wave of memory washes through me, stripping my thoughts to the bone – I feel myself crumbling. Because her eyes, as I remember them, show nothing: nothing.

I slept on. Perez, Lucille, Jacqueline and Charvillefort sat on chairs next to the bed. Natalie Drax, as agreed, was in a side-room with Georges Navarra.

Then at four o'clock, Marcel Perez, who had dozed off by the bedside, woke up. He had been dreaming about Louis, he told me later. Louis had come to see him in Gratte-Ciel, and they'd talked. He couldn't remember what about, but they had been glad to see one another. Piecing the dream back together from the fragments it left around him when he woke, he had an idea – an idea so simple that when he voiced it, it struck him as bizarre that he'd not thought of it before. There was no need for pen and paper. Marcel Perez would simply address Louis the way he always did. He cleared his throat.

— Tell me, Louis, he said softly. — What happened on the mountain?

And I opened my eyes and began to talk.

Mohammed came, in Alcatraz, but we kept him in the boot while we ate the picnic.

— What did you eat? asks Fat Perez, because he's into eating, which is how he got so fat and called Fat Perez instead of Monsieur.

— Food, duh! Has your brain shrunk to the size of a pea or something?

— What kind of food? he asks. (See what I mean?) — Can you remember?

— You want a list? OK, here's what was in the picnic basket, Monsieur Perez. I bet it makes you hungry. There was bread and pâté and cheese and *saucisson sec* secretly called donkey dick, and wine for them and Coke for me. And lots of *non-harmful bacteria*, cos food's always swarming with non-harmful bacteria and sometimes the harmful kind too, that's how I got salmonella once. And Maman said I should slow down or I'd get tummy ache, that's what she's always on about, scared I might puke up, or swallow a screw by accident, that can happen. I once ate a three-centimetre screw by accident, you ask her. She'll tell you I'm not a liar.

— I know you're not a liar, Louis. Tell me more.

— About food? You want more food?

— About anything.

— There was birthday cake. Chocolate. And you had to make

a wish. Maman's wish was that I'd be hers for ever and that nothing bad would happen to me.

— And your wish?

— That Papa was my real dad, so he'd stay with us.

— Aha. And did you tell them your wish, Louis, or did you keep it to yourself?

— Blah blah blah.

— What does that mean?

— It means blah blah blah.

— Does that mean –

— It means I wasn't going to say it. But I did cos Papa told me off about the sweets.

— The sweets?

— They weren't sweets. He thought they were. I had them in my pocket. I only ate one.

— What were they, Louis, if they weren't sweets?

— Blah blah blah.

— Something that made Papa cross?

— Lady-pills don't even look like sweets. They don't taste like sweets either, you just swallow them. He wanted to know why I had them in my pocket and why I ate one. So I told him I ate one every day.

— You ate a lady-pill every day, Louis?

— Of course.

— But why?

— So I'd turn into a girl.

— And why did you want that?

— So I wouldn't be a rapist. And when I told Papa that he started shouting at Maman about being a *pathological liar* and look what it's led to and blah blah blah, so I tried to stop them by saying the wish aloud. The one I didn't say before, about him being my real dad. If he was my real dad I wouldn't have needed the lady-pills, would I? So it was Papa's fault, not Maman's.

— And then what?

— And so I said I know who my real dad is, he's a rapist called

Jean-Luc and he let Maman down very badly. And she doesn't want me to grow up and be like him. And nor do I cos rapists should have their dicks cut off, and I should too, to stop me growing into one. Maybe I'll cut it off myself one day. I've got a penknife. But before that I'll just eat lady-pills.

— And then?

— Maman started screaming at Papa, so I ran away and she ran after me, and he ran after her and he was yelling at me and saying Jean-Luc wasn't a rapist, and you're not the son of a rapist, and I can prove it to you, Louis, it's something she made up. Just come with me to Paris.

— And did you want to do that, Louis? Did you want to go to Paris with Papa?

— No. I couldn't anyway, cos she grabbed me and we were right next to the edge where it's dangerous, and she was yelling and screaming at Papa. And Papa stopped running. He said, Let Louis go, Natalie. Because we were right near the edge. Let him go.

— And then?

— She wouldn't. She dragged me right to the edge.

— Why, Louis?

— Blah blah blah.

— What was Maman doing, Louis?

— It's allowed you know. That's what Papa didn't understand.

— What's allowed?

— It's a secret rule. It's called Right of Disposal. But then Papa suddenly jumped forward and grabbed us both and pulled her off me and said no, Natalie, never again. And he shouted at me to go to the car and wait there but just when he said that, she gave him a huge push and he wobbled, just like in a cartoon. And blah blah blah.

— He fell?

— It could've been an accident. I know about accidents. It could've been one, you could've thought she was trying to help him.

— But was it an accident, Louis? asks Fat Perez.

— It might have been. I could've thought it was. I could have.

— What did you do then, Louis? whispers Fat Perez. His voice is cracking up like an old radio that's disappearing.

— I did what she wanted, like I always do. She didn't even need to help me, not this time. It was easy. I'm always doing it. It's what I do. But it wasn't her fault.

— What wasn't?

— What I did. Because I did it myself. I chose it, and she says if you make a choice then it isn't anyone else's fault. It's yours, and you mustn't go making up stories about it to impress people. You have to live with the choice you made, and you mustn't ever blame anyone else for it.

— What did you do Louis? he whispers. His voice is far away and maybe mine is too. Suddenly there's a pain in my chest, like something's going to burst.

— I walked backwards. I counted the steps. It was five steps. It was easy. One two three four five. And then I thought there might be a six but there wasn't a six. Instead of a six, I fell into the water, and I died.

It was at that moment that Louis Drax stopped breathing.

I awoke abruptly to the sound of a terrible scream. It was Natalie Drax, who had rushed in with Georges Navarra at her heels. It was complete turmoil. At first I couldn't make head or tail of what was going on; I was in a sort of paralysis, between the sleeping and the waking state, but I could remember everything Louis had said, and was reeling from it. Louis' eyes were open. Wide open, just like before. I saw Charvillefort rushing off to get some help, and I saw Jacqueline wheel over a respirator. Charvillefort came back with two more nurses and Jacqueline swiftly connected Louis to the machine.

— We're losing him, said Jacqueline. Her voice was calm but I could feel the urgency behind it. — I'm calling Vaudin. I can't get this thing working.

— No, said Stephanie Charvillefort briskly. — There isn't time. Pascal can do it. Can't you, Pascal?

— I don't know, I wavered. I felt strangely distanced from the scene, as though I was still partly inside the mind of Louis, in quite another place. Somewhere shadowed and lopsided and oddly cold.

— Well I do, said Stephanie Charvillefort firmly. And she slapped me hard – wincingly, shockingly hard – across the cheek. Before I even had time to react, she'd slapped me again on the other cheek, with equal force. I cried out in pain and rage, but the physical insult worked: she'd brought me fully back from wherever I had been. At which point instinct took over. Hauling myself off the bed, I went into overdrive. Louis' lungs had failed, but as soon as I'd clamped the mask to his face and performed a CPR, punching his chest rhythmically to kick-start his heart and lungs, the respirator took over and did its work. I held his wrist and got his pulse, which gradually normalised. Another night-nurse arrived from another ward, along with a porter, and suddenly the bedside was swarming with people.

— Where's Natalie? I asked finally. I had sensed her some-where to my left as we were stabilising Louis, but I no longer felt her presence.

— Oh God, said Navarra, wheeling round to face the French windows. They were wide open. Outside, dawn was breaking. A pale, smoky pall hung in the air. She'd gone.

— Go after her, said Lucille flatly. — Now. You have to get her back.

— I'll call for back-up, said Charvillefort, stabbing at her mobile. — She won't get far.

Marcel Perez was sobbing. Jacqueline patted him on the shoulder and spoke soothingly, as one would to a child. But he wouldn't, couldn't, stop. His chest heaved and the tears ran. When he looked up at me – why did he suddenly look up? – I saw raw agony. It was like being shot in the heart at point-blank range. I turned away from his directness. It felt too fatal. Lucille sat quietly next to Louis, holding his hand with a stunned look on her face. Both of them were as pale as air.

Charvillefort made a quick assessment of the situation. She said Natalie would probably steer clear of any roads, which would make the search more difficult, especially with the choking smoke that was beginning to sweep the landscape. The dawn had risen further, a hectic pink smudged with plumes of pewter gas that wheeled their way up the hillside towards us. Quickly, we agreed to go in separate directions. Stephanie would take a car and follow the road to the village. Georges would go on foot downhill, skirting the *route nationale*, and I would head uphill – also on foot – to the edge of the pine forest.

A car shot up the drive just as we were setting off, then braked hard in front of us. It was Vaudin. He wound down his window and addressed Charvillefort.

— I've just had a call from the fire service, he called. — We've got to evacuate the clinic. Then he looked at me. — What the hell are you still doing here?

— I'll tell you later, I called, and began to run.

I kept stumbling. The rough track that led to the forest rim was littered with stones, gravel, shards of olive branch, thistles, bark. The looming smoke-clouds had recast the landscape so that its landmarks – a stone ruin, a lavender field, a pylon – looked displaced. Tricks of the light that made everything splintered and disjointed. I ran on. Steadily I could feel the line between earth and air blurring, merging the elements into one. There was a moment when I thought I saw a fluttering shape but it was gone so instantly that I immediately doubted it. I scanned the terrain ahead, hungry for a glimpse of her, a sign that she had passed this way. On the lower horizon I saw the distant shape of Georges Navarra running down the slope in the direction of the olive groves to the west of the *route nationale*, but visibility was worsening, and I knew that soon we would be lost to one another.

The flank of trees lurked squat and dense before me. Within its heart I imagined a bomb, heat mushrooming outwards. Still there were no flames, but the smoke was slewed across the sky, a low-slung pulse that sucked and spat and breathed filth. Then, in my peripheral vision, I thought I saw a shape flit across the line of the trees a hundred metres ahead of me, then disappear. The blood drummed in my ears and I heard my own breathing: a forced, painful rasp. For a moment, the world seemed to tilt on its axis.

— Natalie! I yelled. My lungs baulked at the effort and I coughed. The smoke swarmed; thickened with black dust. — Come back!

The figure reappeared briefly from the line of trees. It was her. Although far away, you could see the outline of her face, like it had been cut from paper: a perfect, shocked oval. The shape and colour of terrible innocence. A mixture of feelings – love, distaste, revulsion, pity – rose in my throat like vomit. There was an eternity to that moment, that see-sawing split-second when adoration clung and then lurched, spilling into chaos, rage, hate, anger: the desire to smash and embrace, love and destroy. Betrayal does that. Forces the clash of belief and disbelief. Shows you how worthless love is, when its object is indifferent, ruthless, no more than a machine for surviving.

She saw me. Turned. And ran.

Still dizzy from the temazepam and half-blinded by the sting of smoke, I stumbled after her, keeping my eyes focused on her dress, whose paleness flashed among the tree-trunks like a grotesque moth. A creature that I wanted above all to punish, stub out, be rid of for ever. And yes – save. From herself, from the fire, from my own fury. Reach her, forgive her. Understand. Yes, that ruinous need man has to understand.

I seemed to be sobbing. Vaguely, I registered the whine of a helicopter but there was nothing to be seen in the sky's dark swirl and I knew it was pointless to call out. I lunged on, tripping and scraping myself, until I came to the line of trees into which she had disappeared. I was sure I would reach her. She had gambled by heading into the flames. She must have thought she could lose me, or that I would hold back, but she had me wrong. I was set on getting to her no matter how close we came to the inferno. My survival felt irrelevant, a small detail in a world where I was just a futile speck.

You could see flames now. They shot out from the trees, ribboning across the horizon as though released from a giant canister: a cruel, vital orange. I saw her again, just for a second. She emerged, saw that I was still pursuing her, and was instantly gone, sucked in by the hot forest. Seized by something beyond me, something virulent and wide awake, I stormed into the maw of the heat. The force of it hit my face and made me splutter with pain. To get any closer was suicide, but a kind of madness propelled me on.

This could not end happily. And yet although every cell in my body told me to turn back then – turn back, save myself, fetch help, let the forest decide her end – I followed her screams and went in. Why couldn't I leave her there? Why was it that I found myself – by now sobbing hopelessly, my eyes streaming from the smoke – hurtling on like a creature possessed?

Her screams were one long, high shriek of pain. By the time I reached her, she was a human firework. Her pale dress had turned black and was welded to her body like scorching, textured paint. She spouted flame; it seemed not just to envelop her, but to leap from her. For a second I stood rooted, my eyes fixated on the flaming, mutilated doll that stood before me. She was still screaming, her mouth a wide O of pain. Her whole head was haloed by effervescent flames that darted outwards like shoals of startled fish. Her face, that lovely face. I saw it eaten up, I smelled the stench. I ran towards her, lungeing forward just as she was falling, and caught her burning body in my arms.

Then, hell.

Immediately, before I could think what I had done, the fire fused her skin to mine. I tried to cry out but no sound came. I couldn't shed her. Repelled, and flayed with pain, I hauled her with me across the flaming forest bed. I had no choice.

I don't know how far I dragged her, or how long it was before I fell unconscious. You don't feel your own scorched flesh right away, but you smell it. Our welded bodies – mine still alive, hers perhaps already dead – smelled of charred pork.

— What did she say, at the end? Perez asked me later. — When you reached the stream?

Because yes, she had spoken. I don't know how. I thought she was dead. But there came a few words, squeezed out like bile. Her voice tiny and cracked, cooked by the heat.

—I always saved him, she said. —I never let him die. You have to protect your child. I love my son. I love my son more than anything in the world.

Her last words before she rolled her scorched eyes to face me. They were blind, boiled in their sockets like white eggs. I remember the need to retch. Holding her foul body in my arms in the muddy water, and turning away to vomit. Then blackness.

You plant a seed thinking it's love. It's only when the thing starts putting down roots that you realise it's not growing the way it should. But by then it's too late. It has sprouted foliage, blossomed and borne demented fruit.

What do you do with the sickness in you?

You can embrace it, make it part of your life. Maybe Pierre Drax tried to do that for a while. But by then there was something else pulling him the other way: the knowledge of what he could have had, what he threw away with Catherine. And the knowledge that his son was in danger. You can run away, to the ends of the earth. Or you can confront your worst nightmare. Maybe that's what happened on the mountainside that day in June, when the story of Louis Drax had one of its many beginnings.

A man confronted the truth, and two people paid the price.

I was hospitalised in Cannes with severe burns. When I woke, after three days in Intensive Care, I was in an agony so transcendental that I wondered how I could still be alive, how any human body could bear this much pain. Detective Charvillefort was sitting next to me. Her astonishing eyes looked red, heavy, shocked. I must have seemed like a creature from hell. She told me they taken Natalie's body – what was left of it – to the morgue. I had been lucky to survive. If I hadn't stumbled across the stream, if Georges Navarra hadn't reached me when he did, and dragged me to the field, if the helicopter hadn't spotted us . . .

I too would have been burned to a stump.

I love my son. More than anything in the world. I never let him die.

Louis called it Right of Disposal, according to the report that Marcel Perez wrote for the police after Natalie's death, when he had pieced the fragments together. Louis used to kill his pet hamsters, because he claimed there was a secret set of rules. The rules no one talked about. And under these rules, a pet-owner has the right to kill his pet. If you own it, you control whether it lives or dies. And how. This was knowledge Louis had grown up with because that's what Natalie believed about her child. His life was property: hers.

When he was small, she had injured him herself. Perhaps even tried to kill him, but lost her nerve. Then, as Louis grew older, he soon learned what she wanted, and responded to her needs. So he did it himself. Having heard what Louis had said from his coma, Perez was sure of it. She didn't need to touch him. She just had to be there. He'd have an accident, and she would save him. It would strengthen the bond between them. She loved him, she hated him. She wanted to be with him for ever and she never wanted to see him again. She couldn't live with him and she couldn't live without him.

And Louis colluded.

When Sophie turned up, tearful and scared, I told her everything.

— I'm sorry I wasn't there for you, she said. — The girls are on their way.

And then neither of us knew what to say. Despite all our years of marriage, there was an awkwardness, a formality. It felt as though we were strangers who would have to acquaint themselves, slowly, with the new people we had become. She put her hand on my arm and I saw a terrible expression on her face: not love, but pity.

— Will you come back? I asked. There was a long pause.

—I don't know. I don't really know if I can live with what's happened to you. I don't mean the burns. I mean what's happened in your head.

When she said that, I wondered if I could either.

I came out of hospital in November, and began to work at the clinic again part-time. I was still weak. In August, after the post-mortems, both Pierre Drax and Natalie's funerals took place. Natalie's, in Paris, had been a small affair, according to Lucille, who'd visited me regularly, bringing me news of Louis, and the outside world. Natalie's sister Francine came, and the mother whom Natalie had always claimed lived in Guadeloupe. She did not. Had never even been there. She was in sheltered accommodation in Étampes, south of Paris. She'd looked weary and drawn and strangely resigned to what had happened. Though she had known nothing, she said, understood nothing. After Louis was born, Natalie had broken off all contact. There had never been a stepfather, with or without Parkinson's disease.

December brought me a visit from Detective Charvillefort and Marcel Perez, who was off the bottle. Stephanie Charvillefort was dealing with a case of fraud in Cannes, and Marcel Perez had joined her for the ride. Both of them had wanted to take the opportunity to visit me, Louis and Lucille. I was delighted to see them, delighted that they had made this detour – a whole trip, in Marcel Perez's case – to visit me. If they were shocked at the change in my appearance, they hid it well.

—And how are you, Pascal? asked Marcel.

—I don't look very attractive in the nude, but Sophie says I never did anyway.

—She's come back, then? asked Stephanie searchingly.

—Sort of. It's very delicate. Some days we're OK and other days we aren't.

—Give it time, said Marcel Perez. Treat it like bereavement. There are stages to it.

— She's still doing anger, I said.

— Then let her.

— Shall we walk in the garden? I suggested.

— I'll sit with Louis for a while, said Marcel Perez. — I've got things to say to him. I'll join you.

When he saw Louis, his face lit up, then darkened. He took the boy's hand in his and squeezed.

— No change? he asked sadly.

— No change. We keep on hoping.

I needed two sticks to walk. Even with their help, I couldn't move fast. Everything hurt. I explained to Stephanie that the burns would take a long time to heal, and I might need some further surgery on my chest and legs. My hands were mending slowly.

— Come on. I'll show you the roses. Winter roses. They're just in bloom. As we left the ward, Stephanie reached for her cigarettes, and I picked up an empty plastic specimen jar to serve as an ashtray, knowing that Monsieur Girardeau would never forgive me if I didn't clean up after my visitor. We walked for a while in silence under a sky dotted with white clouds. The seagulls spun above us.

— Have you lost your faith in women, Pascal? Stephanie Charvillefort asked abruptly. — I'm interested.

I thought for a moment. I'd never asked myself this. I wondered why. The question was so obvious.

— Perhaps I should have. But no. Actually, I refuse to. On principle. It's more that I've lost faith in my own judgement.

What I couldn't say was that I wasn't over Natalie Drax. That a sick, tortured part of me hung on, yearning for her still. Stephanie took out a cigarette and lit up. I winced at the flame.

— Sorry, she said. — I didn't think.

— And what about you? Can one ask the same question of a woman?

— No, because it's different. You can't lose faith in your own sex. That would be a kind of abdication. But you know what your own sex is capable of, and what it can sink to. I may not be a typical woman, she said, shooting me a wry glance, — but I do understand the female psyche.

— And the male psyche?

— To some extent. Men want to think the best of women, especially if they're attractive. Isn't there some truth in that? That we attribute moral goodness to attractive people? And to those who present themselves as victims? Natalie made a very convincing victim, she mused. — I was taken in too. Despite being female.

I had a sudden flash of memory: Natalie's scorched figure screaming and on fire. It was recurrent. Five times a day on average, I saw that small frail frame, running away from itself, from me, from the world. Hurtling into hell. Saw the once-pale hair on fire, a ghastly halo around that blackened, eaten-up face.

We had reached the roses.

— Aren't they stupendous? I asked shakily, pointing a stick at the yellow mass of blooms. I forced the image of Natalie back into the corner of my mind where it lived and lurked.

— A very striking colour, said Stephanie, stubbing out her cigarette before grinding it into the earth with her heel. — Didn't Louis mention lupins? Do you have them here?

— Hundreds, I said, pointing to what remained of them. — Highly toxic.

At this she grew serious again, animated. — What's so puzzling to me is that Natalie's way of thinking comes from another era. From the time when women really were helpless, when they really did have to manipulate men.

— A throwback, I murmured. — Some kind of relic. But to hurt her own child and call it love . . .

— Every day, a woman somewhere kills her own child, said Stephanie Charvillefort bleakly. — Believe me. We watched as Marcel Perez stood on the balcony with Jacqueline, then descended the steps towards us.

— But I don't want to believe you.

— No one does. But it's the truth. It's the easiest kind of murder to cover up, because it's the kind most people would prefer not to contemplate.

— Which makes us accomplices, I said slowly, allowing the thought space. — Because we've colluded without knowing.

— That was the end-point. But it all began with something very small. Natalie's first mistake was negligible. It was easily understandable. It was even forgivable, if you're into forgiveness. She wanted a man who didn't want her, so she tried to trap him by getting pregnant. It's the oldest trick in the book.

— One of the oldest tricks, said Marcel, joining us as Stephanie took out another cigarette. This time she turned away from me to light it. — There are actually many. What lovely roses.

— All of them listed somewhere in a psychology book, right? said Stephanie. He smiled and we walked on, rounding the corner and stopping by the ornamental pond. It struck me that Stephanie and Marcel must have spent some time discussing the case of Natalie Drax. I felt oddly out of the loop.

I watched the tiny rainbows shooting up from the fountain. My legs were hurting and I had to stop for a moment.

— It may be a morally questionable thing to do, said Stephanie, — but it's not evil. It's not even illegal. It's just a dirty trick to play. Talk to any man who's been caught out that way. He's furious, he's resentful. Women can be their own worst enemies.

— But why invent a story of rape? I asked. I still didn't get it. — It's so – so *drastic*. How could anyone come up with an idea like that?

Marcel Perez sighed. — That's where I went wrong. I never doubted it, when I heard that story. You don't, do you?

— No, I said — You don't. It's too . . . indecent. Indecent to question it, but the idea of making it up's indecent too. No one with any pride –

—Oh, but it came from pride, said Marcel. —Look at it this way. She could hardly tell the real story. It didn't make her look good. But she could have come up with something that didn't make her look so bad – some kind of halfway version. Most women in that position manage to. But she was too proud for that. And cunning. She took it a step further. The rape story gained her a sort of sick cachet.

—It was actually quite inspired, said Stephanie dismally. —It made her a sort of holy martyr. Three cheers for the female mind.

This thought depressed me. I didn't like to think of women like that. Most are not. Surely, most are not?

—That's why I asked you if you'd lost faith, she went on. —Because in your position I might. But I don't want you to.

I smiled at her sudden seriousness. I could see Marcel smiling too. When I felt a little steadier, we walked on slowly, Charvillefort smoking and talking, Marcel and me mostly listening and thinking. I remembered at one moment, with a kind of shock, that I had rather disliked Stephanie Charvillefort when I first met her. Or at least not taken her seriously.

—I got you wrong, I said suddenly.

—I know, she said, turning sharply to look at me, and then smiling.

—People do, Stephanie, said Marcel. —It's the way you come across. Perhaps you should wear a bit of make-up.

But I couldn't join in their laughter. My feelings – would they ever leave me? – were too strong, too recent, too excruciating. The three of us sat down on the bench near the azaleas and looked at the garden in silence for a moment, each absorbed in our thoughts.

—She loved her son, said Marcel Perez. —But she hated him too. There was an eternal conflict. It was more complex than Munchausen's syndrome by proxy. The murderous instinct really was there. She said she never let him die. But she took

218

him to the edge time after time. A part of him wanted it too. It was a game they played together.

A sleek koi carp glided into view beneath the surface of the water, its scales smooth. Another followed, and then a third. I watched, mesmerised as their cool shapes swirled in the depths.

It was February. Winter had laid everything bare. The mountains, capped with snow, rose dark and primaeval from the plain below: a desolate, almost lunar landscape. Huge rocks lay scattered like a handful of dice flung down by a petulant giant. There were hardly any other cars on the road, but the occasional HGV rumbled past, its tyres shooting up swathes of slush. Somewhere, in this emptiness, they took deliveries.

After Ponteyrol the road narrowed; it took me another hour, from there, to reach the spot where the Drax family had gone for their picnic. It was higher up, more remote, than I had pictured.

I parked in a clearing nearby and picked my way slowly along the track that led through tall dead grass spangled with frozen cobwebs. Stephanie had given me the police map which showed the landmarks: a bent fir tree, a clutch of birch trees, two boulders. There were odd patches of mist; despite my thick coat, I shivered. The scars on my chest and hands ached as I struggled with the brambles that caught at my clothing. Slowly, I became aware of the sound of rushing water. I limped to the edge of the ravine and stood at the spot where Louis Drax fell.

It was a few minutes before I summoned the nerve to look down. The drop was sheer and unrelenting. A wave of nausea overtook me. Vertigo. The trick is to breathe slowly, quell the panic. Unthinkable, that anyone could have survived such a fall.

You could see a thin ribbon of silver far below, with a cloud of spray rising from it.

I stayed there for a long time, just breathing. Breathing, and wondering if I would ever make sense of the dance that Louis and his mother danced together for nine years, the rituals and acts of complicity that led to him walking those five steps back. Or if I would ever know where Louis was wandering now. The mind is infinitely larger than the world it inhabits. There is more to the human brain than machinery or meat. I believe in the soul, I thought suddenly. Everything I know about the brain tells me not to, but I believe in it still. I believe in Louis' soul. I felt myself swaying.

To try and put a lid on things, I wrote about the case of Louis Drax. But despite the proof of a telepathic interchange – the CCTV footage, the witnesses – my article was rejected by all the major medical journals. In my heart of hearts, I had always known it would be. It was too bizarre. The editors indicated, gently, that publication would discredit me. That it would not help my career to be seen as any more of a maverick than I already was.

Vaudin made sympathetic noises, but I knew he agreed with them. He didn't disbelieve the proof, but he was cautious. I considered writing about it in a newspaper, but that would have involved telling more of the story than was wise. There was still a chance that Louis would emerge from his coma. It would be unfair.

So I kept quiet about it, went on with my work, tended to my bonsais.

Sophie returned, but she left every weekend to stay with the girls in Montpellier. I didn't try to stop her. We were coming to a slow rapprochement But it was painful.

Coming back to life can be as slow as dying. Slower. But there have been a few small signs of encouragement in Louis' progress at the clinic. I still tend towards optimism, still believe just as firmly in the power of hope. I have changed in many ways, since the fire. But on that score, I am the same man. And so – unlike some of my colleagues – I like to think that whatever the evidence to the contrary, in a few months' time, Louis Drax will have fully emerged from his coma.

And then I think about the life we will have, far in the future. Yes, I sometimes – often – allow myself to dream about things like that.

We will make an odd family. Perhaps by then Sophie and I will have reached an understanding of sorts, and be rebuilding a life together. Not the one we once shared, and which I shattered, but a new one, with a new shape and a new voice, new feelings. A wary tenderness. Lucille will still be suffering bad health in the wake of her son's death, and although she will have come to live in the village, she will have asked Sophie and I to consider Louis our son. When she smiles, which is rarely, you will notice the effort it takes for her to summon the right muscles.

Sometimes I will even call Louis 'son'. It will be a joke, but a joke we both need. My daughters will adore him, and come to stay at weekends from Montpellier, with boyfriends in tow, and spoil the kid rotten with computer games, videos, trips to McDonald's. Sophie will cook huge meals for all of us, just like she used to, and when Louis eats, she will watch him maternally, and I will watch her watching him and think of how precarious life is, how swiftly and irredemably it can be knocked sideways. How there are certain types of pain that never really go away. Certain things that are best left unspoken, even when a boy has started to ask questions.

Lucille will keep Pierre's memory alive for Louis, but none of us will talk of Natalie Drax. It will be best that way, if there is a 'best' in such circumstances. Louis will know that she loved him. That's enough. Some memories you do not need. The brain is vaster than I ever realised, its workings more subtle and strange.

When a part of you is cauterised, the mind compensates. The weirdest plants are the ones that grow out of ashes.

Marcel Perez will come to visit once a month, and with his help, Louis will make visible progress. Marcel, Sophie and I will discuss how he is doing, always a little wary, always on the watch for signs that his memory is stirring. For we will be nervous, all of us: nervous that despite all the healing, despite the normality that now surrounds him, the past might find a chink through which to slip, and flood his soul.

Don't think that I didn't grieve, when Natalie died. Don't think that I had stopped loving her. I hadn't. Even now, I am not sure that she's out of my system. Maybe that's what Sophie can see in me. Maybe that's why we still have separate bedrooms, and why despite the tenderness, the new grace we have learned, she stays watchful.

Yes, however misplaced they were, the disturbed emotions Natalie Drax stirred in me still linger, still renew themselves in tiny daily stabs of pain and shame and guilt and sorrow. Surely I might have been able to save her from herself? Surely, with the right kind of love, she might have . . .

— No, Marcel Perez tells me. — She wasn't cut out for love. Love was never going to bring her happiness. Her agenda was different.

One day I will be purged. The day will come when I wake up and do not think of her. But in the meantime, the best of her lives on. Her son. Who perhaps one day will be ready to reach out and re-enter the world – a different world from the one either of us knew before, a world where he has a place, and where I will do all I can for him. All, and more. And maybe one day, almost by accident, I will stumble into redemption.

Let us imagine all that, as we stare at the creature, the two of us. It is a marvel, huge and milky-mauve with long pink tentacles adorned with suckers the size of saucers. It's in a massive tank, and everyone at the museum seems, like us, to have become lost inside it. It hangs in suspended animation, a thing that nobody had believed in before.

They once said that sailors invented them, even though the sucker-marks found on whales proved they must have existed in the dark bowels of the ocean. Deep down, they had hidden for years but now here they are, triumphing in the new climate, breeding like no other creature on earth, silent messengers from those shadowed chambers of the world we had imagined eternally locked, remote, unreachable. The miracle is not that we discovered them by breaking into their world, but that – washed-up and dead – they broke into ours.

In his wheelchair, his head clamped in place, wide-eyed and unblinking, Louis stares and stares, so silent and blind and perhaps also so in awe that you can barely hear him breathe. And suddenly it is a stupendous marvel to me that creatures such as this exist, and that alongside, there can be a boy like Louis who might yet come back from that huge and unknown place beneath the surface of things.

You shouldn't think 'oh poor Louis Drax.' Because it doesn't suck too badly. True story. I don't mind staying here.

Lots of stuff sucked before. It's not easy being a Disturbed Child or accident-prone. Seeing Fat Perez sucked, and Maman and Papa hating each other sucked and school sucked and being called Wacko Boy sucked and even the Mohammeds sucked.

This doesn't suck though. See, what Fat Perez didn't understand is, I never thought hospitals sucked. I just said that. I like them. I like it that people take care of you all the time. I like it that you can just lie there and think and stuff, and you don't have to worry that they're fragile or if they're playing Pretend You Don't Hate Him. I like it that you can just think about *La Planète bleue* and you can dream about people like Gustave and listen to Pascal reading to you from *Les Animaux: leur vie extraordinaire*. It's even better than being asleep because you never have to wake up. All you have to do is just lie there and breathe. You don't even have to talk. And the bits you don't like, you can just switch off and sleep through them. I'm good at sleeping through the bad bits. I like Dr Dannachet, I like Jacqueline Duval and Marianne and Berthe and all the other nurses, I like Mamie coming to sit next to me and telling me about all the different dogs she had and what happened to them, and all the places she lived when she was young. I even like Fat Perez coming to visit.

All my life I have been waiting for this hospital. Nine whole years. Nine's my lucky number, cos this is my ninth life, and my ninth life is the best one. True story. I could stay here for ever. I don't need a Papa or a Maman cos I've got Gustave and Dr Dannachet. Every night he comes and reads to me. And when when he says goodnight, he whispers, You can wake up whenever you want to, Louis. I would love to take you to Paris to see miraculous creatures pickled in tanks. But he doesn't understand cos he's a bit dumb. He doesn't get it. He doesn't get that I can already swim underwater, and I can see as many giant squids as I want to, and any other animal or any other thing, anything I want in the whole world. I can go anywhere I want and do anything I want.

Anywhere in the world, anything.

You'd have to be mad to swap that for being Louis Drax again.

That's what Dr Dannachet doesn't get. But Gustave gets it. Gustave knows. My choice is I say, no thanks, Dr Dannachet. I like you. I like it here. My ninth life is better than the other eight, I promise you. I've been thinking and this is what I think. It's OK to be here. So I'll stay put. *If you make a choice, and it's wrong, you have to live with it. Everyone has to live with the consequences. You chose, Louis. It was your choice.*

— So is it OK with you if I stay put? I ask him.

— No. I'm not sure it is, Louis.

But it's not Dr Dannachet's voice. It's Gustave's. Papa. I haven't heard him for ages. I thought he'd gone. He's very faint.

— You don't have to stay, says Gustave. Says Papa. — You can wake up and live. If you want to. Do you want to?

— No. Maybe. I don't know.

He doesn't say anything for a long time. I can't see him any more, did I tell you that? Ever since we went to the cave together and he showed me my name and the name Catherine in blood on the wall and unwrapped his bandages so I could see his face for the last time, I've lost him. He's just a voice in my head now, like a dream.

— It depends how curious you are about what comes next, he

says. — There might be good things. You know, by the time I'd been stuck in that cave for three days, I wasn't curious, I just wanted it to end. It's different for you.

— The rest of life might suck, too.

— It might, said Papa. — And it might not. But there's a way back, if you want it, you know that.

— And you?

— I have to stay here.

— So you're dead?

— I thought you knew. With all the things you know . . . all your Amazing Animals Facts and your poisons and the way you follow the instructions when we're making aeroplanes . . . I thought you knew, Lou-Lou. I died in the cave. Think about the world, Young Sir. Think about how it might not suck. But we have to say goodbye now. It's time.

And I turn my head to the window. You can feel it getting light outside and you can hear birds. Seagulls. And I know he isn't lying to me because he's the only one who never did. And I know something else. I know that one day, if I want to, I can do it. I can take one step forward.

And then another.

ACKNOWLEDGEMENTS

I would like to thank The Authors' Foundation and the Arts Council of Great Britain for awarding me grants that allowed me the space and time to write this novel. I am also grateful to Paul Broks for his book *Into the Silent Land*, and to Clare Alexander, Gail Campbell, Polly Coles, Gina de Ferrer, Humphrey Hawksley, Carsten Jensen, and Kitty and John Sewell for their comments, support and advice on the manuscript.

READING GROUP GUIDE

A free guide to *The Ninth Life of Louis Drax* for reading
groups is available to all UK readers. The guide
contains discussion topics, background to the writing of
the book and suggestions for further reading.

To order your guide, please send an email to:
readersgroups @ bloomsbury.com
or log on to: www.lizjensen.com
or write to:
The Ninth Life of Louis Drax Reading Group Guide
Bloomsbury Publishing Plc
38 Soho Square
London
W1D 3HB